The Halo Revelations

J. S. Colley

Published by: VIPER Press

Copyright

Dedication

This book is dedicated to Joe, Will, and Grace, who are the loves of my life.

And to the SETI Institute whose mission is "to explore, understand and explain the origin, nature and prevalence of life in the universe."

Content

D oug felt the deep rumble before he heard it. The ground swayed in a slow rhythmic motion. He turned and looked at his guide. The ground heaved, and suddenly they were several yards apart, instead of just a few feet. A sharp crack snapped through the gauzy mountain air. Giant boulders thundered toward them. The sound was like nothing Doug had ever heard. The roar so uniformly loud, it was like pure silence. Pebbles danced beneath his feet, shooting his legs out from under him as if he were stepping on marbles, and slammed him to the ground. He felt his heavy backpack rip from his shoulders as he slid down the incline.

No, he thought, *I can't lose it now!*

He wrenched his body to the side, ignoring the jagged rocks that gouged into his skin, and stretched his fingers out to try and snag the strap, but the backpack moved away from him as if it were on a conveyer belt.

Doug watched Genjo claw at the rubble in a futile attempt to stop his progress down the mountain. Through blood mingled with dirt, Genjo looked toward the loose backpack and then over to Doug.

And then he was gone.

CHAPTER 1

H enry stared at the tattered red knapsack lying atop his desk. A jade hunter had awakened his old friend, Jian Lin, early one morning. As Jian stood sleepy-eyed in the doorway, the man offered him the pack. The hunter expected nothing in return, only the hope that his good fortune would continue. He smiled a toothless grin and turned to show Jian a large white stone strapped to his back with ropes.

Now, Henry touched the dusty red fabric. His fingers came away feeling as dry as the brutal Himalayan air it had been exposed to for over a decade.

Has it really been that long? he thought.

After all this time, Henry still couldn't rid himself of the feeling that he had been responsible for Doug's death. It was the earthquake that killed him. Who could have predicted that? But it was Henry who had put him in harm's way. He thought of Doug's wife and two children, especially his son Nicholas, who had only been five years old at the time. A young man now. *A boy shouldn't have to grow up without a father*, he mused, as he finally moved to unzip the bundle.

A few hours later, Henry listened as the video camera whirred and a sharp tone announced the rewind was complete. He reached out with a shaky hand and pressed the play button again.

* * *

The video went viral on YouTube in less than a week.

Nick could still hear the kids at school. *The great archaeologist Doug Farraday*, they mocked, waving their cell phones at him.

Nut-job Farraday.

He wanted to slam his fist into their gaping pie holes but, truth was, he was beginning to think the same thing. He couldn't believe the man in the video was his father. He looked more like a lunatic—some crazed UFO hunter—or a druggie.

His close friends were sympathetic but, in general, the entire student body thought his father was fair game for ridicule. None of them considered how Nick might feel, but what did he expect? It was mostly the so-called popular kids who taunted him. When he was younger, his mom told him those kids would end up being losers with a capital L. Little good it did him now.

Trust me, she said, *what goes around comes around.* His mom was full of platitudes, one for every occasion. She wasn't perfect but she was the only parent he had, and now he was grateful that she tended to be overprotective; he was in no mood to face the kids at school again. She had asked permission for him to be absent so he could attend the memorial service. That gave him a little time, but he would have to go back after Thanksgiving break. *This too shall pass.* Nick hoped she was right and the jerks at school would get bored with the video by then.

He sat in front of his laptop and clicked the video for the umpteenth time. Only one person could have leaked it: Henry Applegate. And the realization made Nick feel as if he'd been punched in the gut. He let the video run to the end and then slammed the lid closed.

As if my life didn't suck enough already, he thought.

Lately, when he wasn't thinking about how the video had ruined his life, Nick spent most of his time thinking about Henry. He couldn't believe his friend, and his dad's old partner, would do this to him—or to his dad.

But the evidence was hard to deny.

* * *

Liz was the first to notice his limousine glide up to the curb opposite the tall front gates of the cemetery. As the window slid down, Henry heard her snarl at the police officer stationed at the entrance.

"Your job was to keep the riff-raff away."

Liz had changed very little over the years. Henry had been surprised when he first realized she was shorter than him. She gave the impression of being tall.

"Ma'am," the officer called out to her as she hurried past. "Please wait."

She waved him away when he moved to get between her and passenger side window of the sedan.

"What brought you out of your little hole?"

"Lizzie, so good to see you again." Henry reached his gloved hand toward her but she swiped it away.

Her remarks reminded him of his weakness—his fear of being outdoors—and he felt the familiar twinge of panic settle in his chest and then spread outward, until he broke out into a fine sweat. He welcomed the cold air that fell in through the open window.

"Please, Lizzie, I need to speak to you."

"Your needs don't concern me."

Henry realized the recent events must have intensified her incessant anger toward him, and his guilt kept him from attempting any form of defense.

"At least let me say hello to Nicholas."

"Say hello to Nick? After you've smeared what was left of his father's memory?"

"You know I had nothing to do with that."

"Do I?"

"Lizzie, we need to talk."

"You've said and done enough already. And please stop calling me Lizzie! You know I hate it."

Henry started to speak again, but Liz held up her hand.

"Sorry, Henry. I appreciate that you made all the arrangements to get Doug's body back home. I really do. I know how much trouble it must have been for you, but one good deed doesn't wipe out everything else you've done."

"But Lizzie ... Liz." He lowered his voice. "We're all in danger."

Henry noticed Nick standing by the gate, keeping his distance. He missed the boy. Other than the occasional customer, Nick was one of his few contacts with the outside world. He imagined Nick walking over to speak with him, but the boy stood alongside his sister, his hands shoved deep inside his pants pockets.

"Real life isn't like one of your conspiracy-theory books, Henry. And don't try to drag me into your little PR stunt. I'm not falling for it."

"PR stunt? You're making—"

"Please tell your driver to leave, or I'll have you arrested for disturbing the peace."

The police officer was standing a few yards behind Liz, keeping a close watch. The idea of spending even a few minutes in jail terrified Henry, but it was important he convince her the danger was real. *If only she would be reasonable.* He noticed her glance toward the white satellite TV news van that sat lurking down the street.

"Please, Henry." She nodded toward the vehicle.

If he couldn't get through to Liz, perhaps he could warn Nicholas. They had made a pact long ago that Henry was never to call him. Liz would see Henry's number on the phone bill and their visits would have to stop.

It didn't seem to matter now.

Henry leaned his head out the window and called out to him. They locked eyes for a moment. Nick made a slight movement forward, but his sister touched his arm and he didn't come any closer.

"Henry, please! If you have any decency left, you'll leave and never bother us again."

Henry pulled his hand inside the car. As the window moved back into place, he instructed the driver to take him home.

* * *

Mount Avon Historical Cemetery sat on two square blocks of land in the middle of the old residential district. Nick's mother had to get permission from the Rochester Historical Society for her husband's body to be interred there; but since Douglas Farraday was the city's most famous prodigal son, and since his family had been among the original founders of the city back in the mid-nineteenth century, the decision had been easy for the council.

Even though the discovery of the archaeologist's body warranted an article in the local newspaper and a spot on the evening news, only a few invited guests attended the funeral service. The sheriff anticipated a large group of onlookers, but the crowd mainly consisted of media.

The Farraday home sat across the street from the north side of the old graveyard, on the corner of Castell and Third. The house had been in the family for generations. Police cars kept the reporters at a distance as the dark-clad group made the short walk to the house for the wake, but Nick could still hear them bark at the camera operators in front of them.

"Farraday was best known for his research in the controversial field of archaeo-astronomy, which is the study of how ancient people interpreted what they saw in the sky and how it shaped the way they thought and their culture. During the last years of his life, he had formed a dubious association with our own famous—and equally controversial—author, Henry Applegate. The release of a video on the internet showing Douglas Farraday during the last hours of his life has cast some doubt on his mental stability, and the validity of some of his previous studies."

"Immediately preceding his death, he was conducting research into the mysterious Drōpa Stones, first uncovered decades ago in the Kunlun-Kette region of the Himalayan Mountains. UFO conspiracy theorists believe the Drōpa Stones were

left by an alien race that crashed landed in the area thousands of years ago."

Nick shoved his hands deeper into his pockets and rushed ahead of the group, eager to be out of earshot of the reporters.

* * *

"Why do you keep watching that thing anyway?"

Nick and Emily had taken plates of food upstairs in an effort to avoid the over-attentive adults. There was a small landing situated between their rooms that served as a study/TV area. Empty plates sat on a small table near the stairs. Emily lay sprawled across a beanbag, cell phone in hand. Nick sat at the small desk in the corner with his laptop.

"Do you really think Henry posted it? For an old guy, he's not bad with computers, but I'd be surprised if he even knows what YouTube is."

In all the times they'd spoken, Henry never mentioned the site.

Emily continued staring at her phone, thumbs working the tiny keypad.

"Maybe I should go ask him," Nick said.

It was more of a statement than a question. Nick felt confused, one moment hating Henry for deceiving him and, the next, positive he would never do anything to tarnish his father's reputation just for the sake of promoting a new book. Maybe there was some other explanation.

Emily put aside her cell phone. "Mom would blow a gasket."

"Well, she doesn't have to know everything." Nick teased his eyebrows at his sister.

All his life, Nick felt like his mom kept things from him, especially things concerning his father and Henry. Turn-around was fair play. The only thing Nick knew about their relationship was what Henry had told him.

Emily smirked at him and then shook her head. "I don't think you should see him anymore. Why would you still want to be friends with him anyway?"

His sister was the only person who knew he had been secretly visiting Henry these past few years.

"Because maybe he didn't leak the video," Nick said.

"Who else would benefit from releasing it? And who else would have access to it?" She looked hard at her younger brother. "Think about it, Nick."

She shrugged in that annoying you-know-I'm-right way of hers.

He really didn't know what to think. He'd overheard people try to comfort his mom by saying it must be such a blessing to know her husband was finally home and at peace, but finding his dad's body hadn't given him any peace. In fact, it was just the opposite. Sometimes he wished his father's body had never been found, but as soon as he had the thought, he regretted it.

"I never understood why Mom hated Henry so much."

"Dad's career was going great then, all of a sudden, he hooks up with Henry for some reason." Emily waved her hands around her head. "The crazy, ancient-alien-conspiracy-theory guy. Everyone figured it was because Applegate had deep pockets."

Henry came from a wealthy family and made lots of money selling his books. Except for the fact he used a limo service because of his panic attacks, no one would ever know it.

"Everyone assumed Dad sold out, and he lost some of his professional credibility because of it. But Mom says he did the work for Henry so he could finance what he really wanted to do. I don't know if it's true, or if that's just her way of coping."

Nick wondered how Emily knew all this stuff and he didn't.

"So that should make Mom mad at our dad, not at Henry."

"Maybe she thinks he put Dad in the wrong place at the wrong time." She drew her eyebrows together. "And there's more stuff. You shouldn't judge Mom too harshly."

"What stuff?"

"Girl stuff. I'm not sure I should tell you."

"Come on, Em. You can't say something like that and not tell me!" *How much more didn't he know?*

Emily sighed. "Listen, you can't mention this. *Ever.* Mom doesn't even know that I know, but I've listened in on conversations."

"What?" Nick wanted her to spill it already.

"Mom thought Dad was having an affair."

Emily almost whispered the last word. Hearing it, Nick felt a rush of heat spread up his face.

Emily continued, "With one of the women on the expedition. An Asian woman. From the conversations I've overheard, she was an acquaintance of Henry's."

An Asian woman? Something stirred in Nick's brain. He glanced at his father's journal on the desk next to his laptop. He didn't say anything for a minute.

"That can't be true." He shook his head. "From what I've read in his journal, Dad was always thinking about Mom while he was away. I just can't believe it."

Nick was trying to hold on to a good image of his father, but it was getting harder and harder. He was only five years old when his father died, so he didn't have much to go on. Emily had been eight, so she remembered a lot more about their dad than he did.

"If it's hard for you, think how hard it must be for Mom to not know the truth. And, right or wrong, whenever she sees Henry, it reminds her of something she'd rather not think about."

But, whether Henry was to blame for any of it—the video or his mother's unhappiness—the damage was done, and Nick believed Henry was the only person who could undo it.

CHAPTER 2

Except for the person, or persons, who posted it, Henry was the only one who knew the video on the internet had been edited. The original video was over twenty minutes long. The posted video was less than four. Someone wanted to discredit Doug, and they had done a superb job. The edited version left out all the important details, but left in the parts where Douglas seemed incoherent and, Henry thought, crazier than a loon. The oddest thing was that Doug acted as if the viewer could see what he appeared to be witnessing. But they could not. The effect was disconcerting.

The implications of what Doug said were startling in their possibilities. For most of his adult life, Henry had searched for real evidence that extraterrestrials visited Earth in the ancient past. He wondered if the object sitting on Doug's head was really the proof he had been seeking; or was it merely what it looked like—an ancient crown of sorts? But it was more than a simple crown. It gave off an iridescent glow, leaving the impression of a dim halo surrounding Doug's head. The three medallions circling it looked like miniature replicas of the infamous Drōpa Stones. In the center of each was a smooth, rounded nugget of white jade.

Had Doug found the proof?

A bookshelf sat against the wall on the side of Henry's desk and he looked at it, studying the titles: *Earth Visitors and Ancient Sites*; *Earth Visitors and Mythology*; *Earth Visitors and Strange Rituals*; *Earth Visitors and Unexplainable Geoglyphs*. He reached for the last book and opened it to a page showing the Nazca Lines—the straight lines etched on the flat surface of the Peruvian desert—and read the caption below: *Ceremonial prayer lines, or ancient airport runway?* He turned the page and looked at the other huge glyphs found in the area: outlines of a monkey, spider, hummingbird, and even a whale. Archaeologists dated the glyphs to about 400 and 650 AD. Modern man first discovered them in 1927, after a pilot observed them while flying over the area. Henry had found other, but smaller, glyphs all across the globe—including drawings that depicted beings dressed in what looked remarkably like modern-day astronaut's garb. All these things the mainstream archaeological and scientific communities ignored, or explained away as something far less obvious.

While still an undergrad, Henry became interested in mythology. He went on to study comparative religions in grad school and began writing about his alien visitor theory in earnest. There were just too many similarities between the planet's geographically widespread religions for it to be a coincidence. The more he studied, the more questions he had, and the more startling his conclusions.

Henry's first book series was a huge success. The books had been printed in almost every language in the world. He could have stopped then, but he continued his investigation, traveling to other ancient archaeological sites in search of the evidence that would prove his theories beyond any doubt. He was convinced that the written depictions of encounters with the gods in ancient religious texts were not accountings of sightings of the Supreme Being—the creator of the universe—but merely beings from another planet. This did nothing to sway his own personal belief that there was a Divine Creator, but his vision of a creator was far different from that represented by the various religious dogmas.

Henry replaced the book he was holding and touched the spines of the others, remembering all the amazing things he had seen and done. How he missed it! He only stopped after contracting lime disease. The disease weakened him physically and allowed the phobia, which he had managed to hold in check for so many years, to take a stronger hold on him. As if by miracle, he found Doug. They were a perfect team; their partnership was both financially beneficial and a personal pleasure.

But had his passion led him to do something he would later regret?

If Doug really had found the proof they were searching for, he knew Doug would agree that the end justified the means. But Liz was another matter altogether. She would be furious with him, he was certain—and perhaps rightly so. How could he have thought it was a good idea? But he couldn't think of any other way. He wanted desperately to tell Liz before things got out of hand, but now they'd already had the funeral.

He never wanted it to get this far.

Henry leaned back in his chair. He wished Nicholas would come for a visit. He had a lot of things to explain to him.

A loud bang came from somewhere downstairs. *Isis?* Had she knocked something over? His head snapped toward the small rug beside the radiator. The Persian was curled up in oblivious content. Henry's heart tapped in his chest. He was certain all the doors were locked, and he wasn't expecting any clients.

* * *

Emily's comment about the Asian woman intrigued Nick. He was sure he'd seen several references to her in his dad's journal. Thinking about the possibility that his dad might have cheated on his mom made Nick feel a little creeped-out. No kid ever wants to think about his parent and *sex*, much less about them having an affair, but Nick didn't really remember his dad. Try as he might, he could never conjure up any memories. That made it a little easier to deal with.

He picked up his father's journal and carefully leafed through it. The journal was covered in well-worn leather and its pages were fragile from years of being exposed to the weather. Nick was pleased, but surprised, his mother had given it to him.

A few days after receiving a package from Henry, she had walked into his room and stood in the doorway.

"This was your father's."

"What is it?"

"His journal from his last expedition. I thought you'd like to have it."

"Don't you want it?"

"I've already read it. I thought it would be something you'd like to have. I know you've always been interested in his work."

Nick was an amateur astronomer. His mother had bought him a telescope a few years ago for his birthday, and he spent many nights studying the nighttime sky. One of his favorite things was spotting satellites whizzing overhead.

His mom was right. The universe fascinated him, and he was interested in the work his father had done. Whether he would have been interested as much if his dad were still living, Nick would never know, but it was a way to stay connected, and that's all that mattered. Since his friendship started with Henry, Nick had also become interested in the search for life on other planets. Even if he didn't buy into all of Henry's crazy theories, the idea that extraterrestrials might have visited Earth in the ancient past wasn't out of the realm of possibility.

Anything is possible. It sounded like one of his mom's clichés or the cheesy slogan of some motivational speaker, but it was true.

Nick had read the entire journal as soon as his mother gave it to him. Now he carefully turned the pages to the last entry.

June 15, 1999
This is the last expedition I'm conducting for Henry before the new antiquities law goes into effect next year, a necessary law but yet another bit of red tape to make my job more difficult.

Just two days ago, my spirits were low. I was having little luck and was anxious to get off the mountain. Most of the caves I explored had already been pillaged and there was little left to see, so I sent the rest of the crew back to the village and only Genjo and I remain.

Reminder: Ming Lin did a great job in assembling an expert crew. I mustn't forget to tell her when I get back.

Ming Lin. That was the person his dad had mentioned several times throughout the journal. Was this the Asian woman Emily was talking about? His mom had read the journal. Was that why she'd given it to him? She couldn't bear to read about her?

While Genjo waited, I decided to explore a low-ceilinged cave one last time. I ventured farther into this cave than I had ever gone before. About forty yards toward the back, I stumbled upon several more discs, much the same as I found a few days ago. They are similar to the Drōpa Stones first discovered in this area during the late 1930s, with markings that spiral inward toward a center hole. I am only mildly interested in them, but finding them has given me hope. Perhaps a burial site is nearby.

I haven't had time to study the markings etched on the stones in any detail, but some of the drawings found in the cave clearly depict the Pleiades constellation. Many ancient cultures held this constellation in high regard.

Here, high on this mountain, away from mo-dern civilization, I can begin to understand our ancient ancestors' fascination with the stars. Having no artificial light to block them out, they must have been glorious in the night sky, just as I see tonight. No wonder they were so drawn to the heavens.

That no one stumbled across these stones before now is remarkable. This mountain pass is teeming with treasure seekers. Perhaps they are not interested in something so mundane as dry, old discs. They are hunting for the much sought-after Kunlun-Kette jade, a much more profitable commodity. The Chinese prize it for its color. I would love to find even a tiny gem to take back to Elizabeth.

If my dad was having an affair, Nick thought, *would he be thinking about bringing Mom a piece of prized jade?* He couldn't bring himself to think his dad didn't love his mother. She was wrong about him, he was certain.

With my newly found hope, tomorrow I will explore the cave a little deeper using what little time I have left. Unless I find a burial site before it is time to start down the mountain, Henry will not get the DNA samples he so hoped for. He will have to be satisfied with the enigmatic discs and their curious markings.

His father hadn't mentioned anything about a crown, only the stones. Did Henry know about either the video, or the crown, before his father's body was found?

Later that afternoon, while Nick was still mulling over the idea of confronting Henry and they were saying goodbye to the last of the guests, two ominous-looking black Cadillac SUVs pulled up to the curb opposite the Farradays' house.

"Is that Mr. Applegate again?" Emily asked.

"No, it isn't Henry," their mother answered.

"Then who?"

"FBI?" Nick offered, half joking.

But he was wrong. It was the NSA.

CHAPTER 3

"I'm Agent Vagnetti."

A short woman lifted her pudgy arm toward her partner. "And this is Agent Nelson. We're with the National Security Agency. We'd like to ask you a few questions."

The difference between the two agents was startling. The male agent was physically fit, tall, dark-haired, and good-looking. The female agent was anything but fit and, next to her partner, unremarkable in looks. Her mostly-silver hair was cropped short, and she wore a zippered navy blue cardigan with what looked like crumbs from this morning's toast still clinging to the front. The only thing young looking about the woman was her eyes. They twinkled a sparkling blue. Liz couldn't help but wonder if the NSA required physical fitness tests.

Once inside, Liz led them to the living room and stood with her arms folded across her chest. She stole another glance at the tall agent. Handsome or not, it had been a long day. She wanted this interview over with.

One minute of patience, ten years of peace, she thought.

"Please, why don't we all sit down?" Agent Vagnetti suggested.

Everyone took a seat except the female agent. Instead, she waddled to the end of the room and stood facing the fireplace. She studied the decorations on the mantel for a moment before turning around to address the three Farradays now clustered together on the sofa.

Agent Nelson sat to the left on a black-lacquered Oriental armchair.

"First, let me say that we're sorry to bother you today, but I'm afraid this can't wait."

The agent had a trust-me-this-will-be-painless kind of look on her face that irritated Liz.

"We only have a few questions." The agent seemed distracted.

"Could you please get on with it?" Liz blurted out. She had been on edge since her confrontation with Henry at the cemetery. "I appreciate your attempt at niceties, but we've all had a long day."

"Yes, you're right, Mrs. Farraday. Or would you rather be called Elizabeth?"

"Liz is fine. And you? Agent Vagnetti? Or just Agent?"

Beware of wolves in sheep's clothing. Liz couldn't believe she was being so rude, but didn't she have a right after the month she'd had?

Liz felt the agent's eyes on her.

"Did you find anything unusual in your husband's belongings?"

"Unusual?" Liz fidgeted with the hem of her sleeve. "What do you mean?"

"Anything you wouldn't normally expect."

"I didn't expect any of it."

The agent gave a consolatory smile. "Was there anything that didn't fit in? Perhaps an artifact?"

"Are you suggesting I received illegal antiquities that I'm not reporting?"

Liz noticed Nick and Emily glance at each other. They were both sitting with their hands folded in their laps. Except that Nick's hair was dark and Emily's was chestnut, they looked remarkably alike. Even with their difference in age, Nick was almost the same height as his older sister. Their eyes were golden amber with long, thick lashes. Every time Liz looked into them, it was as if she was looking into Doug's, and she would get that old, familiar ache.

"I'm not suggesting anything. I'm just asking a question," Agent Vagnetti said.

"Perhaps you should be asking Henry Applegate. He's the one who arranged for everything to be returned to the States."

"Yes. We're aware of that. But we'd like to know if you found anything unusual in his belongings."

"I really don't know what you're getting at, but I'm sure Doug's belongings were searched before they left China. If there was anything of value or importance, the Chinese authorities already discovered it. And Henry always follows the law concerning transport of antiquities."

At least Liz could say that much for him.

Agent Nelson moved forward in his chair and rested his elbows on his knees. "We are aware of the video. Do you have it in your possession?"

Liz turned to the distinguished-looking agent. If circumstances had been different, she might have been attracted to him. She'd felt a twinge of... something...

when she first locked eyes with him. Now she found herself involuntarily glancing at his ring finger. It was bare.

"If I had it in my possession, it wouldn't be posted on YouTube. Again, why don't you ask Henry? I'm sure the video is all part of a publicity stunt to sell one of his new books. If I didn't know better, I'd accuse him of staging the discovery of Doug's body to coincide with the release date, too."

"He's about to release a new book?"

"I suspect so, but you'll have to ask him. I haven't spoken with him in years."

"Yet he was at the funeral this morning," Agent Vagnetti said.

Liz's head snapped around. "You were spying on us?"

"Not spying. Just observing."

* * *

Nick squirmed in his seat. He was starting to get nervous. If the NSA was observing them, then maybe they knew he visited Henry. The last thing he needed was for them to say something to his mother. He hadn't been there in weeks. If they had just started watching, maybe they didn't know. If they did, he prayed they wouldn't say anything to incriminate him.

"Spying. Observing. Same thing." Liz sneered. "If you were observing, you'd have noticed he didn't stay long. Except for a few brief phone calls regarding the arrangements for the return of my husband's body, that's the first contact I've had with him since shortly after Doug went missing ten years ago. "

"What about the diadem?" Agent Nelson interjected.

"Diadem?" Nick asked, to no one in particular. He'd never heard the word.

"The thing on your father's head in the video," his mother explained. "The crown."

So why didn't he just say crown? Nick thought.

"It wasn't in Doug's things, if that's what you're getting at. Again, why don't you ask Henry? If it's in the States, he would be the person in possession of it, not me."

"What about this?" Agent Vagnetti pointed to a decorative plate displayed on the mantel.

As if seeing them for the first time, Nick studied the plates. What he'd just read in his father's journal was fresh in his mind. He realized they looked exactly like the discs his father described in his journal.

"A gift from my husband from just before his death."

Agent Vagnetti raised an eyebrow.

"They aren't real. It was made from a plaster casting. Doug often made casts of objects for reproductions. I would paint them to make them look old, and Henry would sell the reproductions in his shop. I kept this one. For sentimental reasons."

"I'd like to take this for study if you don't mind. "

"Study? I told you, it's a reproduction. It's fake. I antiqued it myself."

"I believe you, Mrs. Farraday, but we'd like to take an X-ray of it."

"X-ray?" His mother reflected for a moment. "Oh, I see. You think there is something inside."

The agent shifted her weight, then nodded.

"You think my husband was a smuggler? Certainly not drugs?"

"Now that you mention it, did your husband have a drug problem, Mrs. Farraday?"

Nick noticed a vein bulge in his mother's forehead.

* * *

Liz was outraged by the question. Her interest in the good-looking agent was quickly starting to wane. Although the same thought had crossed her mind when she first viewed the video. Perhaps her husband had been offered a hallucinogen by the locals and was curious about what the experience would be like—more information for his research—but she had discounted this notion and certainly wasn't going to share her initial concerns with the agents.

To accuse him of drug smuggling? Ridiculous.

"No! I'd never seen my husband take any type of illegal drug. Why is the NSA interested in a ten year-old video anyway? Obviously, my husband was under great stress and had a breakdown. There. Are you happy now? Do you want me to spell it out for you? And now some UFO fanatics think what they see on the video is somehow proof that aliens have visited Earth. Well, it's a load of garbage. As much as I hate to admit it, the truth is my husband lost it up in those mountains. He flipped out up there. And, on his way back down, he was killed in an earthquake."

She was shaking now, remembering Henry driving up in his limo. "He would have never been there if Henry hadn't poisoned his mind with his crazy theories. Doug was a respected archaeologist before he started working for Henry. Now everyone thinks of him as a lunatic—all except for a few other lunatics."

Liz was instantly sorry for her outburst in front of Nick and Emily, but she couldn't take it back now. She'd felt like she was going to come out of her skin ever since the day she got the call from Henry that Doug was finally coming home. And now she had to deal with all this. Her nerves were shot. But she knew that was no excuse.

She turned back to Agent Vagnetti. "So why are you really here?"

"We're here for two reasons. The primary one is to protect you, Mrs. Farraday. And your children."

"Protect us from what?"

"From people who would like to find the object in the video."

"Why? It's just a prop used by a man obviously pushed over the edge." She glanced at her children.

"We understand your position. And we certainly would like to get a better understanding of the situation. But it really doesn't matter what we think. The people who are looking for this object believe it is real, or want others to believe, and they'll do anything to get what they want. They are known to perpetuate frauds that result in the loss of huge sums of money for their victims. And they aren't above violence. We've had run-ins with them before. That's our second reason for being here. We'd like to catch them before they can victimize anyone else."

In the end, Liz let them take the decorative plate, even without a warrant.

CHAPTER 4

It wasn't difficult for Nick to sneak out of the house. After the agents left, his mother had been so upset she went into the bedroom and closed the door. Emily was in her room, either texting or on Facebook or Twitter. By now, she would be totally oblivious to everything else around her. It was only once he was outside the house that Nick might encounter a problem.

His bedroom window looked out over Third Avenue and was directly across from the cemetery. A dark sedan had been parked there ever since Vagnetti & Company had said their goodbyes a few hours ago. He could see the profile of a man's face in the faint light of the streetlamps.

He looks a little old for a field agent, Nick thought.

Nick suspected Agent Vagnetti had posted the operative to keep a watch on them. He didn't know if the agent was trying to be obvious, or if he was just bad at his job. Whether he would follow Nick or was just there to keep an eye on the house, he wasn't sure. But he wasn't going to take any chances.

Once outside, Nick thought about his options. What difference did it make if the NSA agent followed him? Probably not much, but it was the principle of the thing. As far as he was concerned, the NSA was on a need-to-know basis. And they didn't need to know he was visiting Henry.

Nick could see down the length of backyards almost all the way to University Drive. Dimly lit and scattered with shrubbery meant to provide privacy, it would be the perfect escape route. He wound his way along the backs of several houses, then cautiously made his way to the street. He peered down the length of Castell Avenue, to where it dead-ended at Third. No agent in sight.

Man, this is way too easy. The thought didn't give him much comfort. He crossed over Castell and ran through the side yards until he had crossed two more streets. Then he turned right to make his way back to Third, leaving the agent far behind.

By the time he reached the heart of the small town, the shops were all closed. Unlike the nearby malls that stayed open until nine, the retail shops in town closed at six. The only businesses still open on Main Street were the restaurants. Kruse & Muer and The Rochester Chop House had Cadillacs, Beemers and Jags lined up by the valet. Toward the southern end of town, groups of young college students from the nearby university stood outside Main Street Billiards smoking cigarettes.

Technically, Henry's shop, The Antiquarian, was never open. You needed an appointment to get in, and Henry only left the doors unlocked when he was expecting someone. He not only made a living from writing controversial books about ancient aliens, but he also dealt in the sale of antiquities—including rare books—and by providing appraisals. In particular, he was an expert in religious artifacts, but his knowledge of antiques in general was vast. Despite his unorthodox views of the ancient past and his controversial books, both the affluent collector and week-end antique hunter sought his opinion.

The Antiquarian was the kind of shop you walked into and felt transported back in time. It looked more like a library or a museum. The thing Nick liked most about it was...everything. The walls were covered with floor-to-ceiling shelves crammed with books and scrolls and the occasional piece of pottery or figurine. Low glass cases, containing all sorts of objects, made neat rows near the outer walls. In the center was a long, worn oak table where Henry conducted most of his business. When you opened the door the aroma of old leather greeted you. It was a comfortable, welcoming smell.

Nick decided to use the rear entrance. He turned down the alley and sprinted to the far end. He almost bumped into a couple heading toward the rear parking lot across the alley from one of the posh restaurants. The Antiquarian was the second building from the end of the long cobblestone alleyway. Nick glanced up at the small window of Henry's upstairs apartment. The light was on. Not that he expected Henry to be out, but the glow from the window confirmed he was still up.

Nick was far from the streetlamps surrounding the nearby lot, and the alley went suddenly dark. There was no moon. The meager light cast from the second-floor kitchen window did little to penetrate the blackness. He made his way to the back door and was ready to press the intercom when he noticed a narrow strip of light coming from the doorjamb. The door was open. Odd. Nick knew that Henry always checked and rechecked that the doors were secure before going upstairs for the night. It was a ritual brought on by his phobia.

Just as he eased opened the door, Nick heard a crash coming from inside. He hesitated. Someone groaned. Was that Henry? Suddenly Nick found himself flying through the air as someone rushed past him. He hit the rough pavement with a thud and a sharp pain shot up his left arm from his elbow.

It took a minute for him to catch his breath and sit up. He rubbed his elbow and grimaced. Sweat beaded on his forehead then, just as quickly, he turned cold. He rolled over, waiting for the inevitable. The food he'd eaten at the wake churned in his stomach. After a few seconds, the feeling went away, and he sat up and looked both ways down the alley. From the far end, an undisturbed circle of light from a streetlamp filtered down to the pavement. The alley was deserted. Whoever had shoved him was long gone.

Nick scrambled to his feet. *Henry!* Even after all his doubts about the old man over the last few weeks, he was still concerned.

The security nightlight inside the shop gave the small back foyer an eerie glow. It was quiet. Then Nick heard a raspy sound come from near the stairwell.

"Henry?"

"Over here! Is that you, Nicholas?"

Nick ran to the bottom of the stairs where Henry sat slumped against the bottom step.

"What happened?"

Henry coughed. "Someone...I heard a noise. And when I came downstairs to investigate, someone shoved me. I hit my head on the edge of the banister."

He reached out his hand and touched Nick's arm. "I'm so glad you came." He raised his hand to his forehead. "I think I'm bleeding."

An inch-long horizontal cut showed above his right eyebrow. A trickle of blood flowed down the side of his nose and cheek.

Nick felt queasy again. "Yes, you are."

He turned and looked in circles, as if there was someone else in the shop who might help.

Henry said, "Go upstairs and get a towel. I'm going to sit here for a minute longer."

Nick started up the steps.

"Wait! Did you notice if the door was damaged?"

"It didn't look like it. It was just opened."

"Go close it and try the lock. I don't want that thug getting back in."

Nick didn't see the point. If the lock didn't stop the thugs the first time, it wouldn't stop them now either. But he did what he was told.

After wiping the blood off his face, Henry folded the towel and put pressure on the cut.

"You don't look so good,"

"I don't feel so good," Henry said.

Nick reached in his pocket for his cell phone.

"I'm calling 911."

He noticed a missed call from his mom and made a mental note to call her when Henry was settled.

"No, please. Don't."

"You need stitches. And you might have a concussion."

"If you call emergency, there'll be too much commotion. The entire town will be out watching."

"Can you call your driver? He can take you to emergency."

"I'm NOT going to the hospital!"

Nick didn't understand what the big deal was. He'd go to the hospital, get a stitch or two and maybe an X-ray, and that would be that.

"Come on, Henry. You can't just sit here bleeding."

Nick's arm had been numb from the whack to his elbow and now it was starting to tingle. He shook it out and rubbed his forearm.

Henry pressed the towel harder against his wound.

And then they both jumped at the sound of loud banging at the back door.

* * *

If Liz was angry with Henry for showing up at the cemetery this morning, now she was lethal.

She had gone upstairs to talk with her children, still feeling awful about saying those things about their father in front of the NSA agents, but Nick was nowhere to be found.

"Where's Nick?" Liz asked her daughter. Even if he didn't always ask permission, he never left the house without at least letting her know he was going out.

Emily looked up from her phone. "He's not here?"

"No, I've checked everywhere."

"Well, I don't know where he is." Emily shrugged and went back to keying in a message on her phone.

Liz reached into her pocket and pulled out her own cell phone. She let it ring until it went to voice mail.

"Nick, please call me when you get this. Where are you?"

She turned back to Emily. "Today, of all days, he has to pull something like this. Like I don't have enough on my mind!"

She glanced at her daughter. Like a body language expert, she could read her children, and she knew her daughter was not being honest with her. "What's going on?"

Emily shrugged. "I don't know. I'm not Nick's keeper."

"I'm really in no mood for this today. If you know where he went, then tell me!"

Liz realized her kids weren't angels. They sometimes didn't tell her everything, but today she needed—she demanded—to know the truth. And even though she hated to admit it, Henry's warning at the cemetery still rang in her ears.

When her daughter didn't answer, she said, "Emily, if you know something, you have to tell me. Even though I don't trust Henry as far as I can throw him, at the cemetery he said we're all in danger, and now he's made me paranoid. I'm worried about Nick."

Emily rolled her cell phone around in her hands. She seemed to be weighing what she would say next. Then she blurted out, "I can't believe he still went after I talked to him!"

"Talked to him about what?"

After more coaxing, Emily told her mother everything.

Nick was probably at Henry's, Emily confessed. He'd been visiting him in secret for years, and he'd been talking about confronting Henry about the video all day.

"How could you have kept this from me all this time, Emily?"

"I felt sorry for him, Mom, growing up without a dad. It's hard on me, but I imagine it's even harder on Nick. He just wanted to hear stories about his father. He wanted to feel close to him. And he knew you wouldn't approve. I'm sorry. I just didn't see the harm in it before now."

Liz banged on the door again.

"Henry, open up! I know Nick is in there."

She stood in the dark alley. On Fourth Street a young couple walked by, heading home from a night out. A group of rowdy youths turned down the alley and walked toward the rear parking lot. They didn't notice Liz standing in the dim recess of the doorway to The Antiquarian.

The door creaked open. Henry stood in front of her with a bloodied towel to his forehead.

She drew in a breath of air. "Where's Nick? What's happened?"

"Don't worry. He's okay. Its only me who's been damaged."

Liz gazed over Henry's shoulder into the dark shop where she saw Nick's shadowy figure leaning against the long oak desk. He was holding on to the edge with both hands.

"You," she pointed at Nick, "are in a heap of trouble."

"Mom, I—"

"Don't. Just don't. Not today." She'd have a long talk with him later. Right now, she just wanted to get him home. "Did you get the answers you were looking for?"

Nick stared blankly at her.

"I thought not. You'll never get a straight answer out of this one." She jerked her thumb at Henry. "One day you'll learn."

"But Mom!"

"Not now, Nick. Let's go."

Henry didn't move from the door. "Liz, I've been understanding up to now. But I really have to say you're being rather unreasonable."

"Me? Unreasonable?" she snorted.

"Your stubbornness will get you in trouble. I'm only trying to protect you."

"Like you tried to protect Doug?" It was a harsh thing to say, she knew. She couldn't seem to help herself.

"Nothing you could possibly say would be any worse than what I've been saying to myself over these last ten years," Henry said. "And you know it. Can't we set that aside for now? "

"Very noble of you. Now please get out of my way."

"Look around you, Liz. The shop has been ransacked and I got this," he lifted the rag from his forehead, "when I got in the way. You and your family will be next, I'm sure. Until they find what they're looking for, we're all in danger. I tried to warn you at the cemetery."

"Whoever tried to break in could have been looking for anything. How do you know what they were looking for?"

Liz was starting to wonder—first the NSA and now Henry being attacked. Maybe there was more to this than she first thought. But the NSA agents never claimed the object was anything special, only that some people thought it might be. All this could still just be the result of some convoluted plan-gone-wrong of Henry's. And she wasn't going to allow herself or her children to be dragged into it.

Before Henry had a chance to respond, she asked, "And who, Henry? Who are *they*?"

Henry's arm, with bloodied towel in hand, dropped to his side.

"Everyone. The entire world it seems." A trickle of blood slid down his forehead and he pressed the cloth back into place.

"You're not making any sense."

She motioned to Nick. She'd had enough of his conspiracy theories. Just more nonsense.

Henry managed a smile. "Aren't medical professionals required by law to help out in an emergency?" He waggled the bloodied towel.

During her long medical career, Liz had treated many unsavory people. She didn't always like her patients, but it wasn't her place to judge, only to perform her duties to the best of her abilities.

"You could go to the emergency room."

"You know my aversion to hospitals."

"Mom, you have to help him. He's bleeding."

Liz looked into her son's pleading face. She had been shocked and angry when Emily told her that Nick had gone to Henry's, and even more shocked when she had admitted to her that Nick had been visiting Henry for a few years. How could she not have known? *Just another thing to make me feel like a failure.* But deep down she knew Emily was right. Nick was looking for a replacement for his father. And Henry was as close to Doug as he could get. Sometimes she felt guilty about not remarrying, about not providing her two children with a father, but she had never found the right person. As angry as she had been that Henry had turned her once-respected archaeologist husband into little more than a UFO hunter, and even with all her other suspicions, she had still loved her husband very much, and she tried to raise their children to the best of her ability.

"I'll take a look at it."

CHAPTER 5

"You have ten minutes of my attention," Liz told Henry, who was sitting in a chair in the kitchen while she poked around at his wound.

"I really don't know where to begin."

"Make it fast, Henry. Ten minutes."

"Alright," Henry took in a deep breath, "just before Doug died, he told me he had found something astonishing."

Liz's hands stopped moving. "Why didn't you ever tell me this?" She started to mention the NSA agents, but thought better of it.

"Really, Liz, when did you ever give me a chance?"

She couldn't argue with him there. She went back to nursing his wound.

"It was just a few days before the earthquake. Doug sent word over the ham radio that he was going to send me a video he had made and then we should talk about what to do next." Henry sighed. "But, of course, we never got a chance. I spent several years searching for Doug's body—as you well know—and for whatever it was that he had found. In fact, I only gave up just a few years ago. At the time of his death, there had been rumors within the archaeological community about the nature of his discovery.

Other ham operators had probably been listening in on his transmission. But it seemed whatever he had been talking about was lost forever."

The corner of Henry's mouth curled up. "It's hard to keep secrets, even high in the Himalayan Mountains. So, naturally, the rumors resurfaced when word got out that Douglas' things had been found. And the search was back in full swing for his great discovery."

He looked at them. "And that lead them to me... and to you."

Henry winced as Liz vigorously scrubbed the cut on his forehead. The peroxide bubbled pink as she rubbed.

"Must you be so rough?"

"Keep talking, Henry. Your time is running out."

"At first I thought someone found the video before the camera was sent to me, but then I thought why wouldn't they just keep it? So I believe someone hacked into my computer recently and found the video there."

Liz stood back and took a hard look at Henry.

Before she could respond, Nick said, "So you didn't post the video." It was a statement rather than a question.

"Of course not, Nick. And I'm surprised you'd think I'd do such a thing."

Nick grinned.

Liz snorted and started to apply a butterfly bandage that she had found in Henry's first-aid kit to the now clean and dry wound.

Henry grimaced at Liz's rough handling and then continued, "No one would have known, except me, the true nature of Doug's discovery—that it was the Halo—until the video surfaced on the internet. Now they have something specific to search for."

"Halo?" Nick asked. "You mean the crown?"

"It's more than a crown, wouldn't you say? I think Halo describes it well."

"Wait a second," Liz said, "so you're trying to tell me that someone who was looking for this discovery hacked into your computer and found the video—a video that showed the discovery—and then posted it on the internet for all the world to see? That doesn't make any sense either."

"On the surface, it might not. But if you think about it—about motivation—then it makes perfect sense." Henry first looked at Liz and then at Nick, who had leaned forward in his chair. "They effectively neutralized the discovery before it could be announced. By showing Doug looking like some kind of loon in the video, they cast a shadow of suspicion over it."

"Disinformation," Nick said.

"Exactly!" Henry slapped his knee.

Liz shook her heard. "But why would someone want to neutralize," she rolled her eyes at the word, "it? If it were neutralized, then how could they benefit from it?"

"It's obvious, Mom. They must think it is the real thing, but they don't want the public to know."

"And, again, who are they?"

"Who else?" Nick said. "The *government*."

"Or governments." Henry added.

"That's why—"

She cut Nick off, thinking he would mention the NSA, and she didn't want Henry to know they'd been asking about him. If they questioned him about the crown, or the video, she didn't want to give him a chance to rehearse his answers.

"See what you've done, Henry? Now you've got Nick thinking like a conspiracy theorist!"

Liz snatched up the used cotton balls and wrappings and tossed them in the trashcan underneath the sink. She took her time washing her hands while Nick and Henry continued their discussion.

Was she wrong? She was starting to feel confused, and when she was confused, she felt panicky. And she didn't like the feeling one bit. She turned back to face them and interrupted Henry in mid-sentence.

"The question still remains, what makes this artifact more special than any other one you've ever found? Why do you think it isn't exactly what it looks like—an ordinary crown? Maybe a very old crown, and one that emits a glow, but still just a crown." She had noticed a faint aura surrounding it when she'd watched the video, but hadn't thought much about it until Henry called it a Halo. "You can't be sure that Doug didn't have a breakdown. That he wasn't delusional, just like it looks on the video." She glanced at Nick, looking for his reaction. Then she looked back at Henry. "Unless you have it in your possession? Unless you've already studied it?"

Henry shook his head. "Unfortunately, no. I don't have it in my possession, nor have I ever."

Liz wasn't sure she believed him.

He slapped his palm on top of the table and she jumped at the loud thud, certain he had read her mind.

"Doug was no fool and he wasn't delusional! As his wife, how could you think such a thing? He is... or was, as sane as you or I. He had to believe it was the genuine article or he would have never told me so."

"How do you really know, Henry? Why are you so sure?"

Henry's eyes narrowed. "Because I've seen the entire video."

"The video. That damned video!" Liz motioned to Nick. "The video proves nothing, Henry. Until someone has studied the *Halo*—someone with credentials—until then, no one can be certain of anything!"

"If you watch the video, you'll be convinced of its authenticity, just as I am."

She had no desire to watch the rest of the video. It had been painful to watch her husband acting so irrationally, and she certainly didn't want Nick subjected to it again.

"You believe because that's what you want to believe, Henry. Or because it is beneficial to you."

She'd had enough. She was suddenly very tired and just wanted to go home.

"Okay, your ten minutes are up. I've listened to you, but you still haven't convinced me of anything. For all I know, you talked Doug into being a part of some kind of crazy publicity stunt, and then he got caught in the earthquake. And now the video has conveniently resurfaced."

She nudged Nick toward the staircase. Without glancing back at Henry, she said, "Why let a good conspiracy go to waste? Even ten years later."

* * *

The drive home was quiet. Nick dared not say a word for fear his mother would fly into a rage. He was surprised she had been so calm. In fact, it kinda scared him, but at least he had his answer: Henry hadn't leaked the video. He had no real reason to believe Henry. But he did.

His mother parked the car in the garage. Before she had time to take the keys out of the ignition, Nick hopped out and was already at the back door. It wasn't until he was standing inside the kitchen that he realized the door hadn't been locked.

His mother never left the house without locking up.

It took another few seconds before he realized the kitchen had been ransacked.

"Nick, could you please move?" He stood blocking the doorway.

"Mom. I think—" But he never got a chance to finish.

"My god! What happened?" His mother pushed past him and stood for a moment assessing the scene in front of her. Then she began to grab the scattered contents of the room and put them back in place, as if doing triage in the emergency room.

Then, she stopped. "Emily!" she cried out.

CHAPTER 6

I n their shock and confusion, they had forgotten about Emily, and now Liz ran through the hallway and raced up the stairs to Emily's room, not stopping to consider that the burglars might still be inside the house. Nick heard her footsteps pound down the hallway and the door smack against the wall as she flung it open.

"Emily!" Liz let out a wail.

His mother screaming Emily's name would make no difference, Nick already knew she was not in the house. He was looking at the screen of the computer, oddly untouched in the disheveled room, sitting atop the desk—the catch-all of their lives, where his mom kept the bills and expired coupons, where the drawer held the all-in-one handy home tool, the lonely stamp and random paper clips, a ruler, a pair of scissors—all the ordinary things of life that seemed so foreign now and that lay scattered across the room. The internet was opened to the page containing the video of his father, his grimacing face frozen on the screen. The glowing crown was wrapped around his forehead. Next to the video was a digital sticky-note electronically pinned to the desktop.

DON'T CALL US

WE'LL CALL YOU

YOUR DAUGHTER FOR THE ARTIFACT

DON'T CALL THE POLICE!

"Mom!" Nick ran to the bottom of the steps. "She's not here. She's gone. Come downstairs."

"Emily! Emily!" His mom ran from room to room. Nick knew she'd heard him, but she wasn't ready to accept the obvious.

His mother came to the railing. "Where is she?" As if Nick knew the answer to that. He could feel his heart squeeze in his chest, and he couldn't seem to get enough air in his lungs.

"Come downstairs and look at this. They left a note."

"They! They again! Who the hell are they?" She came almost tumbling down the steps and they both ran back to the kitchen.

Nick pointed to the screen.

Liz collapsed into heap on the floor and then she lifted her head and screamed, "Damn Henry to Hell! Look what he has gotten us into now!"

"Henry? What about the NSA? They said they were going to protect us. So where are they now? I thought they were keeping an eye out for us!"

Nick thought about the operative sitting in his car. Was he still there? Nick hadn't noticed.

"Everyone is just out for themselves. I never thought they were really concerned about us in the first place. They're just using us for their own purposes. Like everyone else." Liz shook her head. "Henry. The NSA. I don't know who to blame."

"The NSA practically said they were using us as bait! At least Henry was trying to warn us."

"The NSA might be using us, and Henry might have tried to warn us, but he's the one who got us into this in the first place."

Nick rubbed his eyes with the back of his palms.

"Mom, please, none of that matters right now. What are we going to do to get Emily back?"

"The note says they'll call us." Liz turned her palms up. "I... I'm not really sure. I don't know what else to do but wait for them to contact us."

He watched her twist her hands together and the creases deepen in her forehead.

It was true, that's what usually happened in the movies. The loved ones of the victim waited patiently for a phone call about what to do next. But Nick didn't feel like waiting.

"We could call Agent Vagnetti."

Even if they hadn't done their job, maybe the NSA was their best bet under the circumstances.

"They said no police."

"I know but..."

Nick watched his mother stare into the nothingness before her. She sat quietly for what seemed like a long time. Then she pulled herself up. He noticed her hands shaking as she reached for the chair. She pulled it out and sat down to study the screen, as if just staring at it would somehow give her answers.

"If she's hurt..."

"Don't even think about it."

"Emily in exchange for the crown. That should be easy enough. I know Henry has it."

She brushed a tear from her cheek as she pushed up from the chair.

"Let's go. We're going back to Henry's."

* * *

But when they got there, he was gone.

The back door was unlocked, just like their door had been. Liz tentatively pushed it open.

"Henry?"

There was no answer. She blindly reached her hand out behind her and took hold of Nick's arm. The security light faintly illuminated the vast room. The Antiquarian looked much the same way as they had left it only a little over an hour ago—everything in disarray.

Liz turned to look at Nick and she could see the fear in his eyes. In silent communication, they moved toward the back stairwell leading up to Henry's apartment. Liz led the way as they walked up the creaky stairs. It took a moment for her eyes to adjust to the light after Liz opened the door.

She let out a gasp. "Nick, look!"

She pointed toward the radiator. Isis' body was spread out in an awkward pose; the antique Aubusson carpet beneath her head was stained red.

"Isis!" Nick ran over to the dead cat but didn't touch her.

Liz had been clenching her teeth so hard that now her jaw ached. She wanted to grab Nick and run, but she knew they had to check the rest of the apartment.

Henry was not there. They found his wallet on top of the desk that acted as a divider between the living room area and the kitchen. His pills that helped control his agoraphobia were still on his nightstand next to his bed, and they both knew he would not have willingly left without them.

"Do you think the same people who took Emily took Henry too?"

Liz felt bile rise in the back of her throat and she swallowed to keep it down. "I don't know. But I don't think Henry left on his own accord. And we both know he didn't go out for a late night stroll."

"If they were going to kidnap him, why didn't they do it the first time they broke in?"

"You interrupted them, remember?" She stared blankly for a moment. "And maybe it wasn't the same person. Or persons."

Liz's chest felt like a Mac truck was sitting on it. *Oh, Emily*, she thought, *I'm so sorry. We'll get you out of this.*

"Come on, Nick. Let's get back home. Maybe they're trying to contact us."

They again. Now even she was starting to say it.

"What about the cat?" Nick said.

Liz wrapped the cat in a large towel. She was accustomed to blood and to death and she performed the task in a clinical fashion, but inside she was trembling.

* * *

They drove back to the house in a panic and then up-righted the chairs and sat at the kitchen table surveying the disarray all around them. His mom's mascara had smudged. She looked as if she'd aged five years in the last few hours, and Nick felt a sharp cramp in his gut. They had left Isis' body outside where it was cold. Liz laid the sad bundle on a shelf in the garage. They would give her a proper burial later.

"Police or no police, when the kidnappers find out we don't have the crown, they're not going to be happy. We don't have a choice. I think you're right Nick, I'm going to call Agent Vagnetti."

The agent had given Liz a business card before leaving. Feel free to call at anytime, she had said. *Well, now's the time,* thought Liz.

Nick's head snapped around. "I don't know, Mom. I've been thinking. Henry said the Government might be in on it. Maybe it isn't such a good idea after all."

Normally she would have laughed at Henry's paranoia but, after tonight, she wasn't sure of anything anymore.

"No matter what I said before, Agent Vagnetti did say they were trying to protect us. Maybe they can help. And, besides, they might have a good idea who's behind this and…and I really don't know what else to do. With Henry missing we have no hope of finding that damned crown and without it Emily is…" She couldn't bring herself to complete the sentence.

Liz jumped to her feet. "I left the card on the desk. It could be anywhere now."

It seemed as if the entire contents of the kitchen were on the floor. Papers and cookbooks and phone directories that were once neatly stored in the desk were strewn everywhere.

They sifted frantically through the mess. Nick could sense his mother's increased irritation when they didn't find it right away; and he could feel his own frustration nearing a breaking point when he spotted something.

"Found it!" he cried out, and held up Agent Vagnetti's business card.

CHAPTER 7

Henry tensed as he watched shadows move across the light seeping through the bottom edge of the door. Someone was coming. *Better to be alone in the room*, he thought. He had experienced a major panic attack when they first shoved him onto the floor and locked the door behind them. At least they hadn't tied him up. He sat on a mattress on the bare floor. There were no windows, only one door, so they probably felt there was little chance for him to escape.

And they were right.

When first locked in the room, his heart pounded unmercifully for only a few minutes before it finally settled into a more normal rhythm. Henry had been told by many a medical professional that if he let the panic have its full rein—if he didn't fight it—it would subside on its own. He had never had the courage to try, but even though his heart had stopped galloping, he still felt waves of panic and dizziness every now and again. *If only I had been able to grab my medication...but they were so quick!* One minute he was standing at his kitchen sink, the next he had a cloth over his head and was being dragged out of the shop into a car waiting in the alley.

Now, he heard the faint click of the lock and watched the door to his cell open. His pupils had dilated in the dark room and he could only see a silhouette in the bright background of the open doorway. The door snapped closed behind whoever had entered and Henry stood and blinked, still blinded by the sudden light.

"Mr. Applegate."

He detected an Asian accent.

"Who are you? What do you want of me?" Although Henry already knew the answer to the last question.

As if reading his mind, the Asian said, "You know what we want."

"Perhaps you should tell me anyway, so there isn't any confusion."

Henry surprised himself with his bravado. He had never thought of himself as being particularly courageous. In fact, his agoraphobia left him feeling cowardly and impotent much of the time, but now that he was faced with a real and tangible danger, his fear dissipated. It was as if he'd been training all his life and now his body and mind were in peak condition to handle the situation. The thought intrigued him.

"The object, Mr. Applegate. Where is it?"

Henry would have liked to continue to ponder his new-found courage, but the Asian standing before him couldn't be ignored. There was no use pretending he didn't know anything about the Halo. The video was all over the inter-net, so he simply said, "I have no idea."

The man—the disembodied voice certainly sounded like a man's—shifted his weight.

"Please, Henry, we both know that isn't true."

"What makes you think I have it?"

"We have our sources."

The man was definitely Asian. Had one of his contacts in China betrayed him?

"Well, your sources must be wrong. They've led you on a wild goose chase, I'm afraid. The Halo is still buried beneath tons of rubble in the Himalayas. There is really little hope of ever finding it."

"Halo?" The man nodded as if agreeing with Henry's assessment of the object. Then he said, "Mr. Farraday's body was found."

Henry stiffened. "Yes, it was. By pure luck."

"Yet, it happened."

Henry's hands went suddenly clammy and he felt as if the floor was shifting underneath him. It seemed his new-found courage was fleeting.

"I'm not well." Henry changed the subject. "I need my medication."

Any kidnapper worth his salt would have done some research on their victim, Henry thought. *What good is a dead hostage?*

* * *

The NSA agents had set up a command post in the living room.

"What if they're watching the house?" Liz asked. "What if they know you're here? They said not to call the police."

Agent Nelson grinned. "They always say not to call the police." He shrugged. "We were careful not to be seen. Our equipment truck is parked down the street. We just have to take our chances."

The agent was dressed in blue jeans and a golf shirt. Camouflage for an NSA agent, Liz supposed. The casual outfit made him look even more handsome, if that were possible, than at their first meeting. Even though Liz was frantic about her daughter's safety, the thought involuntarily flicked though her mind.

They—Agent Vagnetti, Nelson, and another agent Liz had never seen before—had sneaked in the night before. Even though Liz didn't have a landline phone, they said they could monitor the situation better from the house than from a remote location. Another group of agents were stationed at The Antiquarian. There was no one there for the kidnappers to contact, but they might try to come back to have another search. Neither Liz nor Nick knew of any close relatives of Henry's. As far as they knew, Henry was the last of the Applegates, so there was no one except them to worry about him going missing.

Whoever kidnapped Henry must not have done it for a ransom. Agent Vagnetti —*please call me Ronnie*—had assured Liz their office was doing everything it could to find out who might have taken Henry and Emily. They were going over the video from the security cameras placed around Mount Avon Cemetery in hopes they might see some activity in the neighborhood that would help with their search.

"So you have an idea who might have done this?" Liz asked.

"We have our suspicions. As we said, there are a number of people interested in getting their hands on the object."

At least it was something to go on, no matter how small. Liz felt the gentle pressure of Agent Nelson's hand on her shoulder. "We're following every possible lead, Mrs. Farraday. We want to see Emily come home as much as you do."

Rummaging through her nightstand drawer the night before, Liz had found a bottle of sleeping pills she hadn't needed in a long time and popped one in her mouth. She hated the idea of it, but she couldn't stop shaking and knew she needed her rest in order to cope. She offered Nick a tablet. At first, he refused, until she insisted. He brought his sleeping bag into her room and laid it on the floor next to her bed. Neither of them wanted to be alone. The agents had taken turns napping on the couch or slumped in the comfortable overstuffed reading chair by the bay window in the living room.

The other agent, Brian Conner, had hooked up a laptop to the computer in the kitchen in case the kidnappers tried to contact them through email. They all agreed this was a likely possibility, even though the note said they would call.

The coffee brewer had not been damaged and Liz was able to make a strong pot the next morning. They all sat in the living room now, drinking their coffee and eating what was left of an almond coffee cake.

Liz jabbed a piece of the pastry with her fork but could only look at it. Her stomach was a tight, twisted knot. The fork dropped with a clatter onto her plate.

"What now?" she asked.

"We wait."

* * *

Emily had never been so scared in her life. *What was going on?* Thankfully, they had taken the duct tape off her mouth before they dumped her into the trunk of the car. She had gagged and almost choked to death on her own bile before they ripped the tape from her mouth. Then she felt the cold metal of a gun at her temple as one of them warned her not to make a sound or else they would tape her up again. The thought terrified her, even though she knew they could do much worse.

No, she would not scream.

The bile matted her hair, and now the stink of it woke her from her fitful sleep. For a moment she didn't remember where she was, but when the memory slowly seeped back into her brain, she shot upright, her heart pounding.

The room was sterile and small. It didn't have any windows, with no way to tell day from night. A twin-size box spring and mattress was pushed up against the sidewall, and a portable children's toilet sat in the opposite corner. She looked at the ceiling. There was one long florescent light fixture hanging from the center. Her first thought was that she was being watched, that there must be a camera hiding somewhere in the room. Well, if they thought she would go to the bathroom with them watching, they could think again. No way. But she was already feeling like she had to pee and she didn't know how long she could hold out. She shoved her hands between her knees.

From what she could tell, there were four of them, three men and a woman. Asian. Not Japanese, she was fairly certain. From underneath the door, she could hear country music playing. *Must be the woman.* The thought gave Emily a small amount of comfort. Emily remembered hearing her humming a country song when she brought her food the night before. She never saw the woman's face. They wore black knit masks whenever they came into the room.

She had overheard them talking in a mixture of their own language and English, and knew this was all about the video. About the crown in the video, or whatever it was. She didn't think they had planned to kidnap her; she just happened to be in the wrong place at the wrong time. She was standing at the top of the stairs listening to music on her MP3 player when she first saw them. The man had just pulled his mask up over his mouth.

"I can't breathe under this thing," he said.

They were startled to find her standing there, and the man quickly pulled his mask down. They thought the house was empty, she realized. And for some reason, that made Emily even more frightened.

CHAPTER 8

Nick watched the postal carrier stride effortlessly up the stairs and slip a bundle of envelopes in the mailbox attached to the wall next to the front door. Even the most familiar of events seemed odd to him now. Everything was colored in a different light. He wanted his sister back. He wanted Emily safe and sound up in her room texting or updating her status on Facebook or posting brainless comments on Twitter.

He wanted things back to normal.

His mother was too preoccupied to notice that the mail had arrived, so Nick opened the door and reached around to pluck the bundle of letters and advertisement flyers from the box. He let the screen slam shut behind him as he nudged the front door closed with his foot and robotically flipped through the stack. The last envelope was a different shape than the others, not your typical business-letter size, and was addressed to him. *Another sympathy card*, he thought. The funeral seemed such a long time ago, he had almost forgotten about it. He tossed the rest of the letters in the wooden bowl on the foyer table and went up to his room with the card in hand.

He flopped on his bed, stared blankly at the envelope, and then set it aside. He had gotten angry with Henry all over again when they first discovered Emily was missing, but when he realized that Henry had been kidnapped too, he softened again. It wasn't Henry's fault that people were after the Halo. He hadn't leaked the video. There was really no one to blame. Nick ran his arm across his face, wiping away tears that seemed to appear out of nowhere. He took in a big gasp of air in an effort to stop crying, something he hadn't allowed himself to do in front of anyone. The envelope was still on the bed next to him and he rubbed his fingers over the surface as a distraction. He picked it up. At least it was something to keep his mind off things for a few seconds. He pushed his finger behind the loose end of the flap and ripped open the edge.

The initials HA were overlapped on the front of a beige card in gold leaf. Henry's stationary. Nick had seen it on his desk many times. Henry must have sent him a sympathy note right before he went missing. He flipped opened the thick folded paper. Taped to one side was a micro-flash memory card with the words "Song of God" printed neatly underneath and, on the other side, a small flat key. Nothing else was written on the card. No signature. No note, as he had expected. He picked up the envelope. There was no mark over the stamp. It hadn't gone through the post office. His heart picked up a beat as he stared at the strangeness of the envelope and the card, then he jumped off the bed, bounded down the stairs, and ran into the kitchen.

"Hey," Agent Conner greeted Nick as he came around the corner.

"Hi. Could you excuse me for a minute? I need to get something out of the drawer."

The three agents had helped them put the kitchen back together the night before, after they had dusted for finger-prints. While they helped, the agents looked for evidence, anything that might help track the criminals down. In the end, they hadn't found anything. His mom had slowly put the rest of the house back together that morning, along with the help of at least one of the agents at all times, in case they'd missed something earlier.

Agent Brian was studying the agency's laptop that was connected to their home computer, but he leaned aside so Nick could get access to the drawer. Nick rummaged through it until his hand felt what he was searching for.

"Thanks, man," he said to the young agent, but didn't wait for an answer. He bounded back up the stairs with a USB card reader in hand.

* * *

The first interrogation by his captors had been brief. Henry had no idea what their strategy might be, having never been involved in a kidnapping before. His only knowledge of the subject was gained from the occasional thriller he watched on TV. Maybe they were going to do the good cop/bad cop routine. He'd certainly seen that approach many times before. The black-clad Asian assured him they would get him some kind of medication for his nerves.

"Do you have any other life-threatening conditions we should know about?"

"I would say just being here might be one."

"I'll take that as a *no*." The man turned to leave the room.

"Wait! You might get me some clean bandages for this cut." He touched the bandage over his eye. "Perhaps a butterfly bandage, if you could manage that?" Since the man had probably been the one to inflict the wound in the first place, Henry thought it was the least he could do.

Henry's panic had diminished again. Having faced imaginary threats for so long, the real thing didn't seem quite so terrifying. *The unknown is always more frightening than the known*, he thought. But, still, he was glad they were getting him something for his unfortunate condition. He would only take it if absolutely necessary. He needed to stay on his toes.

Keeping his mind preoccupied always helped. It kept at bay all those horrible "what-ifs" that kept popping into his head. If he thought about something that was interesting enough, nothing else could penetrate. While waiting for his captors to return—as much as he dreaded that thought—he decided to contemplate crowns and halos in an effort to keep his imagination in check. He settled himself on the mattress, propping up the pitiful pillow his captors had given him, and leaned back against the wall for support.

The first thing that occurred to him was that, just as the world's religious myths had been very similar over a geographically widespread area, so had been the use of crowns to symbolize royalty—someone with power over ordinary man. A power purportedly granted by God. The Egyptians, Celts, Romans, and the dynasties of China all used the crown as a symbol of power.

He knew the experts would say this was logical—the widespread use of crowns as a symbol of power and authority. In much the same way they explained how the practice of pyramid building had begun at relatively the same time in history across the far reaches of the globe. From an engineering standpoint, it was the simplest and most logical way for the ancients to build upward. Our ancestors had been fascinated with the night sky and the heavens; it was logical that they would want to try and touch the sky with their buildings and monuments. The fact that different societies just happened to start this practice at approximately the same time in history never struck the experts as odd or difficult to reconcile.

He also knew what the argument would be regarding imperial crowns. An object placed on the head was easy to see above the masses. It was the most obvious way to distinguish a "royal" from the average citizen.

The practice of wearing a royal headdress was still being observed to this day. Henry recalled watching a documentary of the televised 1953 coronation of Queen Elizabeth II in Westminster Abbey.

...And as Solomon was anointed king
by Zadok the priest and Nathan the prophet,
so be thou anointed, blessed, and consecrated Queen
over the Peoples, whom the Lord thy God
hath given thee to rule and govern...

Another thought occurred to him. Even Jesus had been given a crown, albeit a symbolic one—*The Crown of Thorns*. It was all very intriguing.

Still pondering Jesus' symbolic crown, another idea popped into his head. He pushed himself away from the cold wall of his prison and stood up in his excitement.

All forms of art depicted Jesus and the saints, and often royalty, with halos surrounding their heads. A halo was a symbol of divinity, of being *all-knowing*. Had our ancestors witnessed something they could not understand and, in their limited knowledge, misinterpreted it? It wouldn't have been the first time.

Perhaps Doug's discovery would shed light on some of the things that Henry found to be so paradoxical in the history of man's development. Just as Galileo's studies—that helped prove Earth was not flat—had changed mankind's view of the world around him, the Halo might change mankind's view of its place in the universe.

* * *

Nick pushed the micro card into the matching size reader slot and plugged the USB connection into his laptop. A window popped up asking for a password.

"Great," he groaned.

Why would Henry use as a password? He grabbed Henry's stationary and studied it again. "Song of God" was the only thing written on it, so he tried that as a password, with and without spaces.

Nothing.

He tried Henry's name and initials with no luck either. Nick slammed his fist on top of the desk. It had to be "Song of God!" He tried all lower case, all caps and just the way Henry had written it, with capital S and G.

Still no luck.

The phrase was familiar. Where had he heard it? At school? He tried to remember. Then he googled it: *God songs…a blog about scriptures…The Song of Solomon.*

Then he typed the phrase into the search engine surrounded by quotes.

Bam! There it was: *Bhagavad Gita.*

Of course! He and Henry had discussed this piece of literature a few times. Nick wished he remembered more about the story, but he did remember that it was, basically, the conversation between a Hindu lord and a prince, taking place on the battlefield before the start of a war.

* * *

"We have something to show you, Mr. Applegate."

Henry was disappointed the kidnappers had interrupted his train of thought. He felt he was on the brink of a profound insight when he heard the door creak open once again. At first he thought they were delivering his medication, but he was wrong. He had been wondering why they weren't putting more pressure on him to talk. To tell them where the Halo was hidden. Now he understood why. They had other methods.

The Asian held his cell phone up so Henry could see the screen. In front of him was Doug's daughter, sitting scared and alone in a room that looked similar to his own. His heart sank.

The two others stood in back of their leader. Black knit masks covered their faces, with only slits for their eyes and mouths. The boss was smoking a long thin cigarette and took a slow drag. The Asian held the cigarette up to Henry's face. He could feel the heat from the glowing orange-red end and could smell the acrid smoke that curled up toward the ceiling.

"It would be a shame to mar her beautiful skin." The Asian turned his black eyes back to Henry. "Now. Please tell us where your Halo is."

CHAPTER 9

Nick typed the password: *bhagavadgita.*

He clicked on the only file listed on the screen. It was a video of Henry. He was sitting at his desk, wearing his familiar brown button-down cardigan sweater, his salt and pepper hair in disarray and his glasses pulled down on his nose. He had a worried, faraway look in his eyes.

"Nicholas, if you are watching this, it means..." He looked down at the desk, "it means I'm either dead or in trouble. It also means my password-protection worked and that you were clever enough to figure it out."

"Someone hacked into my computer. I can't be too careful, so I've studied how to add a password to this video card. Thank God for the internet."

So, the old guy was better with computer stuff than Nick thought.

"Hopefully, it will work. I couldn't risk sending it without some obstacle—no matter how small—should the envelope fall into the wrong hands. If the hackers come back, I don't think it will be so easy for them this time. In any case, I won't make the same mistake twice. This video will never be loaded on my computer. I hope these precautions will be enough."

Henry moved his head and now seemed to be staring straight into Nick's eyes.

"Forgive me for involving you, but you are the only person I can trust. I will give Kurt, my driver, an envelope with this video and a key inside, and instructed him to mail it to you should I go missing."

Nick continued to listen as Henry proceeded to tell him things he already knew. That the video posted on the internet was only a small snippet of the original, and about the conspiracy theories they had all discussed while his mother was bandaging Henry's cut. It seemed so long ago that they were all sitting in his kitchen above The Antiquarian.

Then Henry said something that made Nick's heart thud.

"I have something else to tell you. Something that might disturb you. I hope you won't think less of me after you hear it. Hopefully, you will understand why I had to do it."

It was as if Henry was in the room with him, their eyes locked.

"The urn I sent back from China does not contain your father's remains."

Nick sucked in air. *What?* He stared at the video, not seeing or hearing anything as he tried to process this information. After a few seconds, he hit the pause button and rewound the video until he heard Henry repeat: *The urn I sent back from China does not contain your father's remains.*

Then whose body is in it? he thought.

In answer to his silent question, Henry continued, "They never found your father, only his backpack and some plastic storage bins. The urn contains sand. Chinese sand, but sand nonetheless." He paused. "And one other thing."

Henry leaned back in his chair.

"It also contains the Halo. It is inside a lead-lined film guard bag secured to the bottom of the urn. I took this precaution for both security reasons and as a small measure of protection against possible radiation damage when it went through airport security. The urn itself is also covered in lead-based paint, as are many crematory urns. Once airport security sees the X-ray image is opaque, it will require the urn to be shipped in the belly of the plane, where it will go through inspection for explosive devices before it is allowed on board. As further precaution, I had it shipped from China by an airfreight carrier rather than a commercial flight.

"I thought of other ways, but this seemed the best method to get the Halo safely back to the States—to keep it from getting into the wrong hands. Still, it was risky. My contacts went through all the procedures and paperwork very carefully."

Henry exhaled a half-hearted laugh that ended up sounding more like a derisive snort. "Of course they thought they were shipping back cremated remains. Only one man knows even the partial truth, but I trust him with my life."

As Henry talked about the details, Nick was barely listening. He didn't know how to feel. The urn didn't contain his father's remains? What would his mother say? But he didn't have time to think about her reaction right now. He returned his attention back to what Henry was saying.

"What I am going to ask you ..." Henry took a deep breath. "What I am about to ask is too much, I know, Nicholas. But you are the only one."

What Henry had asked Nicholas to do was too much. He wasn't sure he could do it. Nick was to take the Halo to SETI—the scientific institute dedicated to finding evidence of intelligent life in the universe. Henry didn't trust the Government. They would do everything they could to suppress the discovery. If they were to get their hands on the artifact, Henry insisted, the Halo would never be seen or heard about again. Henry was convinced that SETI was their only hope.

Nick was a registered member of SETI@home, a project that utilized the personal computer resources of its members to search for possible radio signals from ET. He was a big fan and knew all about the institute and its work. Until recently, the U.S. Government funded the Search for Extraterrestrial Institute. Now it depended solely on private donations. In years past, the institute's main focus had been searching for radio signals from space, but the institute had expanded to look for signs of other types of technologies as well. Radio signals were not the only signs that might indicate the presences of intelligent life.

"You must get the Halo to Jane Carter, the director of the SETI Institute. It is the only way to learn the truth. I'm certain of it. Revealing the discovery to the world is the only way to render it worthless to those that would use it for evil. As I said, if it should get into the hands of the Government, or any government, it will disappear, and your father will continue to be thought of as a lunatic."

Henry paused and looked intently into the camera lens.

"I don't want you to go through life thinking less of your father. I loved him like a son. I want you to remember him as the great man he was. He deserves the credit for this great discovery, not to be remembered as a man who lost his mind near the end of his life."

Nick paused the video and, for the second time that day, ran his arm over his face to wipe away tears. He couldn't help it, and he was glad no one was there to see him. When he finally restarted the video, Henry was continuing his argument. He kept on with it, as if afraid he had yet to convince Nick.

It was apparent to Nick that Henry was certain the Halo's "special abilities" were extraterrestrial in origin and that was the reason for his passion about protecting it. If Nick believed it too, then he couldn't argue with Henry's concerns. But how did Henry expect him—a fifteen year-old boy—to pull something like that off? He didn't even have his driver's permit yet! And what if, despite Henry's conviction, it turned out to be nothing? What if the object was just an ordinary crown and his own mother's suspicions that his father had suffered a breakdown were true?

Part of him didn't want to know the answer. As long as there was still a possibility the Halo was authentic, then Nick's image of his father didn't have to change. He could still be proud of him, even if the public's opinion was something less. On the flip side, if the discovery were proven to be a fake, a hoax, then both the public and Nick's image would be shattered, with no hope of repair.

In the end, no matter what the truth turned out to be, Nick decided he would rather know than always wonder. And, as Henry said, if his father was responsible for the greatest discovery of all time, then he did deserve to get the credit for it. He deserved better than people thinking he was just some UFO conspiracy-theory nut-job like the kids at school had called him.

Henry went on to explain to Nick that the key taped to the note would open a mailbox at a shipping store a few blocks from Nick's house. Nick was to go there, pick up an envelope that contained a prepaid credit card, a cell phone, and a significant amount of cash.

Then Nick listened to Henry's final words; and, for a moment, he felt as if the ground beneath him had given way.

You will find my driver's business card in the mailbox with the rest of the items. I've instructed him to drive you anywhere you wish to go. I trust him, but don't tell him about the Halo. Be cautious, Nicholas. Trust no one. Confide in no one. Go to the mailbox, then to the cemetery and retrieve the Halo. Then book a flight to Mountain View, California and find Jane Carter. I have faith in you, Nicholas, just like I had faith in your father.

* * *

It didn't take Nick long to walk to the shipping store and find the mailbox. After he shoved the contents into his backpack, he headed for the cemetery. There was only a hint of light left in the sky as he skirted the perimeter, working his way to the southeast corner where he knew there was a large parking lot next to an apartment complex. Entering the cemetery from the main gate, or from across the street from his house with the NSA agents still there, was too risky. Before his sister had been kidnapped, he had never thought about the security cameras overhead, but now he glanced up, hoping he was staying out of their range.

Everything was happening so fast, it was like a dream. Ever since the video had been posted, Nick had been confused, depressed, and angry all at the same time. He hated the idea of his father being laughed at and ridiculed, and he hated the idea that his dad might have been having an affair. It made him sad and angry that his mother could so readily believe that her own husband—and *his* father—had gone mad; but after hearing what Emily revealed to him about their mother's suspicions, Nick understood his mother a little better. Her hatred of Henry blinded her to any other possibility, but Nick was going to hold off final judgment until he had proof. It was practically all he thought about since first seeing the video of his father on the internet, and now he was even more determined after hearing what Henry had to say. Other than rescuing Emily, nothing else mattered to him at the moment.

Getting the urn out of the crematorium would be easy enough. The niche covering the tiny alcove where the urn rested wasn't sealed yet. The covering was only temporary. He had overheard his mother talking to the caretaker about the arrangements to have his father's ashes interred in the family crematorium. He knew it would take several weeks for the permanent covering to come back from the engravers.

It was the rest of his mission that worried him.

CHAPTER 10

It was dark. Whatever meager moonlight might have helped guide him was obscured by the heavy clouds overhead. *Probably better*, Nick thought. The wrought iron fence was low on three sides, only tall at the front entrance, so he would have no trouble hopping over.

He scanned the area. It was too late for after-dinner walkers and too early for college kids heading home from a night out on Main Street. A lone car moved slowly down Wilcox. Nick waited until he saw the taillights turn the corner onto First Street before he grabbed the cold metal railing of the low fence with both hands and swung his body over. It wasn't the first time he had done it. He and his friends used to have séances in the graveyard on Devil's Night, the night before Halloween. They'd grown out of it, but Nick thought of it now as he weaved his way through the headstones and mausoleums. Such innocent fun, he wondered if he would ever feel that way again.

The Farraday columbarium was slightly offset from the middle of the cemetery, sitting closer to Third Street and surrounded by large oak trees. The brittle brown leaves that would cling to the oaks until next spring rustled in a slight breeze and he shivered. Nick could see the corner of the low-slung white marble structure in the distance and quickened his pace.

FARRADAY was arced in large lettering across the top. Nick stood in front of it; now realizing his father's body was not resting there. He was still lost somewhere high in the Himalayan Mountains. It had been nice to think his dad was nearby. Now that comforting feeling was gone, but he wouldn't allow himself to think about it right now. He didn't have time.

His father's memorial niche was near the bottom right. Nick's chest felt tight. He could only take half-breaths. The temporary cover was flush against the front of the crypt, with only a tiny groove to outline it. He curled his fingers and tried to pull the cover off, but it wouldn't budge. All he managed was to scrape and tear at his fingernails. The narrow gap just wouldn't allow for a secure grip. He stood back and studied the cover. Then an idea came to him. Pushing hard against one edge of the plate, the opposite edge moved out slightly, like a door hinged at the center point. Nick let out a sigh of relief. He continued to push on one edge until the other edge swung out enough for him to get a good grip. He wiggled it out of the tight spot and then hugged the heavy block to his chest as he carried it over to the soft grass on the side of the paved area in front of the crypt. Keeping the block close to his body, he bent his knees until he could carefully place it on the grass.

He turned back to the niche. No light penetrated into the deep recess and it took a few seconds for his eyes to adjust. He knew his father's remains were not inside the urn that sat inside, but what he was about to do still felt wrong. He leaned closer, squinted into the dark hole, and then reached in tentatively with both hands. The surface of the urn felt cool and smooth to the touch. When he pulled it out, it was heavier than he imagined. There was a slight tremor in his arms as he carefully sat it down on the hard surface in front of the crypt. It crunched against the concrete apron.

Nick remembered the urn from the memorial service, but he hadn't really studied it until now. It was shaped in a low, wide V with a carved dragon sitting on the gently rounded lid. The finish was finely crackled and light green in color.

Henry might have been convinced that the Halo was genuine, but, before Nick took off on some wild goose chase across the country and risked his sister's life, he needed more than just Henry's assumptions to motivate him.

Nick had to wear the crown.

He put his right hand over the dragon and tried to screw the lid off. It wouldn't budge. He palms were sweaty, despite the cold, so he slid them down his pants and tried again. Still no luck. It just wouldn't budge.

He tried again and again, until he felt a bead of sweat moved down his temple.

Shifting his weight back and forth on his feet, Nick stared at the stubborn urn. His whole body seemed to vibrate. His breathing was shallow and his heart was starting to thud in his chest. He realized what he had to do, but he couldn't shake the uneasy feeling that had taken hold of him. *This urn does not contain my father's remains*, he reassured himself.

The grounds surrounding the crematorium were pristine, with only a stray leaf or two from nearby maples, or nuts that had fallen from the oaks. Nothing he could use to smash the urn. There was only one way. He picked up the heavy container and held it waist high. *This is not my father*, he repeated.

Then he let go.

The echo ricocheted through the nearby headstones. The noise was louder than he thought it would be and it made him jump. His head jerked toward his house. He peered through the tangle of trees and markers and was relieved when he saw only lights in the windows but no movement, nothing to suggest that anyone had heard the dull thud and the sharp ping as the metal dragon bounced on the hard surface. His heart was hammering in his chest now. There was no turning back.

The tip of the film guard bag was sticking out of the mound of sand and broken pottery. Even though Henry told him it would be there, he was still taken aback by the sight. He pulled the bag from the pile and opened it. The Halo felt thinner, less substantial, than he had imagined. It was not a complete circle, but open on one end, like a flexible headband. It was slightly iridescent on the outside surface, but there were lines of gold crisscrossing the inside in a way that vaguely reminded Nick of a computer circuit board. It was cold to the touch. It felt odd to be holding it, and he traced the edges with his finger.

Nick had come to the cemetery not sure what he would do once he found what he was looking for. If he followed Henry's instructions, he knew he might be putting both his sister's and Henry's lives in jeopardy. Up to this point, he had been driven—not by what Henry had told him he must do, because when Henry had made his video for Nick, he didn't know Emily would be involved—but by the notion that he might save both his sister and Henry from the kidnappers; and, in addition, that he might learn the truth about his father's mental state right before his death.

No matter what happened, he still wasn't sure what he would do next, but fake or real, once he handed the Halo over to Agent Vagnetti, she would be in control. Nick wasn't confident he could trust her to do whatever was necessary to save his sister and Henry.

In his confused state of mind, Nick took the crown and moved underneath the oak opposite the crematorium and leaned against the trunk. His hands were trembling as he lifted it to his head, his breathing shallow, and his chest so tight he thought his ribs might crack.

What had his father seen when he had placed it on his head?

Nick was about to find out. He spread the flexible band open and placed it around his temples, like he had seen it wrapped around his father's head in the video.

It took a few seconds before anything happened. At first, he felt a strange tingly sensation. Not unpleasant. Then Nick felt a little dizzy, but he didn't know if that was an effect from the Halo or his nerves.

* * *

If Nick's heart was drumming triple time before, it was now bursting with, not exactly joy, but awe. The shock of it pushed him back against the rough surface of the oak. What appeared before him was like a hologram, but more. It was as if he were there, right in the middle of it all. Weaving between galaxies and sun systems. Skimming the surface of other worlds. Wandering the continents on what must certainly be Earth. Unfolding an entire history in just a few seconds. The visions were astonishing, even if Nick couldn't fully comprehend all of them, but what he did understand explained a lot of things. Answered questions he would have never even thought to ask. No wonder his dad looked like a loon on the video. Nick let out a sound, not exactly a laugh and not a cheer. If he knew the word, he might say he was having an epiphany. But, for him, there were no words to explain it.

It was like being on the best amusement park ride, *ever*. Nick felt exhilarated. It took all his willpower not to shout with joy, to scream as if he were really on a roller coaster. But something out there, something outside the fantasy playing inside his head, was clamoring for his attention.

Someone was coming.

Reluctantly, he pulled the Halo from his head. It took a moment for him to come back to reality. It was like waking from a wonderful dream and he didn't want to let it go. Then he heard the voices again and the euphoria was gone in an instant, as if sucked away by some giant vacuum. He carefully placed the Halo back in the pouch and tossed it into his backpack. The remains of the broken urn were still lying where he had shattered it earlier. He pushed himself up and then pulled his backpack over his shoulder as he quickly moved toward the columbarium.

Working quickly, he threw the broken shards of the urn into the niche and wedged the heavy cover back into place, then kicked at the sand—what should have been the ashes of his father—off onto the grass. He managed to scrape most of it away, but some still remained. It couldn't be helped. Whoever it was, they were getting nearer.

Nick hardly had enough time to hide behind a nearby granite obelisk before he saw two men stop in front of the columbarium. They were both dressed in black. The bigger man spoke but Nick couldn't understand him. He was not speaking English, that was certain. Chinese? He couldn't tell. Why were they stopping in front of his family's monument?

The two men talked rapidly as they studied the structure. One of them pointed to the corner where his father's niche was situated, and they both bent down to look at it. The structure hid them from view, but when Nick saw the shorter man put the niche cover on the grass, just as he had done only a few minutes before, he knew they were after the Halo. How did they know to look there? Nick thought back to what Henry had told him in his video. Could Henry's contacts in China have betrayed him? No matter how careful Henry thought he had been, and no matter how much Henry trusted his contacts overseas, one of them could have somehow discovered what was really hidden in the urn and, once they understood the potential value, followed the urn to the United States. It wouldn't be too hard to figure out where it would end up. Were these men the kidnappers or some other group looking for the artifact?

The two men were almost shouting now. And Nick knew why. They were looking at the crumbled remains of the urn sitting inside the niche.

He needed to do something. Emily's kidnappers could be right in front of him. He thought for a moment, then swung his arm around to the backpack and pulled out his cell phone. The prepaid phone Henry had left for him in the mailbox was tucked deep in the recess of his backpack, along with the cash and, now, the Halo as well. Nick would have to ditch his own cell phone when—or if—he decided to take the flight to California, but now he pointed it at the two men and hit the video icon. If Henry ever had the chance, Nick wanted him to see the faces of the men who betrayed him. Or, if these men were the kidnappers, Nick might be able to get a good enough picture of them to help with identification.

The two men stopped shouting and the bigger man pulled his own cell phone out of his pocket. Nick watched as he punched in a number and waited for an answer. Then he heard the man speak the only word Nick could understand. *Applegate*.

Was Henry in on this? Scenarios flashed through Nick's brain as he tried to make sense of what he was witnessing. Who were these men? Had Henry asked someone to come and retrieve the Halo? Then why would Henry bother to send him the letter with the video and the instructions? Maybe Henry hadn't meant for Kurt to deliver the letter after all. Nick was confused. Then he heard the man speak in English.

"You lied to us, Henry."

CHAPTER 11

Henry didn't know how to feel—happy that Kurt had successfully delivered the envelope to Nicholas, and that the boy had somehow managed to decipher his clumsy code and get the Halo, or frightened at what would happen next. He had to think of something. And fast.

"I didn't lie to you," he said into the cell phone the woman had handed him.

Henry wished he could address his kidnappers in a more personal manner in order to develop a better rapport, but they were being very careful to conceal their identities. They had all been meticulous about hiding their face from him, yet this woman seemed familiar. Henry was sure he knew her from somewhere.

"I fulfilled my part of the deal," Henry continued. "You must release us." He was making a feeble attempt to appeal to the man's sense of honor. If he had one.

"I have to do no such thing. You must know who took the artifact. Only you knew where it was hidden."

Henry thought about Jian Lin. He had been helping support the Lin family for years. For the first time, a hint of suspicion was creeping into Henry's subconscious about his old friend. Until now, Henry thought he could trust Jian with his own life. When Henry had asked for his help with the artifact, he knew that Jian hadn't realized, nor cared, how potentially valuable the object might be. Jian only knew it was important to Henry that it was safely delivered to the United States, and that was good enough for his trusted ally.

Henry quickly removed the seed of doubt he had planted in his own brain. No, Jian Lin did not have the means or the desire to betray him, and so Henry remained silent.

"You know who those others are, and you will tell us, Mr. Applegate. You will tell us or the girl will die. And you will die. Slowly and painfully."

* * *

Even though he was frightened, Nick was still under the spell of the Halo. Yet his mother's words played back in his head, battling against what he had witnessed with the weapon of doubt they created. *If this is an elaborate hoax then it's a pretty amazing one,* he thought. Nick had never seen or heard of a technology capable of producing what he had just experienced—for it was an experience—but that didn't mean the technology didn't exist somewhere. He shook his head. No, it just couldn't be a hoax. It seemed from another world; it was far too advanced for this planet. But he would have to sort his doubts out later. He had a more immediate problem.

Nick didn't understand all of what he had seen but, intuitively, he knew that if it were true it would change the world forever. What would these men, these obviously unscrupulous men, do with the object, with such powerful knowledge?

He didn't have time to think about that either. He pushed all his other concerns aside and only thought of his sister and his friend. They were in danger. Now that he'd heard the men talking to Henry, his first instinct was to step out from behind the obelisk and hand the Halo over to them. It was obvious that Henry had offered up the location to his kidnappers, so maybe Nick should follow his lead.

He hit the stop record icon on his cell phone and tilted his body forward but then stopped.

They weren't wearing masks. Once they realized he had seen their faces, they would never let him go. They would kill all three of them. He shivered and glanced over his shoulder toward his house. Help was so very close. He pictured the agents who had invaded his home, hovering over their laptops or with their cell phones glued to their ears, oblivious to what was happening only a short distance away.

Nick stepped back into the protective shadow of the tall granite. He looked down at his cell phone, wondering if the video he'd just taken would ever be of any use.

Of course! He would send it to his mother's phone. She would have it by her side constantly in hopes of hearing from Emily's kidnappers. Nick tapped out a message as fast as his fingers would allow and attached the video, and then he sent it to his mother's account. The audio or video might not be very clear but, hopefully, Agent Conner could make some sense out of it. He glanced over at the house again, wondering what was going on inside, hoping Agent Conner was still sitting in front of the computer and would see the email instantly.

Should he shout and make a commotion? Maybe someone would hear him, but he couldn't take that chance.

His only hope was that the agents would understand his video and come to the cemetery as quickly as possible. Nick felt helpless to do anything but watch. If the men started to leave, he could follow them to their get-away vehicle. He couldn't imagine that they had taken an evening stroll to the graveyard. If he could get a license plate number, it would surely help the agents track them down if they got away. He hoped it wouldn't come to that.

The men made no move to leave. The bigger man paced in front of the structure, flailing his arms and talking in a low menacing tone to the other man. He stopped and stared at the barren niche. Even from a distance, Nick could see the anger etched across his face. Then suddenly the man in charge swung around and quickly walked away; the other man followed. Zigzagging from one monument to the other, Nick followed them out of the cemetery. Every few seconds, he glanced toward the house. There didn't seem to be any activity. Where were the agents? Why weren't they coming to help?

* * *

Liz could feel the hot breath of the three agents on her neck as they stood over her. She clicked the message.

I'm in the cemetery...need help...send agents!

Her stomach had flipped when she heard the familiar ping of an incoming message. Nick had been missing since this morning, and they still hadn't heard from the kidnappers. Were they sending instructions? The NSA still had no idea where the crown was and, without it, they had no way to negotiate with the kidnappers.

At first, she felt an immense feeling of relief when she realized the email was from Nick. Now she felt as if she had been doused with a large bucket of ice-cold water. She felt dizzy and had to hold onto the edge of the desk. But her son was in trouble; she had no time for paralyzing emotion. She pushed away from the desk.

"Let's go!"

"Wait. Let's take a look at the video first," Agent Vagnetti said.

Liz hadn't even noticed the attachment. She hadn't seen anything but the words her son had typed.

"It doesn't matter what's on the video. He said he needs help. We don't have time."

"Please, Mrs. Farraday, just click on it. It might be of some use. Quickly."

Agent Vagnetti was right, of course. Liz clicked on the video, willing herself to stay in her seat and not run out the door to find her son.

They watched in silence, the figures barely discernible, until the glare from one of the men's cell phones lit up the darkness surrounding them. The audio was only a little better. It took Liz a moment to piece together what she had seen and heard.

"They're going to kill Emily!" Liz moved to get up, but she felt Agent Vagnetti's hand pressing down on her shoulder.

"Let's let the agents handle this. You'll only get in the way."

The agent turned toward the two men. "I'll call for backup. Quickly!" She waved her hand at them.

The two male agents had already opened the plastic bins of equipment they had brought with them and were strapping on bulletproof vests and night vision goggles.

They reached the back door before their boss finished her sentence.

Liz rested her forehead against her palms.

"Don't worry. We'll get them." Agent Vagnetti assured her.

Liz lifted her head. Through red-rimmed eyes she watched the agent punch numbers into her cell phone.

"I don't understand. What was Nick doing in the cemetery in the first place? And why were those men looking for the crown there?"

Everything was happening too fast. She had never been much of a crier but now she felt tears streaming down her face and she couldn't stop them. Her entire life was un-raveling. Finding her husband's body should have been a time of healing. It had been anything but.

Agent Vagnetti pulled a tissue from the box sitting next to the computer with her free hand and offered it to Liz. She took it and blew her nose loudly.

Waiting for her call to connect, the agent said, "I'm confused too, Mrs. Farraday, but we'll get some answers soon. It was smart of your son to send us the video. You should be very proud of him."

* * *

Staying in the shadows, the two agents moved cau-tiously toward the cemetery, their Glocks held down by their sides and night vision goggles in place. They passed the Farraday crematorium and glanced at the vandalized niche. Keeping near the protection of the trees and monu-ments, they listened for movement.

"Over there," Agent Conner whispered. He nodded toward the northeast corner of the cemetery, close to

Wilcox and Fourth Street. Through their night vision goggles they saw three figures, two walking together and another figure trailing several yards behind.

Agent Conner moved to his left and signaled to his colleague that he would get the boy out of harm's way.

Agent Nelson picked up his pace and continued to follow the two men. He watched as they jumped the fence and hurried toward a waiting vehicle in the apartment parking lot.

He wasn't going to make it in time.

CHAPTER 12

Agent Conner watched the green image of the boy through his night vision eyepiece. When the two other men jumped the fence, the boy crouched by the rail. Conner sprinted the short distance between them. He was no longer worried about being quiet. The boy turned his head toward the noise.

"Stay down!" He called to Nick, who stood up just as the suspect's car came roaring out of the lot. He saw the boy hold out his arm toward the street. Did he have a weapon? Then he realized Nick was videotaping the getaway car.

"I think I got the license number," Nick said without turning toward the agent.

Brian was impressed with the young man's cool but he didn't have time to congratulate him. "Stay here," he warned as he ran to join the other agent.

* * *

Gunshots popped through the quiet night air as Nelson and Conner opened fire on the fleeing vehicle. Nick thought the noise sounded more like firecrackers than gunshots, but he knew he was hearing the real deal. Ignoring

Agent Conner's order to stay down, he craned his neck over the fence to get a better view. Hopefully they were aiming at the tires or just trying to stop the vehicle. If they killed the two occupants inside, he might never see his sister and Henry again. Even if he wanted to, Nick couldn't move as he watched the scene in front of him playing out like an action movie.

The two agents continued to advance on the car, firing their weapons as they went. Then Nick heard the screech of tires. Two black sedans suddenly appeared, the back ends swerving ninety degrees until they blocked the street just as the kidnappers' vehicle made the turn onto Third Street.

Moving in closer, the two agents kept their weapons aimed at the occupants inside the stopped vehicle while more agents poured out of the sedans. They flung the doors open and used them as shields as they took aim. Nick's heart pounded in his chest. He was holding his breath, waiting to see if the Asian men would fire back or surrender.

"Exit the vehicle!" He heard one of the agents shout, but the men didn't move.

His heart sank. Then he saw the doors open slowly.

"Put your hands on your head!"

Agents rushed the car and surrounded the two men, pushed them onto the pavement and handcuffed them in one smooth motion. Nick's fear turned to elation. They had them!

Then he heard an unexpected but familiar voice.

"Where's Nick? Where's my son?"

He turned to see his mother running toward the melee.

Nick watched as Agent Nelson comforted her. Standing a few feet away, Agent Conner pointed to where he had last seen Nick. They were talking in low tones now, so he could barely hear what they were saying.

He should have stood up and shown himself to his mother, letting her know that he was all right, but he needed to think.

The object in exchange for Emily.

Nick felt the burden of the decision he was about to make. Like fast-forwarding through a movie, scenarios flickered through his mind in triple time.

Henry's warnings sounded in his head, bringing to the surface his lingering doubt that Agent Vagnetti would ever take the risk of losing the Halo by turning it over to the kidnappers. The capture of the two men changed things. It was obvious to Nick that Henry hadn't willingly sent them to the cemetery. The men were Henry and Emily's kidnappers. And there had to be at least one more. Someone left behind to guard the captives. Would the two men rat out on their accomplice? Would the remaining kidnappers risk an exchange? Nick wasn't sure, but a plan was fomenting in his mind and, if it worked, then it would be a win-win for everyone.

He made his decision and tapped out another message to his mother.

i'm okay mom...don't worry xo nick

Then he backtracked to the family columbarium, using the monuments and wide trees for cover. He placed his phone into his father's burial niche among the sand and broken shards of urn.

Nick circled around the cemetery toward the opposite side from where the NSA had apprehended the kidnappers. He could see his mother and a few other agents starting to spread out, probably looking for him. He turned his back to them, cautiously making his way toward a low area of the fence, and hopped over. Once on Second Street, he sprinted most of the way into the heart of town.

Doubts about his decision were already messing with his head. Had he made the right one? But every time he went over the details, he still came up with the same conclusion.

He crossed over Main and made his way to a small industrial area and searched for Elite Limousine Service. He wasn't as familiar with this part of town and it took, what seemed to him, a long time to find the building. If he hadn't ditched his smartphone, he would have pulled up a map using his internet connection. The cell Henry left him in the mailbox was barebones. When he finally found the building, there was only a soft light coming from the front window. The office was closed.

Nick shrugged the backpack off his shoulder and rummaged for the cell phone and note that Henry had left him in the mailbox. He found Kurt's phone number and dialed.

"Hello."

"Kurt?"

"Yes."

"This is Nick Farraday. Henry told me to call you if I needed help."

"Nick! Yes. Have you found Henry? Is he alright?"

"I'm not sure, but I hope he will be soon." He didn't wait for a response. "I need you to drive me to Metro Airport."

There was a pause. "When?"

"Right now. I'm in a hurry."

"No problem. Where do I pick you up?"

"In front of your office."

* * *

"Thanks a lot."

Nick stood on the wide sidewalk outside the airport and reached his arm into the side window to give Kurt a tip from Henry's cash.

On the forty-five minute drive to the airport, Kurt told Nick he always called Henry on Thursdays to see if he needed him for the weekend or had any pickups. He often did odd jobs for Henry. So when he didn't answer after several attempts, Kurt started to worry. He knew Henry rarely, if ever, left the shop unless he had a driver. Kurt had been working for Henry for years and he also knew Henry would never ask anyone else to help him if he was available. Worried, he drove through the alley behind the shop on his way home just to have a look. He saw lights in the upstairs windows.

"So, I parked and rang the upstairs intercom. Some guy answered and told me to wait there. Said he'd be right down. They let me in and showed me their badges. When I asked them where Henry was they told me he had gone missing. Then they started asking me all kinds of questions. Mostly about that thing on your dad's head in that YouTube video."

Kurt glanced in the rearview mirror with an apologetic look on his face and then continued.

"I wondered why they would think I'd know anything about it," he shrugged. "They said for Henry's safety I shouldn't tell anybody about him being missing or about any of the questions they asked me. I got the impression they weren't asking me either. They were telling me." He shot a wry grin at Nick through the mirror.

"Henry gave me the envelope a few weeks ago, before all this happened. Told me to get it to you should anything happen to him." He shook his head. "The old man must have known something was going down. Anyway, I drove by your house that night and slipped it in your mailbox. I could have mailed it, but I didn't want to take the chance it would get lost. Or take days to get to you. But I didn't tell the agents about the letter."

He glanced in the rearview mirror again and smiled. "I'm sure they didn't tell me everything either."

To his credit, Kurt never asked Nick what was in the letter and Nick was grateful. Nick could understand why Henry trusted him. Now Kurt waved Nick's offer of a tip away.

"Hey, no problem. Henry already took care of me."

Kurt talked about Henry as if he were coming back. Nick was grateful for even that small measure of assurance, because it also meant he thought Emily would be coming home too.

Nick wanted to purchase a ticket beforehand, but since there wasn't internet service on Henry's cell, he had no choice but to wait until he got to the airport. He had noticed a tablet computer on the front seat of the limo and thought of asking Kurt if he could use it, but he didn't want to put Kurt in a position where he would have to lie to his mother, or to the NSA. *No use tempting fate*, he thought. He thought of his mother, and how sorry he was for putting her through the worry of him taking off like this. But it couldn't be helped.

He stood on the cold sidewalk by the skycap's stand and watched the limo pull away from the curb. The last link to anyone he could trust was gone. Suddenly, Nick felt very alone.

* * *

Once the agents handcuffed the suspects, they shoved both men into the back seat of one of the black sedans and drove off. The entire incident had only lasted a few minutes. If any of the neighbors looked out the window, all they would see now was a quiet street.

The Antiquarian had been turned into a temporary command center, and Agent Vagnetti ordered the suspects taken there for questioning. They had succeeded in keeping the local police from sticking their noses into the kidnapping, and Ronnie wanted to keep it that way.

She left Agent Nelson and Liz wandering the cemetery looking for the Farraday boy. So far, they hadn't found him. She had quickly deduced who had taken the object from the niche. The kidnappers expected it to be there, but someone had gotten to it first.

And that someone was Nick.

Henry gave the kidnappers the location in order to protect the girl. But how had the boy known it was there? Had he been in contact with Henry since his kidnapping? That wasn't likely. He had somehow figured out where it was hidden and gone to find it, only to be interrupted by the kidnappers. The boy knew the kidnappers wanted it in exchange for his sister. So, what was he up to?

She walked over to Agent Conner, who was sitting in front of a bank of laptops and electronic equipment, where he was already searching through the data stored on the

Asian men's cell phones. It wouldn't take them long to figure out where they had been, and that would, hopefully, lead them to the location where Emily and Applegate were being held.

"Brian, put a trace on the boy's cell phone."

For a few moments after the shooting, Ronnie had a sinking feeling that Nick might have been caught in the crossfire but, when they didn't find him near the area Agent Conner had last seen him, her instincts told her that he wasn't hurt. They had done a thorough search of the corner of the cemetery nearest the scene and had failed to find him.

"It traces to Mount Avon Cemetery."

No surprise there. She bent over and looked at the computer screen.

"The cemetery covers a few blocks. You can do better than that. Pinpoint the location as close as you can."

After Ronnie called Nelson with a more precise location of Nick's cell phone, it only took them a few minutes to find it in the niche where Nick had left it for them to find. According to Nelson, Liz had been hysterical when she first saw the extent of the vandalism to her husband's burial site. It didn't surprise Ronnie that Liz hadn't allowed herself to suspect that it might have been Nicholas who broke the urn and took the artifact. Ronnie was sure the idea of her own son desecrating his father's grave would send her over the edge.

Now, Ronnie sat at Henry's desk in the upstairs apartment of The Antiquarian. The rest of the agents were downstairs questioning the kidnappers, and she needed a quiet place to think.

Why had Nick ditched his cell phone? The obvious answer was so he couldn't be tracked. The next question was: Where was he taking the artifact?

Something else had been nagging at her. Just as Ronnie was sure that Liz would be distraught if she thought Nick had disturbed his father's remains, she was also puzzled by his actions. The urn was completely destroyed and the contents strewn everywhere. One would expect the boy to have treated his father's remains with a little more decorum. Of course, he might not have had much time and did what he had to in order to retrieve the crown in the quickest way possible. But something about it still poked at Ronnie's subconscious. She stared at her pen as she tapped it against the blotter on the desk, and then it came to her.

Doug Farraday's ashes had not been in the urn.

It had all been a ruse to get the object into the United States. And the boy knew. But Ronnie was certain his mother did not.

CHAPTER 13

"I don't understand. *I'm okay mom? Don't worry?* What is he thinking? What's going on?"

Agent Nelson was driving Liz to The Antiquarian.

Ronnie told him she was going to track down the whereabouts of the object and she didn't know when she'd be back. She had an idea—and when Ronnie had an idea, it was usually a good one. It was obvious Liz needed a distraction from the fact that now not only her daughter was missing but also her son. Agent Nelson knew that the desecration of her late husband's burial place had unnerved her. As undignified as it seemed, he had swept what he could of the spilled remains into a plastic bag that Liz brought from the house, and they took the bag back to the Farraday home for safe keeping until she could order a new urn. He hadn't seen many cremated remains, but what he'd swept into the bag looked like ordinary sand to him. It was curious, but he didn't mention it to Liz. No need to upset her on a mere suspicion.

The NSA might have pulled up stakes entirely and passed this kidnapping case off to the FBI now that there was little chance the kidnappers would lead them to the object, but there was the additional problem of secrecy. If they called in the FBI then there would be questions, and Agent Vagnetti didn't want the FBI asking questions. Agent Nelson was glad, he'd hate to leave the case without seeing Emily and Henry, and now Nick, safely back home.

"I wish I knew," he said.

"And what's going to happen to Emily if we can't find the crown?"

"We never had it to begin with."

"But there was still hope. I thought Henry had it, or knew where it was. Now I'm not so sure." Liz stared down at her shaking hands. "Why would he tell them it was in Doug's grave? Didn't he know what they would do?"

"Maybe he did it to stall them. If he doesn't know where it is, maybe it was the first thing that came to mind."

All they had seen on the Nick's video was the kidnappers accusing Henry of lying to them and threatening to kill the captives. They hadn't seen them break open the urn.

"So thoughtless," Liz shook her head. "But that's Henry for you."

Nelson knew it was possible that the crown had been in the urn, but it was gone by the time the kidnappers got to the cemetery.

"We have their cell phones and we're confident we can find your daughter and Henry. Every cell phone leaves a trail. All we have to do is follow it. And I wouldn't worry about not having the crown for ransom. Did you ever think that perhaps we didn't need to give them the real one? We have the video, we could have made up a pretty good facsimile."

She stared at his profile. "I never thought of that."

Liz looked down at her hands in her lap. "Anyone who could desecrate a grave like that…"

Ronnie hadn't told him everything, he was sure. All he knew was that she was off searching for the object. And he had a feeling that wherever it was, she would find Nick there, too.

"Why was Nick in the cemetery anyway? Something's not right. It's as if he knew the kidnappers would be there."

Frank shrugged. He certainly wasn't going to reveal his suspicions to the woman.

"Do you think he was looking for the crown? You don't think he's foolish enough to try and find it on his own, do you?" Liz asked.

"I'd hope he'd ask us for help."

"Where is he? What is he doing?" She was almost to the point of hysteria.

"He's a fifteen year old boy. Lots of things have happened. Maybe he just needs some time to think."

Liz glared at him. "That makes no sense at all."

Agent Nelson lifted his shoulder. He didn't have anything else to offer.

"I've been doing some thinking. What's the real reason the NSA came around asking us questions? I don't believe for a minute it's only because you think someone might try to use the crown in some kind of elaborate hoax. I could see the FBI getting involved in a fraud case. But the NSA? Something's not right."

He kept his eyes on the road.

"Ask me no questions, and I'll tell you no lies?" Liz said. "Unless there is something special about this crown and what it does." Liz shook her head. "Causes hallucinations. Is a time travel machine. Whatever! Then the NSA

wouldn't bother with it. There's something going on here. Something you aren't telling me."

She turned to stare out of the passenger side window. "Do you have children, Agent?"

"I prefer you call me Frank."

"Okay...Frank. Do you?" She wasn't asking the questions to pry but now that she had, she suddenly found herself interested in the answer. Not that it mattered but, so far, she couldn't tell if Frank was married or not. Perhaps NSA agents didn't wear rings for security reasons. Don't let anyone know you have a family in an attempt to keep them safe.

"No," Frank said. "No children. Not married."

"Well, maybe you can't understand what it's like. I not only lost my husband ten years ago—because of this crown, it seems—but now my daughter has been kidnapped and my son is missing. And I'd like to know why!"

"I'll be as honest as I can, Liz." He turned to look at her. "I don't know if the object is significant or not. I don't know whether it's part of a hoax or if it has some kind of power. It's above my pay grade. But, you're right. The NSA wouldn't be involved unless they thought it was of some importance."

He reached out, and she looked down at his fingers where they touched her sleeve. When he quickly moved it away, she said, "I appreciate your attempt at honesty."

Liz was silent for a moment, then said, "I don't think he trusts you."

"Nick?"

She nodded. "He told me that once we found the crown the NSA would take it, and we would never hear about it again."

"He might be right."

Her mouth pressed into a hard line.

"Don't think too badly of us. What would happen if we made a discovery that had the potential to send the entire population into a panic?"

"You have very little faith in the human race."

"We don't need to go on faith. We have proof. Do you remember Orson Welles' radio production of *War of the Worlds*? Agent Vagnetti and I were just talking about it. Entire families committed suicide. Imagine what would happen had it been real."

"I think people are mature enough to learn the truth, Agent Nelson."

He looked at her and raised his eyebrow.

"Sorry...Frank. That radio production was many years ago. Give us regular folk some credit. And there are many people who believe that Earth has been visited by aliens in the past. It wouldn't be that great of a shock."

"Thinking something might be possible and knowing it as fact are two very different things. The feelings they evoke come from different places in the brain. But we're getting ahead of ourselves. Neither of us knows what the object proves, if anything. We need to study it first. It could still be a hoax. I've seen some pretty elaborate ones in my day."

He smiled at Liz, but she was having none of it. "I don't really care about any of that right now. All I need to know is that my children are safe."

"You should have some faith in your son. He said he was okay. He said not to worry."

"Yeah, right."

* * *

It had been a long day. Nick had been going non-stop ever since he found Henry's letter in the mailbox. He looked at the bank of international clocks hanging over the long ticket counter that covered the entire back wall of the airport concourse. It was two in the morning. He felt exhausted and hungry. There were only a few people in the ticket-line by the counter, but Nick searched for a self-serve e-ticket kiosk instead.

The next flight to either San Francisco Airport or nearby San Jose wasn't until six am. Nick hadn't counted on that. He thought he would be able to get on a plane as soon as he reached the airport. Now he would have a few hours to kill. He thought, briefly, about getting on the next flight to anywhere west of Michigan and then catching another flight to San Francisco, but, for all that trouble, his chances of getting to the SETI Institute any quicker were slim.

Hopefully, he could get in the air before Agent Vagnetti realized where he'd gone. She would eventually figure out he had the Halo, and he was sure she would follow him. The NSA didn't want the truth about it to go public, he was certain. And, the more he thought about it, the more certain he was that they weren't going to just hand the artifact over to the kidnappers either. They'd want to hide it and to continue letting the public think his dad was a nut-job. Well, he wasn't about to let that happen. He was going to save Henry and Emily. And he was going to restore his father's tarnished reputation. He was going to make sure his father received his rightful place in history— as the person who discovered mankind's true past. The people of Earth had a right to know the truth. All this, of course, if Jane Carter was able to prove it was real.

Nick bought a one-way ticket for the next Northwest flight out of Detroit Metro Airport to San Jose International, just southeast of San Francisco. It was only slightly smaller than San Francisco International but nearer to the SETI Institute Headquarters building. Northwest Airlines allowed fourteen year-olds to travel unaccompanied. Since he was fifteen, he should have no problem.

Now that he had his ticket, all he could think about was getting through the security gates and finding a place to eat. He needed food and a place to rest, if only for a few minutes.

Security.

Nick stopped in his tracks. He would have to put his backpack through the X-ray machine. When he broke the urn back at the cemetery, he wasn't thinking about how he would get the Halo to San Francisco. It was still in the lead-lined film pouch, but would security let it go through without looking inside?

Of course, he could always tell them it was a prop for a play or something. A gift for his young niece who liked to play princess? A dozen ideas popped in his head, but none that gave him confidence. Nick felt sick. Why hadn't he thought about this before? His heart started to gallop in his chest. His mind was racing, his thoughts so confused, he couldn't move. Then he spotted a fancy customs shop down the concourse and an idea popped it his head. It was a long shot, but, if they had what he was looking for, it might work.

* * *

Ronnie's weight had never really been an issue with her desk job. Gathering intelligence on unusual archaeological discoveries and phenomenon—discoveries that might have a profound effect on society—was her specialty. It didn't require a high level of physical fitness, only mental acuity.

It wasn't only Ronnie's keen intellect that made her successful. She had thousands of web-bots specifically coded to seek out certain key words and concepts that might appear on the internet. All she had to do was press a button and the bots did all the "data mining" for her. Web chatter was a reliable predictor of future events by providing a snapshot view of the world's current mood at any point in time.

It was starting to occur to Ronnie that this mission might involve a little more physical activity on her part. Being the head of a small covert operation, it wasn't something she had anticipated. Even though this investigation was changing into something more physically demanding, it was something she had started, and she was eager to see it through to the end. Ten years ago, when Douglas Farraday went missing after the earthquake, Ronnie was disheartened. She knew of the object's existence and realized it had disappeared along with him. She, like the rest of her small elite unit at the NSA, thought it might never be recovered, or, even more alarming, that it might have been destroyed.

Lately, her enthusiasm for her job had started to wane. Nothing exciting had come across her desk in a long time. Of all the artifacts she had been privy to throughout her career, the Himalayan artifact had been the most intriguing. Now that it had been recovered, Ronnie was beginning to feel that almost forgotten tingle of excitement. Of course, she hadn't actually studied it yet, but from what she could determine, it was promising. This was different from any other physical object she'd ever encountered. An object whose meaning couldn't be twisted into a comfortable interpretation. According to everything they knew, this artifact's technology could not be explained away, and might provide the irrefutable evidence she had been seeking almost her entire life.

Throughout history, the powers-that-be kept secrets from the masses. They hid them away in places like the Vatican or in secret government archives. Ronnie's job was not only to keep up with the latest discoveries but also to uncover knowledge that had been lost to modern man. To find out what secrets other nations, or powerful men, might have that they weren't sharing with the U.S. She understood the need to hold some things back from the public. Mankind might not be ready to learn they were not alone in the universe. Although every day, she felt, the peoples of the world were getting nearer to a point where they could accept this possibility.

Anyone could hypothesize what might happen when, or if, the speculation ever became a reality. Would people unite? Or would it cause further rifts, each nation vying for a position of power for the time when we would meet the aliens face-to-face? What would happen to the world's religions? What would happen to people's faith in their personal god?

For Ronnie, that wasn't a problem. She wasn't particularly religious, but she did believe there was some higher power, some high concept that man couldn't even come close to comprehending. But for many of the faithful, no matter what religion, it might completely destroy the foundation on which they had based their entire lives. Was it wrong to try and protect these people? She wasn't sure anymore.

Ronnie had no doubt that there was knowledge she had never been given the privilege—or the security clearance—to witness. That's why she wanted to see this mission to the end. It was her one chance to find out for herself. And, if nothing else, she might be able to restore Doug's reputation to his family, even if it meant revealing some of the secrets she had been sworn to keep.

It seemed appropriate that this would be her last job. In a month, she would retire. She would miss it, but retirement would mean she could finally pursue her love of cooking. She had already planned a month long stay in Italy, booked at a different cooking school each week in a different region of the country, starting at the Villa Mangiacane in Tuscany. A retirement gift she was giving to herself. But the best retirement gift of all would be to finally discover the truth.

Immediately after receiving intel regarding the recovery of Doug Farraday's body, the agency had started monitoring all of Henry Applegate's activities. Unknown to Ronnie, Henry had already shipped the remains back to the states and, she realized now, probably the object with it. Whether the artifact was put in the urn in China, or once it arrived in the states, Ronnie had no way of telling.

Henry's plan was so obvious, so simple, why hadn't she thought of it earlier? They had checked out everything else Applegate had shipped from China, but the NSA had been informed only a few days before the funeral. If the kidnappings hadn't occurred, Ronnie would have gotten a warrant to look inside the urn. But things had happened fast, and one of the main objectives, both then and now, was to keep this case as quiet as possible.

So far, they had managed. Barely.

CHAPTER 14

Ronnie stood in the doorway of Nick's room. A red and white Detroit Red Wing poster hung above the bed pushed against the wall, a bookshelf stood opposite. Ronnie noticed a collection of model NASA aircraft scattered between books on astronomy, various novels, and textbooks. A laptop sat on the desk next to a window that looked out onto the cemetery. In front of the window was a telescope on a tall tripod.

She walked over to the desk. Had Henry sent Nick a message? No, they would have known. Brian had been monitoring all their email accounts. An instant message, perhaps? A Web page? Or a message hidden within a blog? She pulled the chair away from the desk. It groaned underneath her as she made herself comfortable. She flipped open the laptop and opened the internet browser. There was nothing unusual about any of the websites Nick had visited in the last few weeks, although Ronnie was mostly interested in the last few days. The last search Nick typed into the browser was "Song of God."

What made Ronnie so good at her job was her instinct, that indefinable thing that made her nerves tingle at just the right moment. Like the specially trained dogs that root out truffles, Ronnie had perfected her already natural talent of sniffing out the important bits of information within a mountain of data.

She followed the digital trail that Nick had so conveniently left her and ended on a page referencing the Bhagavad Gita. Ronnie was familiar with the ancient Hindu scripture. Many ancient alien theorists believed the Vimana machines described in the story to be—not the flying palace of the gods as the text indicated—but rather the flying machine of an advanced alien race. The Hindu text was connected to the missing artifact. But how?

She searched the desk, leafing through the books lining the back, shuffling through the papers and notebooks scattered on the top. She found Doug's journal and leafed through it, but found nothing that would help her. Then she rummaged through the drawers. On the right, in the second drawer from the top, she found a memory card reader with a micro disk still inserted in one of the slots.

* * *

There wasn't any movement outside his room and there hadn't been for a long time. Henry didn't know how far away from the cemetery he was being held. Calculating how much time it had taken the two men to get to the cemetery and to find the crematorium before threatening him on the phone, he determined they should have been back by now.

Did Nick escape? Or had they found him and harmed him? Henry couldn't stand the waiting, the not knowing. And he worried about Emily. How was she holding up under all this stress? Was she being held somewhere nearby or some other place entirely? All he had seen was a video of her in a room. He had no way of knowing where the room was.

Once they got out of this situation—and they would get out; he wouldn't let himself think otherwise—he would have to make this terrible incident up to the girl. He had no idea that Emily would be involved when he first told Kurt to send Nick the envelope should he go missing.

Henry's guilt was almost unbearable.

* * *

Ronnie wasn't cold as she stood waiting in the dark recesses of the rear hospital parking lot. She rarely wore more than her familiar blue cardigan, even in the coldest of weather. She tilted her head and listened. No one would take much notice of a helicopter touching down near a hospital. It wasn't an uncommon occurrence, but it usually happened on a helipad on the roof. Crittenton—the hospital where Liz was employed—was only a few blocks west of the Farraday's. It was the perfect spot. If all went well, the helicopter wouldn't be on the ground long enough to arouse any suspicions. She lifted her head toward the familiar sound of the blades. In a few minutes, she would be at nearby Bishop Airport in Flint where a Gulfstream 650, with a cruising speed of 700mph, was waiting to take her to San Francisco.

She hadn't told Frank that she suspected the contents of the urn had never held Doug Farraday's remains. Some things she would keep to herself. She simply told him she had an idea where the object had been taken, and she was going after it.

When the helicopter finally touched down, no one could hear her wheeze as she struggled her way to the chopper. If the waiting soldier was surprised at the old, overweight agent waddling toward him, he didn't show it.

* * *

Liz sat upstairs in Henry's apartment on his over-stuffed, and surprisingly comfortable, couch. After Agent Vagnetti had searched Nick's room and then told them she would be gone for a while, Liz started to worry all over again.

The realization that there were people determined to get their hands on the crown came back to her more vivid than ever. Was some terrible person following her son? Had he already been captured? He said he was okay, but for how long?

Even though they had captured the two men who were being held downstairs in Henry's shop, how many more criminals were keeping close watch on the crown? And surely those two weren't the only people involved in the kidnapping.

The agents were questioning the suspects and using the information stored on their cell phones to try and pinpoint where Emily and Henry were being held. But they weren't working fast enough for Liz's liking. What was taking so long?

"You're not too fond of Henry, are you?" Frank had made them both a cup of coffee and now he handed Liz a steaming mug. The question was unexpected. It took a second for it to register.

"No," she said without emotion.

"Bad financial deals with your late husband?"

She shook her head. "No, nothing like that. Henry was fair about money."

"But?"

"Henry destroyed my husband's reputation."

"How so?"

"Just working with Henry destroyed it. He pursued my husband relentlessly, trying to convince him his work was important, that his theories deserved serious consideration. Then—I could never understand why—Doug started to buy into them. Of course, none of Doug's peers agreed. The only people who did were the UFO nuts who bought Henry's books in droves. The only thing my husband received for his trust in Henry was a tainted reputation within the archaeological community. And now there is the release of the video to top it all off."

"The NSA isn't convinced Henry released it. What makes you so sure?"

She sipped her coffee and didn't answer.

"Tell me if I'm getting too personal but, with all due respect to your late husband, it seems you should be angry with him rather than Henry. It was his decision after all."

It hit Liz again, that punched-in-the-gut feeling. He was right, she knew.

"There's more." She turned and held his gaze. "But we don't know each other well enough for me to confide in you."

"Ah, too personal, sorry." One corner of his mouth curled up into that charming smile Liz had noticed before.

She shrugged. "It's okay. Maybe someday I'll be ready to share. Just not right now."

She was sorry as soon as she'd said it. Someday? Someday implied they would have a relationship in the future. She could feel blood rushing to her cheeks.

Then they heard the chime of the back door as it opened.

CHAPTER 15

Nick hoped his idea would work.

He walked down the brightly lit aisles of the shop until he found what he was looking for. He took it to the checkout counter.

"Do you have any film that fits this camera?" he asked the girl behind the counter. "And I'll need some lens cloths, if you have any."

He paid for the old style, but expensive, camera, several small boxes of film, and the lens cloths with Henry's prepaid credit card.

Nick made his way to the nearest bathroom and threw away the various boxes. Then he attached the strap, which came with it, to the camera and hung it around his neck. No one else was in the bathroom. As an extra precaution, he used his backpack as a shield while he quickly took the Halo out of Henry's lead-lined pouch and wound the lens cloths around the edges. He replaced the Halo, and then added the film cartridges until it was completely covered. The gray lens cloths blended with the interior color of the pouch and anyone looking would have a hard time seeing it.

When he neared the security checkpoint, Nick made sure one of the guards was watching as he took the camera from around his neck and put it in a bin, along with his shoes, some loose coins, and a couple of paperclips from his pocket.

As he walked through the metal detector, Nick watched the female guard who was monitoring the X-ray screen. His chest felt hollow. He was trying to act normal but it was difficult.

She studied the screen for a moment, and he knew she was looking at the opaque image of the lead-lined pouch. She stopped the conveyer belt and unzipped his backpack.

Nick held his breath.

She glanced inside and half-pulled the pouch, which was clearly marked with a large logo, out of the pack. She glanced at the camera sitting in the bin and then up at Nick, who was now standing across from her. He heard a sharp zip as she pulled the flap open and gave a cursory looked inside. He prayed she wouldn't poke around. He watched with relief as she lowered the flap and pushed the pouch back inside his backpack. She didn't bother to pull the zipper closed before she started the conveyor belt again.

Nick's hands were shaking as he pulled his shoes on and took the other items from the bin. He hung the camera around his neck and walked away as calmly as he could manage.

Once on board the plane, he found his seat near the tail. He was exhausted. Still clutching his backpack, it didn't take long for the loud drone of the engines to lull him to sleep. One of the flight attendants had to give him a gentle nudge when they reached the gate.

Stepping out onto the jetway, Nick felt a cool rush of air against his face. His legs felt wobbly from sitting for so long. It felt good to stretch, and he took long strides down the tunnel. The jetway took a sharp right turn and then flowed straight out into the bright terminal. A crowd of people huddled at the end, eagerly awaiting their loved ones. Nick scanned their faces. He didn't know why he was so on edge. He hadn't seen anybody that looked like an NSA agent, but he stayed alert.

Once out of the jetway, he stood against a post at the edge of the concourse and watched the crowd move like ants in front of him. He couldn't shake the nagging feeling that he was being watched. Suddenly everyone looked like an agent to him: the man reading a newspaper; a woman with a baseball cap adjusting her iPod earbuds; the man leaning against the wall with his carry-on luggage on the floor beside him. They all seemed suspicious.

Shrugging off his paranoia, he thought about what to do next. Now that he was here, how was he going to get to SETI? He needed to hire a taxi. Nick instinctively reached for his cell phone, flipped it open, and then closed it again. He kept forgetting that Henry's prepaid phone didn't have an internet connection. He slipped it back in his pocket. He really missed his smartphone.

All airports had a taxi stand, he realized. All he had to do was find it. He scanned the signs overhead and saw a sign that pointed him toward baggage claim and ground transportation.

Down the corridor to his right, Nick noticed a general goods store lined with shelves filled with books, magazines, and snacks. In the middle of the store was a stand that held a variety of baseball caps and, just outside the storefront opening, was a rack of brochures. He walked over and found what he was looking for: a map of the San Francisco area. As he passed the rack of hats, he snatched a

Michigan State University cap with the Spartan's logo embroidered on the front, and then headed toward the checkout counter.

Nick followed the signs and stepped on the escalator down to the baggage pickup area. He scanned the crowd. Everywhere he looked, he saw someone who could have been an NSA agent, but none of them attempted to follow him. Was it just his imagination? He wasn't sure. He pulled his new baseball cap even further down on his forehead as he scanned the overhead signs for further directions to the ground transportation area.

Taxis should be waiting just outside the wall of doors at the far end of the vast room. Jumping off the escalator, he moved toward them as fast as he could.

A long line of black limousines, yellow taxicabs, and shuttle vans lined up at the curb, waiting for customers. His pulse quickened. He was almost there. Pushing through the doors, he scanned the drivers standing by their taxis. Nick wondered if you could tell just by their appearance which of them would be a good driver. He hoped to pick one who knew the fastest way to the SETI Institute. He stepped out onto the walkway and took a quick look left and right. He decided the nearest taxi was probably as good as any.

"Where to?" The cabbie asked.

"The SETI Institute. Do you know where it is?"

The driver smirked. "Sure do."

"If you could get me there as fast as possible, I'd appreciate it."

"Luggage?"

Nick gave him a puzzled look.

"Do you have any luggage?"

"No." He shrugged out of his backpack. "Just this."

Nick threw his backpack in and settled himself into the back seat. Taxis had a smell all their own, like every person who'd ever ridden in them had left their scent until it all melded into one peculiar aroma. Nick leaned back and listened while the driver checked in with his office, or maybe he was just talking to his wife or girlfriend, Nick really couldn't tell. Whatever. Nick had tuned him out already.

The nagging feeling he was being followed had not left. Every time a car pulled up beside the taxi, he shrunk a little further into the seat. Several times, he stole a look out the back window to see if they were being following. The same dark blue sedan had been behind the taxi ever since they pulled out of the airport lot. Seeing it gave Nick a sinking feeling.

Even though it wasn't a smartphone, the cell in his pocket could still be traced. No matter how unlikely it was that anyone would connect him with use of a phone that Henry had purchased, he didn't want to take any chances. On impulse, Nick pulled the phone from his pocket, rolled down the window, and pitched the phone as hard as he could. It landed hard on the pavement but, to his surprise, it didn't shatter. He turned to watch it bounce across the width of the road into oncoming traffic, until it finally landed in the gutter running alongside the curb.

"Hey, kid, no littering from my cab."

Nick counted out the fare even before they pulled up to the curb across from the SETI building, and then he counted out what he thought would be a good tip. Squeezing the money in his sweating hands, he waited until the driver finally put the taxi in park. He had been forced to use Henry's credit card at the airport, but he wanted to limit how much he used it now that he was in California. He would only use it again if he had no other choice. Nick wondered again if Agent Vagnetti already knew where he was going. Did she know that Henry wanted to get the Halo to SETI? And would she try to stop him from handing it over to them?

"Okay, kid, here you are."

Nick pushed the cash through the partition as he scooted toward the door nearest the curb. The driver was already counting the money as Nick jumped onto the sidewalk.

"Hey, thanks kid." He leaned toward the passenger side of the cab, peering out the window at Nick and waved the wad of cash in the air. "Have a good day!"

Nick didn't reply but bounded for the steps. He had to find Jane Carter before Agent Vagnetti found him.

Through the glass doors, Nick saw what looked like a tour group milling around the reception area. To the right sat a receptionist at a circular desk with a staircase just beyond. Her head was bent over her work. Nick rushed through the door and headed toward the desk. Even with all the people in the foyer, his footsteps still echoed across the room.

He leaned over the counter. "I need to see Jane Carter."

"Excuse me?" The light glinted against the receptionist's highlighted hair when she raised her head and looked at him. She cocked her right ear toward him.

His heart thudded in his chest. *Slow down*, he thought. He took a deep breath and then said more slowly, "I need to see Jane Carter."

"Do you have an appointment?" The receptionist turned to her computer, moving the mouse as she concentrated on the screen.

"No, but it is very important that I see her." He shot a glance back toward the door.

A faint smile came to the girl's lips. "Is that so? And what is your name?" Her eyes never left the computer screen.

"Nicholas Farraday."

He was getting even more anxious. If he didn't get the Halo into Jane Carter's hands before the NSA got to him, then he would have failed Henry and lost any hope of redeeming his dad's reputation. And endangered both Henry's and his sister's lives, all for nothing.

"Please lady, I need to see her right away."

"Could I tell her what this is concerning?"

Nick thought for a moment. "I have a message from Henry Applegate."

For a second, a puzzled look spread across her face, but then she turned professional again. "If you give me the message, I'll make sure she receives it."

"No. I'm sorry, but I have to give it to her myself."

The receptionist turned from the computer to look at him. "Well, then you'll have to make an appointment. I can't promise anything, but if you give me your number I'll try to set one up."

"But can't you just ask her if she can see me right now?"

The girl shook her head. "I'm sorry but she isn't here. She's at the Lick Observatory and will be there for a few more days. I really am sorry, young man, but the best I can do is try to get you an appointment."

"Lick?" He remembered reading about Lick Observatory when he was researching SETI and Jane Carter.

"Yes."

"Oh, yeah, the one on...Mount something. I've heard of it."

"Mount Hamilton Road."

He started to turn toward the door. "The Lick Observatory. Mount Hamilton Road. How far is that from here?" He needed to get out of there fast. If Agent Vagnetti were on to him, she wouldn't be far behind.

"You're not thinking of going there are you? You can't just barge in. It's only open to the public during certain hours. And it takes about forty-five minutes to an hour to get up the road. Why don't you just leave me your number and I'll have her contact you?"

Nick glanced through the glass front of the building. He saw a black SUV coming down the road. He had to leave. Now.

He started backing toward the door. "I don't have a number. Call Jane Carter and tell her I was here, but PLEASE don't tell anyone else. She wouldn't want you to. Tell her I need to talk to her about Henry Applegate. She'll know what I'm talking about. Call her, please! Tell her I'll get in touch with her somehow." He watched the SUV making its way down the street.

"Henry Applegate? Isn't he that author?"

Nick nodded and then rushed for the door.

"Wait," the receptionist called over the crowd as the door closed behind him.

Nick dived under the protective cover of the dense shrubbery along the side of the building and squatted down behind a bush where he waited and watched.

The black Cadillac SUV pulled up to the front of the building, followed by another. Both had darkened windows. He had no idea how Agent Vagnetti got to California so fast, but with the full resources of the NSA behind her anything was possible. Nick watched as the agent struggled to get out of the back seat. Instead of going inside the building, she stood by the curb as if not sure of her next move. Instinct told him he should start running and put as much distance between himself and the woman as possible, but fear kept him immobile. And, if he moved now, either she or one of the other drivers might see him.

The agent seemed to have finally made up her mind and waddled to the front door of the SETI building. Nick lost sight of her before she opened the door, but he could picture her talking to the young receptionist.

Don't tell her I was here, he silently prayed over and over again, hoping the girl would pick up his vibe and not give him away.

It seemed like ages before he saw the back of Agent Vagnetti's navy sweater as she trudged back down the long walkway to one of the waiting cars. Before she slid into the front passenger seat, she signaled the other vehicle. The second Cadillac did a U-turn and parked, while the SUV Vagnetti was in made its way back down the street.

She was having SETI watched! But where was she headed? Did the receptionist tell her he was thinking of going up to the observatory? He thought about going back inside the building to see exactly what the receptionist had told the agent, but he couldn't risk being seen. He had to find a phone somehow, somewhere. He had to get in touch with Jane Carter before Agent Vagnetti could get to her.

Nick fell back on the soft grass, feeling defeated. Then he remembered the map he bought at the airport. He jerked up and reached in his backpack. After a few seconds, he had the map spread out in front of him and was studying the layout of the streets. There were some larger attractions noted on the map, one being the San Antonio Shopping Center. It wasn't close, but was still within walking distance. An area marked as Whisman School Park was only a few blocks away. School park meant a school building. Maybe, if he were lucky, there would be an emergency pay phone somewhere on the premises. It was a place to start anyway. He had a better chance of finding a pay phone there than anywhere else. Or maybe there would be a store along the way where he could pick up another disposable cell phone. Or he might find someone he could ask to place a call for him. He tried to stay positive about his chances. He would keep a keen eye out for a pay phone along the way.

He gave the map one last look and then folded it. Instead of returning it to his backpack, he tucked it in his jacket pocket where his cell phone used to be. He pulled his baseball cap down and peeked through the shrubbery. Then he slowly backed away from the building and weaved his way through the landscaping, until he was far away from the prying eyes inside the black Cadillac.

Once he was out of sight of the SETI building, Nick moved onto the sidewalk. He hadn't noticed anyone suspicious. Only one car had passed him as he walked. He relaxed enough to notice how chilly it was. *I thought it was always sunny in California*, he thought.

He moved south along North Whisman Road, looking over his shoulder every few minutes. He suddenly felt weak from hunger. He found a tree, sat down next to it, took the backpack off his shoulder, and searched for one of the granola bars he had bought while waiting at Detroit Metro. He didn't particularly like granola bars, but he'd grabbed them at the last minute and now he was glad that he had. He ate the bar in a few bites, all the while keeping a watchful eye out for any suspicious activity. He crammed the wrapper into his pack, swung it back on his shoulder, and moved quickly back to the sidewalk. After a few left turns, he took a right onto Walker Drive. The next sign he looked for was Easy Street.

Easy Street, he thought, *just like in Little Orphan Annie*. His mom had taken him and Emily to see it last year. Was Emily safe now? Was his mother worried? He swiped his arm across his face. He didn't have time to think about that right now.

The park was on his right and, just as he predicted, a school building sat on the corner. With a new surge of energy, he broke into a jog and headed toward the portico leading to the front doors. He searched for a pay phone hanging on one of the walls, but there wasn't one. Disappointed, he walked to the glass doors and peered in. There was a pay phone in the entry area between the outside doors and the inner foyer. Nick grabbed the door handles and pulled, but they were firmly locked. Wasn't it a school day? He couldn't remember. He had lost track of what day it was. He automatically reached for the cell phone to look for the time but stopped short. *No cell phone*, he reminded himself. There was about a three- or four-hour time difference between Michigan and California and the flight had taken about five hours. It was probably around six or seven in the morning. Maybe no one had unlocked the building yet.

Leaning his head against the cool glass, he slapped his open palms against the uncooperative door. The park was his last hope. He walked cautiously along the north side of the building. Nearing the end, his eyes were drawn to a recessed area at the back corner. Was there something there? He quickened his pace until he was standing in a little alcove with a set of double doors at the end. Probably the gym entrance, he surmised. A pay phone hung on the wall. For the first time in a long while, a smile crept across his face.

Nick hurriedly scrounged around for any change that might be in the bottom of his backpack. A sign over the phone stated it was fifty-cents for local calls. Was Mount Hamilton Road a local call? He didn't know. He only had about eighty cents in coins and a one-dollar bill. All the rest of Henry's money was in larger bills. Not wanting to waste the change on trying to find the number to the observatory, he put the receiver to his ear and pushed 1-800-FREE-411 on the keypad. He'd used the toll-free information number before and hoped it would work in California. When he heard the recorded voice on the other end, he let out a sigh of relief.

CHAPTER 16

It took him a few minutes to get through the voice recognition routine, but he finally heard a phone ringing on the other end. Another recorded voice greeting him, telling him he had reached Lick Observatory and gave him a list of departments he could be connected to. Did Jane Carter have an office at Lick? He doubted it, and he was right. The recorded voice didn't give her name as an option. He listened to the recording again and, on a hunch, chose the Telescope Operations Manager.

Of course no one answered. While the recording went through yet another speech explaining how to leave a voice message, Nick thought of what he would say.

"My name is Nicholas Farraday. This message is for Jane Carter. I'm at the German International School next to Whisman School Park on Easy Street in Mountain View, California. I'm calling from a pay phone located in back of the school. I have a message from Henry Applegate. It is very, very important that I speak with you. I'm asking if you can please come and get me. And, if an Agent Vagnetti from the NSA asks about me, please don't tell her I called you. You have to trust me. Please!"

He had spoken fast, but tried to enunciate so he would be understood. Nick paused and looked out toward the empty park, still holding the receiver to his ear.

"Whoever gets this message, please contact Jane Carter. And ask her to hurry."

He paused again, for the second time today finding himself close to tears, and then said a barely audible, "tThanks," before hanging up the phone. If anyone was monitoring calls coming into the observatory, then they could trace the call to the pay phone. He knew he had taken a risk, but he had no other options.

* * *

"Why am I here?" Emily asked the woman who pushed a tray of fast food toward her. Emily hardly ever ate fast food and, whatever this was, it smelled over-processed and greasy.

The woman looked up through the eye-slits in her black hood and Emily thought for a moment that she was going to say something, but then she turned and left the room. The door clicked shut behind her and Emily heard the tumbler fall into place. The room was starting to push in on her, making it hard to breath, and the smell of the food was making her nauseous.

There was really no need to ask, Emily knew why she was being held against her will, but she had wanted the woman to confirm it. She wanted someone to say some-thing—anything. The entire time she'd been there no one had said a single word to her. The last time any of them spoke directly to her was warning her to keep quiet while she was in the trunk. She'd finally given in and peed in the little port-a-potty, but she tried her best to pull her hoodie down over her knees while doing her business. The thought of someone watching creeped her out, but she couldn't hold it forever.

Had she been there a night and a full day? She had no way of really knowing. All she knew for sure was that she needed a shower.

Emily grabbed the cold waxed paper cup of soda and sucked on the straw until it was almost empty, but she didn't touch the food.

There had been a shift in the last few hours. Something had changed. She could feel it. The woman seemed jittery when she'd brought in the food, and she'd heard the muffled sounds of a tense conversation outside her door.

Emily was leaning back against the wall, trying to do some calming Yoga breaths, when she heard loud noises—frightened and urgent—coming from behind the door. Things banged against the walls, and the sound of running feet seeped through the door. Sitting on the narrow mattress directly opposite the door didn't seem like a good place for her to be, so she rushed toward the wall to the left of it and squatted in the corner. If anyone came in the room, at least she would be shielded for a few seconds.

More noises and banging and shuffling. Emily's heart did a funny little flip in her chest. She breathed in through her nose and exhaled, slowly pushing air over her lips.

The tumbler clicked and she watched the doorknob turn, as if in slow motion. The door did its job. It hid her from sight, but it also kept her from seeing who entered. Whoever it was, they had a gun. She saw the tip of it peek from beyond the edge of the door. Emily curled into a tight ball, wrapping her arms around her head, like a school kid from the 1950s in a nuclear attack drill. She closed her eyes and made a silent plea.

"Emily Farraday?" A gruff voice sounded above her.

Afraid she would look up into the barrel of a gun, she didn't move.

"We're here to take you home."

With those words, she moved her hands from around her head and turned her eyes upward. The man standing in front of her didn't look all that different from her kidnappers, dressed head-to-toe in black. The whites of his eyes showed through the slits in the hood that covered his face.

Emily had never been so happy in her entire life; even as he grabbed her arm so tight, she was sure it would leave a bruise. He lifted her, hurried her out of the room, down a corridor, and then out a door to a deserted parking lot. The feel of the fresh air against her skin almost made her cry. An armored vehicle was parked just a few feet ahead. A hooded man standing at the rear practically threw her inside. He was in a hurry, that was for sure, but so was Emily. She didn't mind one bit.

Emily glanced out the back of the van before the door closed. She knew exactly where she'd been held; an old industrial building that was mostly empty but occasionally used for furniture warehouse sales by local retailers. She had been very close to home all along.

* * *

Parents were starting to pick up their kids at the curb in front of the school and the parking lot was filling. When the students had come out for recess at noon, Nick left the alcove and moved to the periphery of the playground near the trees behind the baseball diamond. Another energy bar from his backpack provided him with his own meager lunch. He had positioned himself so he could still watch the parking lot. If he were older, perhaps someone might think he was a pervert, but either no one noticed him, or they thought he belonged. Now he was back in the alcove, waiting. Several times during the day he thought about hiring a taxi to take him up to the observatory.

Had the NSA succeeded in tracing the kidnapers' activities and finding his sister? Time was slipping away and he was getting anxious. He wanted to learn the truth about the Halo, but not at the expense of his sister's life. His plan was to deliver it to SETI as quickly as possible so Jane Carter could study it. Then he would contact the NSA to see if they still needed it for his sister's safe return. He hadn't counted on a delay.

Maybe Jane wasn't going to come after all. Then he heard the crunch of tires. His head jerked up from where it had been resting on his bent knees. The vehicle moved slowly in front of him, but all he could see was the side of an army-green Jeep. Was it Jane? He wanted to be sure before he moved into the open. He stood up. There was a tomboyish woman with short blonde hair and a worried look on her face sitting in the drivers seat. She was scanning the parking lot. The woman certainly resembled the pictures he'd seen of Jane Carter on the SETI website. Taking a chance, Nick stepped forward and removed his baseball cap. The Jeep stopped and the woman lowered the passenger side window.

"Nicholas?" she said.

He nodded.

"It's me, Jane."

Nick was still not certain. Was it really her? Maybe the NSA had somehow intercepted his call and this was an imposter. Or maybe it was another kidnapper, someone who was after the Halo. He had no idea who that could be, or what they might be capable of. But he was hungry and tired and he wanted to believe the person in the Jeep was really Jane Carter. Still, he couldn't bring himself to move.

"I got the message you left at Lick, and Ashley, the receptionist at SETI, told me you came looking for me today." She seemed to have read his mind.

Nick thought for a moment. This woman knew the receptionist's name. But so did he, for that matter. He had read the nametag pinned to her suit jacket. Nick decided to trust his instincts.

"Yes," he said, more to himself than to her, as a feeling of relief swept over him.

He was glad to be in the warm Jeep and sitting on the soft seats. His backside was sore from crouching on the hard cement all day. He had never ridden in one before and he liked the feel and smell of it, just like the leather saddle when he had gone horseback riding with his friends last summer.

Jane didn't move the car but turned to look at him.

"I couldn't come right away. An agent from the NSA came to pay me a visit at the observatory."

"Agent Vagnetti?"

"Yes, the one you mentioned on the phone. So, you know her?"

"You might say that. Listen, Mrs. Carter—"

"You can call me Jane."

Nick's mom had raised him to call adults by their last name, but he wasn't going to argue with the woman.

"Did you tell Agent Vagnetti I called you?"

"No, actually, I hadn't gotten your message from Bernie yet."

Nick looked puzzled.

"Bernie. The telescope operation manager." She said. "Your message was left in his mailbox and it took a while to get to me."

"She'll be following us."

"Us? Who? The agent?"

"She'll put a trace on your cell phone and your car. If she hasn't already."

"What?" Jane let out a soft laugh.

"She knows I'm looking for you. You have to ditch your cell and your car."

Jane raised an eyebrow at him. "Oh, is that all? My cell *and* my car?"

"I know it sounds crazy but, trust me, if you want a chance to study the artifact—and, believe me, you do—then you'll do it. It'll be totally worth it."

"So, this *is* about that object Henry Applegate's been hounding me about." She seemed to be talking to herself. To Nick, she said, "Do you have it with you?"

Nick hesitated a minute. She sounded eager to see the Halo, but from what Henry had told him, she wasn't interested at all when he'd tried to contact her about it. What had changed her mind? Maybe this was a trap. Maybe Agent Vagnetti had put her up to meeting him; and, as soon as he revealed the Halo, the NSA would come out of nowhere to arrest him. He did a quick scan of the parking lot.

"Well, do you have it or not?" Jane pressed.

"I know where it is." Suddenly he felt uneasy. His confidence vanished like a fragile leaf caught on the wind, and he was hesitant to reveal anything more to this woman.

"I'm not getting rid of my things unless I have a good reason," she said.

"I told you the reason. We're being watched."

Jane didn't respond for a moment, and then said, "Listen, you called me, kiddo. I didn't have to come, but I did. Because you sounded so desperate on the phone, and I knew you'd been waiting here a long time. My motherly instincts took over. Maybe I made a mistake not telling that agent about you in the first place."

Nick turned to stare at her profile. "So you plan on turning me in?"

"I never said that. Listen, you've got my attention. I'm willing to look at this thing, but I'm not going to get involved in some kind of spy game with the NSA."

"Why *did* you come?" Nick was starting to get angry. She wasn't taking him seriously. When she didn't respond, he pushed her for an answer. "Why *didn't* you just call Agent Vagnetti as soon as you heard my message?"

A crooked smile appeared on Jane's face.

"For one thing, I assumed you'd rather turn yourself in to me than to a bunch of agents with guns pointed at you. But, you're right, kiddo." She shifted in her seat to get a better look at him. "I guess I'm starting to get a little curious, and your message sounded so...sincere. If you want the truth, I wanted to see what all the fuss was about. I was intrigued. Even more so after the NSA came to visit."

He opened his mouth but stopped. He felt close to tears again.

"Did Henry Applegate put you up to this?"

He nodded.

"He sent you in his place?" She didn't wait for an answer. "I'd like to give this Mr. Applegate a piece of my mind. Sending a young boy to do his work for him."

"He would have come himself, but he's kind of tied up right now." She didn't seem to hear the irony in his voice. He shrugged. "Besides, I'm fifteen."

That didn't impress her.

"Another reason I didn't turn you in to the NSA, aside from the fact that I'm curious, is that I recognized your last name." She glanced over at Nick. "You're Douglas Farraday's son?"

He bobbed his head.

"Then I suppose I don't have to ask how you got involved in all of this. Your father worked for Mr. Applegate, is that right?"

"Yeah."

"Is he your guardian?"

"No. I live with my mother."

"Does she know you're here?"

"Probably."

"Probably?"

"It's a long story. And I'll tell it to you once we ditch your cell and the car." He smiled at her.

"I'm not doing anything until I see the artifact."

Nick looked around the parking lot. It was empty.

"I'd feel better if we were someplace more private, but …" He shrugged and pointed to the far end of the lot, where the branches from a large tree hung over the asphalt.

"Park over there."

From that spot, he could watch if any cars pulled in.

CHAPTER 17

"I'd like to rent a four-wheel drive vehicle, please."

Jane hadn't been able to wear the Halo for long, but it was long enough for her to find out about the dinosaurs. A carload of teens had pulled in to shoot a game of hoops at a net set up very near where they were parked. Nick had reached over and yanked the Halo off her head when they started to get too close. They drove out of the lot and Jane ditched her cell phone in a garbage can not far from the school. Then she parked her Jeep at the mall, which was two blocks away from the car rental office. She could come back for the Jeep later, but the phone was another matter.

"I've had my eye on a new one, anyway," she'd said.

She had called her husband before she ditched the phone and told him she hadn't been able to find the boy after all. And, no, she didn't know what he wanted.

"Since I'm here, I'm going to pick up a few things at the mall. I'll be back as soon as I can."

As she threw the phone into the garbage receptacle, she said to Nick. "I don't normally lie to my husband, but I think he'll forgive me. We'll save telling him about you and the Halo until we get to the observatory."

Jane was starting to get into all this espionage stuff. Nick smiled.

Before they walked the two blocks to the rent-a-car office, they went inside the mall and purchased a disposable cell phone. They ended up using Henry's cash for the transaction so neither of them would leave a credit card trail.

"Could I please have your driver's license?" The vehicle lease agent was busy filling out forms.

Nick shot a glance at Jane. She shrugged. There was no getting around it, but they would use Henry's dwindling money to pay for the one-day lease on the vehicle. It might not stop the NSA from learning of their transaction, but it might at least slow them down.

Once they were settled into the new vehicle, the enormity of everything that happened struck Nick. Since seeing the men at the cemetery, he had been in escape mode. All he had been thinking about was getting the Halo to SETI. He hadn't forgotten what he'd seen while wearing it, but he had put it in the back of his mind.

"You look tired and hungry," Jane said. "As much as I'd like to get to back to the observatory to study the Halo, I think we need to get you something to eat."

They were sitting in a Chipotle's parking lot. He hadn't said a word since Jane handed him the bag of food. She was right. He was starving. He wiped his fingers on a napkin and took one last gulp of his drink, then stuffed the empty cup and wrappers back in the bag.

While he ate, Jane had been staring out the window, her right leg bobbing up and down. She couldn't seem to sit still. She glanced over at him at the sound of the bag crumpling.

"Feel better?" she asked.

He nodded.

"Suppose you give me a little more background on this Halo."

Suddenly, the entire story spilled out of him. He started from the beginning, when he first decided to visit Henry against his mother's wishes, and ended with him deciding to get on a plane to California. He didn't tell her much about what he had seen when he wore the Halo; it would have taken too long. Besides, she was going to see for herself anyway.

"That's quite a story, Nicholas."

"Everybody calls me Nick."

"And, as I said, everybody calls me Jane." She looked over at him as she pulled out of the parking lot. "What did you see when you wore it?"

Nick could tell she was anxious to wear the Halo again.

He shook his head. "Incredible stuff. Unbelievable stuff. I don't understand some of it. But it's more than just what's on it, it's how it's shown."

"Yes, I know."

Every time he thought of it, he felt the same sense of awe as when he had first watched the hologram unfold in front him.

A yellow traffic light flashed in the intersection but Jane didn't slow down. Nick grabbed the door handle and glanced up to see it turn red before they were barely through.

"And the pictures of the universe..." He turned to meet her stare. "It was fantastic."

Jane stepped a little harder on the gas.

They drove for a few minutes in silence, and Nick began to wonder if she had forgotten he was in the car. Then she suddenly turned to him. "You took a great risk coming here by yourself. You should have called me before you flew here."

Nick shrugged. "Henry had already tried to contact you by phone, remember? But you weren't interested. He said we'd have to come to you."

She nodded her head. "Yes, I suppose I might have refused to see you."

He looked out the side window. "I had to try, no matter what. I was going to do whatever it took to convince you to speak with me."

"Well, you've certainly got my attention. But, as intrigued as I am, I'm still not sure this isn't some kind of hoax concocted by your friend Henry to stir up publicity for his new book."

She turned to look at him again. He wished she'd keep her eyes on the road.

"I don't know if you'll understand this fully but SETI has lost its federal funding. We have to count on contributions from private citizens who want to see our search for extraterrestrials continue. If we get caught up in some scandal, this will hurt us. Our credibility will suffer. Do you understand?"

"Yes, I understand." Nick said, keeping his eyes on the road. "I don't know if it's a hoax either. But I saw it. I experienced it, just like you did. And it just doesn't seem like something Henry would be able to create. But I'm still not sure. There are a lot of people out there who believe it's real. And now Henry has been kidnapped and so has my sister. No matter what, I can't believe he wanted that to happen."

Nick didn't speak again for a few seconds and then he blurted out, "I need to find out the truth. And quick! If the NSA can't find my sister, then I'll have to turn it over for ransom."

A look of alarm spread across Jane's face. For the first time since he'd stepped into her Jeep, Nick was confident they were both on the same page.

"I don't want to hurt SETI, or your research, or your reputation. I just need to know the truth and this...you...are my only chance." He turned to face her. "And what if it *is* real?"

She was quiet for a moment and then said, "I'm glad you came to me, Nick, but we have to keep our heads. You know there is a chance we can't verify its authenticity? We might not be able to say with confidence one way or another and, even if we could, it might take us more time than you have."

But Nick knew she believed and, for the moment, that was all he needed.

* * *

"Ming Lin?"

Henry and Emily were seated in the back of the armored van when an agent helped a handcuffed woman into the vehicle. Her black hair was cut fashionably short. She looked young and fit, like someone who went to the gym on a regular basis.

"Mr. Henry."

Henry was shocked to see her. Ming Lin was his old friend Jian Lin's daughter. When she was a young girl,

Henry had arranged for her to learn English; and, when it was time for her to go to college, he had made arrangements for her to get a student visa and sent her to the United States for an education. She had graduated with Honors from Brown University. Afterward, she worked for him as a translator and had been working with Doug on that last expedition, negotiating with the locals for supplies and transportation. Henry lost touch with the girl after the earthquake, but he'd heard from Jian Lin that she obtained a position working as a translator for the UN several years ago.

"I don't understand."

The young woman hung her head and didn't say anything more. The agent guided her to the bench opposite of where Emily and Henry sat and handcuffed her to the metal grid behind the seat.

His voice low, Henry said, "I think you owe me an explanation."

The woman turned her head and started to weep quietly.

"Ming Lin?"

"I didn't know they were going to kidnap you! You must believe me. I only thought they wanted the artifact."

Henry sighed, lost in his own thoughts for a few minutes. Then he turned to Emily.

"I'm so sorry. I hope you weren't hurt in any way."

If she could have, Henry thought Emily might curl up into a ball. He reached out an arm toward the girl and she fell onto his shoulder and clung to the lapel of his scratchy woolen sweater. Their rescuers pushed another man inside the vehicle, handcuffed him next to Ming Lin, and signaled for the driver to start moving.

Henry turned his face from the small Asian woman sitting across from him and concentrated on comforting Douglas' daughter.

* * *

Nick couldn't see much of the countryside as they made their way to the observatory. He knew they were climbing, and the road was winding; in fact, he was getting a little nauseous from the back and forth of the switchbacks and hairpin curves. The arc of the headlights illuminated the road ahead, leaving the shoulder in almost total blackness. Even inside the Jeep he could tell the air was changing, becoming thinner and cooler. Jane kept glancing in the rearview mirror to see if they were being followed, but unless someone was driving without lights, they were all alone on the road. When they first started up Mount Hamilton Road, a few vehicles had passed going the other direction, but they hadn't seen another car for at least fifteen minutes. The Mexican food he'd eaten just a few hours earlier might not have been a good idea. Nick's stomach churned as they took another curve.

Jane said, "I take it you've never visited the observatory."

"No, I haven't." Nick could tell she was concentrating on her driving now. He was glad. The road continued to twist and turn. He wondered if it would ever stop. "This is my first visit to California."

"Well, you'll like it, I think. It's is one of the oldest observatories in the country. We—SETI that is—use their optical telescope in our research. Most of our work is done from remote locations via computer, but my husband and I have been up here doing some observations this past week."

Nick turned his eyes from the road and looked at Jane. "You're searching for some kind of signal from outer space? For a sign?"

"Yes, for life. Somewhere out there." She waved her hand skyward. "There has to be. Right?" She smiled. He noticed her glance at the backpack on his lap.

"Right." He clutched it and felt for the outline of the Halo beneath the fabric. After what he'd seen while wearing it, he was more than convinced. He looked up at the sky and saw more stars than he had ever seen before, a mass of tiny dots against a blue-black background.

"The universe is so vast. There has to be another planet out there that will support life, and probably one with—not just life—but intelligent life. We just have to find them," Jane continued.

Maybe they've already found us, Nick thought. He said out loud, "But what are you looking for *exactly*?"

"If ET is going to communicate with us through the vastness of space, then it will be by sophisticated signals. Signals generated with purpose, with patterns. Something unmistakable as being intelligently designed."

"But how will you know for sure?"

Jane turned and smiled broadly at him. "We'll know."

Nick was beginning to wonder. Was his dad's discovery real? Was it an unmistakable signal of sorts? Or was it fake? *We'll know*, she'd said.

He hoped so.

When they neared the summit, Nick scooted down in his seat.

"What are you doing?"

"The NSA is staking out the SETI building, so they're probably staking out the observatory too."

"Well, unless they have people up in the trees, then there's really no place for them to hide."

Nick knew better than to underestimate the NSA, but he hadn't put much thought into how he would get into the observatory unnoticed until that very minute.

Jane pulled the vehicle around to the back and parked as close to the building as she could. They would be better concealed there. He pulled his baseball cap down and his hoodie up over it.

He kept his head down so his face was hidden from the security cameras. If anyone was watching from the trees, they could only tell someone was entering the building with Jane, but they wouldn't be able to identify him with any certainty. Jane hurried him through the door.

Once they were safely inside the building, she dropped Nick's arm and reached into her pocket for the disposable cell phone and punched in a number.

"Stan, it's me." She paused. "I'll explain in a minute. Meet me in the library. And hurry!"

As they raced to the library, Nick noticed the images of space that lined the long corridor. He would have liked to stop and study them, but Jane didn't slow down as she turned off the phone and slipped it back into her pocket. She directed Nick through doors leading to a small room lined with books and a few long tables sitting in the middle. They had only been in the room a few seconds when a tall man with sandy-colored hair came bounding into the room.

"So what have we here?" He turned to address Nick.

"Nick Farraday, meet my husband, Stan."

Stan's mouth fell open but, before he could speak, Jane said, "I lied."

She saw a crease form between her husband's eyebrows. "I know I told you I'd let the NSA know if I found him, but that was before I heard his story. And that's why I ditched my phone and bought this." She pulled the disposable cell phone out of her pocket.

"Jane, have you lost your mind?"

CHAPTER 18

They were sitting around one of the long tables, Nick on one side and the Carters on the other.

"We'll that's quite a story." Stan leaned back in his chair. "It seems you've gotten us mixed up in something that could get very messy."

"Yes," Jane interjected, "it is quite a story. And yes, it could get messy. But it doesn't have to. I promised Nick I'd take a look at his device because I agree with him. If the NSA gets hold of it, we'll never be able to study it. Now is our only chance. And I can't really see how any of this is illegal. The Halo is property of Henry Applegate until proven otherwise. And Henry, in essence, left it for Nick to protect. This has been my life's work. You're asking me to give up the chance to discover what I've been searching for my entire life? But if we *are* going to do this, we need to do it quickly."

Stan shook his head in confusion.

"Aren't you the least bit curious?" Jane asked.

'Of course I'm curious. But, no matter if it's true or not, it seems the NSA thinks it belongs to them. And, besides, if this does turn out to be a hoax—which in all likelihood it is—and somehow the media gets hold of it ..."

"I know. But the Halo is already here. We didn't ask for it. It came to us. And the reward outweighs the risk."

Jane gave her husband an encouraging smile. "Nick and I are confident that once you take a look at the device, you'll understand. If the NSA still needs it for ransom, then we'll hand it over, but this might be our only chance. Even if all it does is to lead us in the right direction, gives us a hint to where we should be looking in this vast universe, wouldn't it still be worth it? In any case, we need to make a decision. There are people being held ransom for this thing. We either take time to study it, or Nick makes a phone call right now."

Stan stared down at the table. "The possibilities of it being the real deal are highly doubtful. But on the slight chance it holds some useful information, then I suppose it is worth the risk. No matter what happens to it later, the government can never take that knowledge away from us," Stan raised his head and smiled. "They'd have to kill us first."

The three of them went suddenly silent. The smile fell from Stan's face.

"I never considered that possibility," Jane said soberly, "but it's too late to think about it now!"

Jane watched the scene progress in front of her. It was breathtaking. She traveled through space and approached Earth. When she neared the singularly beautiful blue orb, a double helix DNA hologram appeared, and a beam of light pointed to Earth, signifying this as the genome of the intelligent beings there. Another double helix appeared and a beam of light traveled back across the universe to a planet in the Pleiades constellation. She recognized the unmistakable cluster of stars and watched in awe as the beam of light shifted and pointed to different spots on Earth, just as Nick described. The beam of light flashed to Stonehenge; to the pyramids in Egypt; to South America; to the Andes; to the Tibetan Plateau—near where the device had been found—then to the Nazca lines in Peru; and to places no one would associate with great archaeological finds. Everything was revealed to her in symbols and pictures. Jane thought of the saying: *A picture is worth a thousand words.* Pictures and symbols were the perfect tool to communicate in the absence of a common language. Finally, the beams disappeared and Jane was left staring at the rotating double helixes.

The scene changed to what resembled math equations and, even though she didn't fully understand them at the moment, Jane could instantly see patterns in them.

"There, look, that could easily represent Einstein's Theory of Relativity. They're not using symbols common to us, but we can make the connections. It might take some time, but I'm sure it can be done."

Jane, just like Doug reacted so many years ago, didn't seem to remember that no one else in the room could see what she was witnessing. Again and again, equally fantastic images, with messages she either understood instantly or realized it would take time to understand, came up in a 3D hologram and filled the space surrounding her.

"This is incredible!"

There were other disturbing scenes that almost knocked her off her chair. Scenes that made her heart race and her stomach flip. Stan had already taken a turn wearing the Halo. He was equally stunned.

"Incredible is right, and some of it rather disquieting. But what this shows is irrefutable evidence that aliens have visited Earth."

Now it was Jane's turn to be practical.

"If it is authentic, Stan. Let's not get ahead of ourselves. As much as I'd like to believe it, we still lack absolute proof. Remember? We can't jump to conclusions." Jane was trying hard to control her own enthusiasm.

They looked at the Halo sitting between them on the long table.

Stan gave a heavy sigh. "I know we have to be cautious, but my God! If this is real, if it isn't a fake, then..." His eyes went blank, reflecting his introspection. "It pointed to 21 Tauri, Asterope, in the northeast corner of the Pleiades." Stan stated. "Wouldn't you agree, Jane?"

"Yes...yes, it did."

"Astounding."

"This will change the World's view of itself. Everything will be seen in a different light."

They both seemed to forget that Nick was still in the room. Stan paced the floor. Nick could almost hear the tension coming from both of them, like the pluck of a taut wire.

"All the great ancient monuments. Everything is explained. And the Grand Canyon! Amazing."

Nick remembered seeing scenes of a mining operation being conducted in a deep canyon but didn't realize, until Stan mentioned it, that what he was seeing was the Grand Canyon and how it had been formed. Not by erosion, as so many geologists claimed, but by strip mining—leaving behind strangely shaped rock monoliths when the operation was abandoned.

There were other things that Nick didn't understand at all. But he understood enough to know that the ancient ETs had an advanced understanding of cloning. Some of what he had seen was gross, but he put that out of his mind. He would think about it later. Restoring his father's reputation—in his own mind as well as the public's—and freeing Henry and Emily, was all Nick could concentrate on at the moment.

"The only reason I'm not jumping around like a lunatic at this very moment is that we don't know if this is real or not. It is just mind blowing! I'm...I'm speechless," Stan said as he slumped down in a chair.

* * *

The van door flew open. Liz blinked a few times and then caught sight of Emily. Her daughter leaped up and rushed out of the rear of the van.

Liz folded Emily in her arms and squeezed as tight as she could. "Are you okay?" She pushed her away and held her at arm's length, running her eyes down the length of her daughter's body, searching for any telltale signs of abuse.

"I'm okay. I just want to go home."

Liz pulled her daughter close again and looked up as Henry struggled to step off the bottom ledge of the vehicle. When she caught sight of the woman still inside, she gasped. "Ming Lin?"

The woman turned her head to the front of the van, avoiding Liz's gaze.

"What are you doing here?" Then she saw that Ming was shackled to the iron grate on the inside wall of the van and everything became clear. Liz felt her hand curl into a fist.

"Why, Ming Lin? Wasn't seducing my husband enough? Now you had to kidnap my daughter too? What kind of monster are you?"

Ming Lin stared at Liz. "This wasn't supposed to happen." There was a catch in the woman's voice. "What I did here was wrong. But if it makes any difference to you, I didn't know kidnapping was part of the plan. And, just to set the record straight, I didn't seduce your husband." There was no spite or bitterness in her voice.

"What's that supposed to mean?"

"It means we weren't having an affair. I know that's what you thought, but it wasn't true. We were just friends."

"Friends?" Liz waved her arm at Emily. "This is how friends act?"

The agent took Liz's arm and tried to lead her away from the van. "Sorry, ma'am, you have to leave. Now!"

* * *

"Before we get ahead of ourselves," Jane said. "Nick needs to make his phone call."

They glanced at Nick.

"We've both worn the Halo. It would be nice to have more time to study it, but at least we have something to go on. You need to make your phone call. If your sister and Henry are okay, then...well, then you can make a decision."

Nick nodded.

"And I want you to let your mother know that you are doing this on your own. You are underage, you know. Stan and I are putting ourselves in a precarious situation, in more ways than one. You can call her from the prepaid cell. But, remember, the NSA probably has your mom's cell tapped and will hear what you're saying."

"I know. I'll be careful what I say. I just hope everyone's okay." He thought about Emily and Henry and a tight knot formed in the pit of his stomach.

Jane reached in her pocket and handed him the phone.

* * *

"Nick? Where are you? Agent Vagnetti went to search for you! I've been scared to death!"

"I'm sorry, Mom. I'm alright."

"Where are you?" she repeated.

"I'm safe."

"Tell me where you are and we'll have the NSA pick you up and get you home."

"Listen, Mom, I don't have much time. Have they found Emily yet?"

"Yes, you're sister is here. She's good. Still a little shook up, but okay."

Nick let out a sigh of relief.

"What about Henry?"

"They're both okay. I don't know what you think you're doing but you need to come home."

"No, Mom, I can't do that. I don't want to do that. Maybe in a day or two…"

"Day or two? I want you home now."

"I can't just yet."

"I don't believe this. You—"

"Listen, Mom, I promise I'll be home soon. I just have some stuff I have to take care of."

"Take care of? What could you possibly need to take care of? You need to come home!"

"I need to get some questions answered about the Halo."

Liz had reached the limit of her patience. She wanted her son home, but mostly she wanted to never see or hear about that damned crown again. She wanted her life to get back to normal, if that was even possible. Then it dawned on her.

"You went to SETI, didn't you? Henry put it in your head to go there!"

"I just wanted to let you know I'm okay and to check on Emily and Henry. And to tell you I can't come home yet."

Liz's heart sank. "Nick, your sister was kidnapped. Doesn't that tell you something? You could be in danger too. I want you home!" Her voice was getting shrill. "I can't stand thinking you're so far away and all alone."

"I'm not alone. I'm with people who will make sure I'm safe. And I need to tell you that what I'm doing, I'm doing because I want to. No one is forcing me to do anything. Do you understand?"

"I...I'm not sure."

"It's important you understand I'm safe. That I'm in safe company, and that I'm making my own decisions."

"Okay, I understand." If he had gone to SETI, then maybe the woman Henry had mentioned was helping him. That thought gave her a small amount of comfort.

"I'm just trying to find some answers."

"You don't need answers, Nick. You just need to come home."

"Yes, I do, Mom! Don't you? Emily is safe now. We don't need the Halo to save her. This is our only chance. If I don't find out now, it might be too late. I'm so close, just another day or two. Can't you trust me?"

"Nick, are you saying you have the crown with you?"

He didn't answer right away. "I didn't say that. I just said I needed to get some answers about it. Don't you?"

She shook her head, knowing he couldn't see her. Yes, she did want answers and from what Frank had confided in her, they were not likely to get any from the NSA. She knew how important it was for Nick—for her—to learn the truth about Doug. But at the risk of her son's life? That certainly wasn't her first choice, but it seemed she didn't have a say in it. Nick was determined to follow this through. Frank's words rang in her ears. She had to trust him.

"Yes, I trust you, Nick. And, yes, I want to know the truth." There was no talking him out of it. "Just be careful and get home as soon as you can...and please try to keep me posted! Call me whenever you can."

"I will. I've gotta run now."

"I love you, Nicholas."

"Love you too, Mom. And tell Emily I'm glad she's home."

Liz hit the "end call" icon and turned to bury her face in Frank's waiting arms.

CHAPTER 19

L et's look at some facts," Jane offered. "Applegate claims Doug Farraday found the Halo in an undisturbed burial alcove, behind a sealed stone slab. He claims the excavation of the device was well documented, and that other items found inside the alcove, prior to Farraday's finding the artifact, were carbon dated back hundreds of thousands of years."

"The Drōpa Stones."

They both turned to face Nick.

"Stones?" Jane asked.

"That's what was carbon dated. My dad found some stones while he was looking for a burial place of the Drōpa people."

"The Drōpa?" Jane asked. "Are you telling me your dad was looking for evidence of the *Drōpa*? The aliens who supposedly crashed landed on Earth and couldn't get back home? Henry never mentioned that."

Jane looked at Stan. He twisted his mouth, shook his head, and looked down at his shoes.

"Henry believed they existed. He wanted my dad to try and find an undisturbed mummy in order to study their DNA. He wanted to prove that either the legend was true, or that they were just humans whose abnormalities had been passed down through the generations."

Jane said, "The mummies found in that area were, most likely, ancestors of the Sherpa, who are indigenous to the Himalayans. The Sherpa were small in stature, but they definitely weren't alien."

"When I looked up 'Drōpa' on the internet I found out that the ufologists—"

Jane raised an eyebrow.

"UFO conspiracy theorists," Nick explained.

"I know what it means, Nick. Those crazies will write anything and say it's a fact."

When Nick first looked it up on the Web, he thought anyone with half a brain cell would realize the legend of the Drōpa Stones was a hoax perpetuated by people who were either out to make money, or the delusional: The *True Believers*, those who saw evidence in anything and everything that might support their unwavering belief in alien visitation to Earth. Nick was sorry he'd mentioned them now. It clearly hadn't helped his cause. He needed to turn the conversation around, and quick.

"My dad wrote some stuff about what he was looking for in his journal."

"What journal?"

"He was keeping a journal. They found it with his things, and my mom gave it to me as a keepsake. Anyway, my dad wrote about all this in the journal."

"Yes," Stan encouraged Nick to continue.

"Henry wanted my dad to try and find mummies, but also to study the cave art and, if he found any of the stones, to study them too. The original Drōpa Stones had hiero-glyphs etched in a spiral."

His dad had written that some people believed the stones held recordings—like an old-time record album—left by ancient extraterrestrials, but Nick decided to leave that part out.

"My dad found drawings of the Pleiades, too. Henry said lots of ancient civilizations depicted that constellation in their art. And he said my dad confided in him that, right before he died, he found something else, something that would even shock Henry. It must have been the Halo."

Stan said, "Let's get back to these websites. Do you know when they were first created?"

Nick's attempt to move the conversation away from the ufologists hadn't worked.

"I'm not sure, but I think most of the articles were dated about ten years ago."

"About the same amount of time your father has been gone."

That was why Nick had remembered the dates. He realized what the implication would be before Stan said it.

"One more reason to think this could be a hoax concocted by Applegate. It could mean this entire Drōpa Stone UFO theory was a plant to make the Halo seem more credible. It could mean that Henry had it all this time and created some of those websites himself, in a very patent, and patient, attempt to add credibility to the hoax," Stan said. "Once your father's body was discovered, it created the perfect opportunity for him."

"A little too perfect, if you ask me." Jane said.

Nick was silent for a moment before he stated: "But my father's body was never found."

* * *

Four wallets and four cell phones sat on the desk in front of Ming Lin. The ringleader of the kidnappers, Bo Zheng and his two male accomplices, Guangli and Niu Chen, were being held in the storage room to the right of the front door of The Antiquarian. They weren't cooperating.

Frank decided to try his luck with Ming Lin and, besides, her English was much better.

"Henry tells me you're the daughter of an old family friend and that he sent you to school here."

"Yes, that is true."

"Tell me how you got involved in this kidnapping."

"I know my rights as an American citizen. I want a lawyer."

"You're not dealing with your local police department, Ming Lin. I could send you to Gitmo this afternoon and no one would hear from you for a long, long time—if ever. But, if you work with me, maybe I can see to it that the worst doesn't happen to you."

Ming Lin fidgeted in her chair and took a moment to consider her options, then she said, "Ask me your questions, and I'll decide if I want to answer them."

Frank wasn't going to waste any time.

"Is Bo Zheng the head of this operation, or is there someone higher up we should know about?"

Ming Lin shook her head. "He's the leader."

"What's your relationship with him?"

"We've been dating for the last five years."

Frank leaned his chair back so that it was rocking on the back legs, his hands clasped behind his head.

"So I take it he learned about the object from you?"

She nodded.

"What made him interested?"

"It's complicated."

"It always is."

Ming Lin sighed. "His brother owns a very successful biological products company in China. I think he's always been a little jealous. So when I mentioned the object, *the crown*—I'd seen the video on YouTube—I told Bo that I knew the man in it and that I had heard a long time ago that he'd found something up in the mountains."

Frank interrupted, "So neither you or Bo posted the video on YouTube?"

"No, I'd never seen it before. I saw a link to it somewhere. Facebook or Twitter. And I took a quick look. That's the first I ever heard of it."

Frank wondered who had posted it. Henry insisted he hadn't, and now Ming Lin denied that the kidnappers had anything to do with it. Something else was curious to him. Whoever had posted it, did it for the sole purpose of discrediting the artifact. It seemed likely that Ming Lin was telling the truth. Bo Zheng wouldn't want to discredit the object, quite the opposite.

Frank nodded his head. "Okay, go on."

"Anyway, Bo got very interested. He was obsessed with outdoing his brother. He thought he could use the crown in some way to make himself successful. If what I'd heard was true, then the crown held information that he could use to create new technologies to outshine his brother. If it turned out to be nothing, then maybe there would still be a way to make money from it, to perpetuate the false claims in order to get others interested and swindle them out of money. If other people thought it was a genuine alien device, then perhaps they would pay big bucks to get their hands on it. If nothing else, maybe Bo could make enough seed money to start a company of his own."

Frank had run a check on Bo Zheng's name and knew all about his brother's successful business. So far, everything Ming Lin was telling him checked out.

"What exactly did you tell Bo about the object?"

"Only that Doug had told Henry he'd made a great discovery right before the earthquake. That he'd found something that contained vast amounts of scientific knowledge, for one thing."

"How did you know this?"

"As you said, my father and Henry were friends. Doug had radioed my father from the mountain with a message for Henry about the discovery. I overheard my father relaying the information to Henry during a phone conversation. I'd forgotten all about it until the video surfaced on YouTube. I realized then that the crown must be the great discovery. At the time, I thought it was just another artifact. Something that would get an archaeologist excited, but meant little to the rest of us. And, frankly, when I first saw the video, just like everyone else, I thought Doug might have lost his mind while up there. The man in the video seemed like a different person than the one I knew. One day I showed Bo the video, telling him all about my connection to the man in it and that his body had just been discovered.

"I had spoken with my father and knew when he was sending Doug's body back to the States. I had asked him about Doug's discovery, if it had been found too, but he told me he couldn't say. I knew he was being loyal to Henry; that Henry must have told him not to reveal anything. But I knew from the sound of his voice that it had been found.

"You have to believe that I never knew kidnapping was going to be part of this. I thought we were just going to break into Henry's and try to find the crown and, if we didn't find it there, then maybe we'd have to search the Farraday's too. I signed up for breaking-and-entering, not kidnapping. Things just got way out of hand."

"Seems like your boyfriend went to a lot of trouble without even knowing if it would be worth it."

Ming Lin shrugged. "Even though I had my doubts after seeing the video, I respected Doug enough to think that he might really have found something up there."

"Did you tell anyone else your thoughts on the object? That there might be some legitimacy to Doug's claims?"

She shook her head. "I only talked to Bo about it. I have no idea if he told anyone else. I know he was determined to keep this a secret. Even the other two don't really know the details; just that we were after an ancient artifact. The brothers owed Bo a favor, and this was their payback."

* * *

Jane said, "Henry claims he discovered the Halo's existence when he was preparing to ship Doug Farraday's body from China back to the United States. Now we know there wasn't a body. So that's one thing we know for sure that he's lied about."

"But he explained to me why he lied. He lied in order to get the Halo through customs!"

"Still, Nick, it was a lie." Jane continued trying to sort it all out. "In any case, the Halo was in a backpack found by a jade miner near where your father disappeared after the quake in the Himalayans. When Henry first discussed this with me, he claimed the man who found the backpack turned it over, with the artifact still inside, to his friend in China, and then Henry's friend sent it to him."

"That's another part of this story that sounds suspicious to me," Stan said. "Why would a poor miner give up a valuable jeweled crown?"

"According to Applegate, the miner who found the backpack had had extreme good fortune that day. Over the years, local legends surrounding the archaeologist and the earthquake had flourished. He was afraid if he didn't return the backpack to its rightful owner, his good fortune would turn into bad luck."

Stan shrugged. "That sounds reasonable enough. The peoples of that region can be highly superstitious."

"Oh, Nick, I'm sorry," Jane said, "We didn't mean to be so insensitive when talking about your father. This whole thing is just so incredible. I think both Stan and I are in shock. We really want to believe it's real. We've been searching for something like this for decades! Except we thought we would find it out there," she pointed upward, "not down here on Earth."

"And, I'm sorry, son," Stan said, "but I still have my doubts. No matter how incredible this hologram device is, the evidence points to it being counterfeit. So, no matter how much we want to believe it, we have to proceed carefully."

"It really isn't a hologram device. You see the images inside your head." Nick said. "But I understand. I want to know the truth, no matter what the truth is." He lowered his head and stared at his shoes.

"Stan, do you know of any technology that is capable of something like this?" Jane asked.

"I'm not aware of any, but that doesn't mean it doesn't exist."

"And even if it did, Applegate would have to pay a fortune for someone to create this device for him. And swear them to secrecy."

"Yes, that does tilt the scale to the other side a bit. And I think we would have heard something about this technology. There would be speculation." Stan moved to a laptop set up in the corner of the room. "I'm going to look up new hologram technology. See if I can find anything similar that's being developed."

"Good idea. Another thing to consider," Jane said, "is why would the NSA be showing such interest if they thought it was a hoax? It seems they are giving it a little too much attention. And we know this for a fact—there are some shady characters looking for this device and willing to kidnap to find it."

"I don't know. I'm starting to get a bad feeling." Stan turned from the computer to look at Jane. "The last thing SETI needs is to become involved and then look like fools when this is proved to be nothing."

"Well, what do we have to lose in investigating it a little further? We've come all this way. Why stop now?" Jane asked.

Stan turned back to the computer screen. "I'm finding some interesting sites on new hologram technology, but nothing that claims they are anywhere near as advanced as this device."

Stan leaned back in his chair, deep in thought.

Jane said, "Well, we can speculate for hours, but one meaningful thing we can do is point our radio telescopes toward the Pleiades constellation. If we don't get any signals, then we will be one step closer in recognizing the device as a possible hoax."

Stan didn't respond right away, then stood up straight and clapped his hands together.

"Great idea! And we can contact the VLA. The Very Large Array," he turned to Nick, explaining the acronym for his benefit, "to get them on board with the search immediately. And the Jodrell Bank, let's get them on board, too! We don't have to tell them why, just that we want to do a widespread search."

"And we can start a laser pulse search here at Lick as well," Jane offered.

"Another good idea. Come on, Nick," Stan said as he headed for the door. "You wanna see something cool?"

Jane scooped the Halo from the table and followed them out the door.

CHAPTER 20

Nick and Jane met Stan in the control room that operated the telescope housed in the South Dome. Stan had everything ready and was standing over a console of computers, getting the software prepared for input. He waved them over as they came through the door.

"We're using the Nickel one-meter reflecting telescope," he said to Nick. "I've pointed it toward the northeast sector of the Pleiades constellation—at Asterope. Right where the hologram indicated. And it's November, and evening, an excellent time to study the constellation. The positioning is perfect."

Stan typed something on the keyboard in front of him. "What we're looking for are laser pulses; more specifically, for photons generated by a quick laser pulse. We've realized for some time now that if ET were to communicate with us, it would be with light." He kept adjusting things, turning knobs and entering data, readying the telescope for the search. "And the use of lasers in the hologram message seems to corroborate that assumption."

Stan inclined his head toward one of the computer monitors, motioning for Nick to take a look.

"The telescope has been equipped with a photon meter. We're going to be counting the number of photons arriving during very short slices of time, about a billionth of a second. If the counter registers dozens of photons per time slice, that's evidence of an intelligent signal."

When both Stan and Jane were satisfied with the software setup, Stan said, "Okay, gang, everyone ready?" He nodded to Jane and she reached over and hit the Enter button.

"Now we wait."

After a while, Stan said to Nick, "I promised to show you the telescope. Want to go take a closer look?"

"Sure, yeah. That would be great!"

Nick's footsteps echoed in the large room. He could feel the cool mountain air falling from the open slit in the high roof of the dome. He looked at the telescope pointed toward the night sky. Attached to the side was what looked like a ship's wheel. *The telescope is like a ship*, he thought, *a tiny ship sailing through the nighttime sky.*

"The observatory is named after James Lick. He wanted to build a monument to himself and his parents. At first, he was going to build a huge pyramid right in the middle of San Francisco, but someone talked him into building the observatory instead. Good thing for us." Stan smiled. "He's buried here, under the large refractor telescope. He died before it was built. The first lens was damaged during shipment. Took years to get a replacement, and they couldn't finish until they had it."

Stan continued to explain the history of the observatory. Nick couldn't believe they could build something like this a hundred years ago. He thought about workers hauling up the delicate equipment along the winding, unpaved road by horse drawn wagons.

Suddenly, the cold air made Nick acutely aware of how much he needed to use the restroom.

"Is there a bathroom nearby?"

Stan told him where to find it and said he'd meet him back in the control room.

When he returned, Stan offered him a cup of coffee from the vending machine. Nick stared at the cup.

"Oh, sorry, I just assumed you drank coffee. You need something to stay warm in here."

"I drink it once in a while. Thanks." He wrapped his hands around the warmth.

Jane turned to Nick, "Stan and I think we need to have a little more discussion about what you're going to do with the Halo. We were in a hurry and never really thought it through. We think it's worth going over all the details, and then you can make a more informed decision now that the situation isn't so tense."

Nick nodded, not really understanding why they needed to discuss it any further.

"Let me preface this discussion by saying that what we are about to say is only important if this object is proven to be extraterrestrial in nature," Jane said.

Nick nodded.

"We, SETI that is, have made an agreement with the astronomical community, and an unofficial agreement with the government, about when and what we would announce to the world should we ever discover a signal. But that agreement pertains to a signal coming from out in the universe. This is an object found on Earth. The fact that it might prove extraterrestrials visited us in the past is irrelevant. I'm not sure our protocol applies in this circumstance or, rather, to this object."

"And I agree." Stan said. "Speaking of the object itself, this is the way I see it: If this was an ancient artifact of any significance, something archaeological, the Tibetan or Chinese government would probably own it, whichever has jurisdiction over the original site. Keep in mind the laws for selling antiquities changed in January of 2009. I'm not sure of the exact laws at the moment, or how they would apply in this situation. I'm sure it's all very complicated because, technically, this item was found well before the change in the antiquities law. And, while I might be relying on a technicality, I don't think this falls under the category of simple archaeological artifact. This is something no one anticipated.

"Jane and I were discussing this very technicality while you were out of the room. We feel this is more of a scientific discovery. And, until we have more time to think about it, perhaps we should consider it a 'found object' and, in that sense, the object belongs to Henry Applegate."

Jane added, "But, no matter what we call it, or who we feel it belongs to, the government will want to seize control. Think of the knowledge and power to be gained from the vast amount of information it contains." She looked at Stan. "Just think of where their math might lead us. They won't be too keen on sharing it with our enemies, or countries with unstable leaders who might abuse the knowledge."

"*If* the Halo is the real deal," Nick said, "then the knowledge belongs to the entire planet, not just us! This could bring nations closer together, rather than further apart! The information wasn't left here for the United States, it was left for the World."

Stan and Jane nodded their agreement.

Nick continued, "I don't want bad people to get hold of powerful information either. I know that much. But I don't think we should hide the discovery, either. There has to be a compromise."

"I think so too," Jane said. "But you must understand, if the entire populace finds out what is on this device, there could be widespread panic. It would instantly change the Planet. Governments, religions...they might all collapse. There has been a lot of discussion and debate about the social effect of contact. Who knows what the reaction would be? It could lead to total chaos. In this instance, I agree we need to practice caution. We're not saying that we shouldn't, or couldn't, announce we found a promising signal. That's well within our rights. It is all spelled out in what we call the Declaration of Principles Concerning Activities Following the Detection of Extraterrestrial Intelligence." Jane smiled. "A mouthful, I know. But to reveal the existence of the Halo to the entire population might be beyond our legal rights and, perhaps, not a wise thing to do in the long run."

"We want to ask you," Stan continued, "even though we don't feel this object falls under the jurisdiction of our agreement with the government, or the astronomical community, and given everything else we've just told you, do you still agree that we turn the Halo over to the NSA after we've studied it? Once we've gathered enough initial information for our own purposes, then it needs to be studied by scientists in different fields; and, in any case, the NSA can take anything they want in the name of national security. We're just fooling ourselves to think we really have a choice."

Nick realized the only way to protect the Halo from coming under government control was to show the entire world the information it contained. Just how they would accomplish that, he didn't know. Everyone would have to wear it to see all the astonishing things it held, unless someone discovered a method of projecting the images on a screen. He was beginning to agree with the Carters. It might not be such a good idea to share the entire story of the Halo. And what individual, or enterprise, could he and Henry trust with the responsibility of this knowledge? That could be just as dangerous—or worse—than handing it over to the US Government. The Halo would need protecting, and none of them had the means to keep it safe.

"Being that you are here on Henry's behalf you are, in a sense, his spokesperson," Stan said. "Are you still in agreement that we hand over the Halo to the NSA? Especially since they've already contacted us about it? If we continue to hide it from them, then we might be asking for trouble. Trouble I don't really want to put myself, or SETI, into."

"I could call Henry and ask him, now that he's been rescued. But the NSA is still lurking around. If I call, they'd know it's here. Besides, Agent Vagnetti knows I have it, she just doesn't know where I am at the moment. I doubt I'd ever be able to get it back to Henry without them finding out."

Nick thought for a moment longer. No matter how much he believed the peoples of the world had a right to know about the artifact, he had to take into consideration everything the Carter's had explained to him. He was grateful they had gone over all the details, so he wouldn't have any doubts about their decision later on. In any case, it seemed they really didn't have any other choice.

He nodded his head in agreement.

* * *

They had been sitting in the control room for over an hour with no sign of a laser pulse signal and no word from the other observatories.

"You didn't really expect to find something right way, did you?" Jane asked.

"No, but I would have thought someone would have picked up something by now," Stan said.

"It's too soon to give up hope."

Nick didn't say it out loud, but he was disappointed. He was starting to get nervous, too. But, like Jane said, maybe it was unreasonable to think they would find it quickly.

The Carters had taken turns wearing the Halo while they let the telescope do its work in the adjoining room. They took notes for each other as one of them wore it and dictated to the other.

Nick must have fallen asleep. He looked at the clock. It was after two in the morning, but it seemed much later.

"Sorry, Nick, it's starting to look like this really might be a hoax," Jane leaned one elbow on the desk and cupped her chin in her hand.

"Damn!" Stan slammed his palm against the desk. "If Henry Applegate was in this room right now I would throttle him."

Nick didn't know what to say, or feel. In the beginning he had trusted Henry, but then he started to have doubts. Big doubts. But, over the course of this evening, he had started to believe again that Henry had been a good friend to his dad and to him. Now it looked as if he had been using Nick all along—using him just like he used his dead father. He could feel his face grow hot. They sat in silence, each feeling betrayed in their own way.

But how could Henry have pulled it off? Nick wondered again. The device just seemed...seemed so out-of-this-world. As Stan said, it could be a technology they hadn't heard about yet. How could they have been so foolish to believe it was anything more?

After a while, Jane said, "We shouldn't give up so soon."

"We've pointed the telescope to the exact area the hologram indicated and everywhere nearby. Even if we were off a little, we should still be picking up something. How much more obvious could they have been? The light beam pointed from practically every important archae-ological site on Earth *precisely* back to Asterope ..." Stan's voiced trailed off, then he jumped up.

"Wait." He started to pace.

"The laser pointed from those sites back to Asterope, and then from Asterope back to the sites. So, maybe, just maybe, what they are trying to tell us is, not just that they had visited those sites, but that they are also sending laser signals back to those points—information—back to those points in particular. That if we are going to pick up signals, we have to physically *be* in one of those places in order to pick up the laser pulses."

Jane said, "Like NASA's GOPEX Project."

"Yes, the Galileo Optical Experiment. NASA sent laser pulses from Earth to Galileo's imaging system. The long exposure images turned out beautifully!"

Nick knew Galileo was the name of the unmanned spacecraft launched by NASA in 1989 to study the planet Jupiter and its moons.

Jane turned to him. "NASA was testing the possibility of optical communication from a spacecraft to Earth. It was a great success."

She was lost in thought for a moment and then continued, "The alien intelligence who left the device could be sending data using a similar method. Maybe they aren't sending us a signal to prove their existence but rather streaming information. This might be the way they communicated with their own people while they were still here on Earth."

Now Jane was standing. "We need to go to one of the places they pointed to. We need to monitor Asterope from one of those sites."

CHAPTER 21

Throughout the night, they discovered that by just thinking about where they wanted to go in the hologram sequence, the Halo would somehow index to that location. They hadn't perfected the technique yet, but it was still better than navigating through the entire hologram sequence until they found what they wanted. As beautiful as it was, they were in a hurry.

"Stan, the nearest location to us is the four-corners area in the U.S., where Utah, Colorado, Arizona and New Mexico meet. What is near there?"

The hologram pulled in tighter, and Jane noticed a reddish patch on the image of Earth. She didn't wait for Stan to answer.

"The Mesa Verde National Park. I recognize the red earth; it shows up clearly on images from space. And the Cliff Palaces of the Anasazi are there! Remember when we visited there a few years back, Stan?"

"Yes. The Anasazi Indians." He ran his hands through his hair.

"And we have our portable optical telescope set-up." She turned to him. "What do you think?"

"It's an awfully long drive from here."

She raised an eyebrow. "We don't have to drive. We can use Hal's jet."

Hal was one of SETI's biggest contributors. "I'm sure I could get him to agree."

"Or, we could take a commercial flight."

"That would take too long. Waste time we don't have. More importantly, I don't trust them with the delicate equipment."

They both turned to Nick and Jane said, "With Agent Vagnetti and the whole of the NSA looking for you, I'm afraid you won't be able to come along. It's one thing for you to be here with us, but we can't cross state lines with a minor. We'll have to make arrangements for you to fly back home."

As if on cue, Stan's cell phone rang.

* * *

Ronnie stood inside the foyer of the Lick Observatory studying the remarkable photos that hung on the long wall spanning the length of the building.

The woman—the astronomer—Jane Carter, admitted she had picked Nick up at a nearby school and brought him to the observatory. It looked as if she was going to deny it at first, but then she turned to her husband and he nodded.

Ronnie was disappointed. They had given up too easily. Her job was to retrieve the artifact and turn it over to her superiors, but on a personal level, she wanted the boy to succeed. She knew his goal was to restore his father's reputation and, in doing so, he needed to authenticate the Halo. He had come to SETI to get the proof he needed.

And Ronnie wanted him to find that proof, if it was there. Because after all her years of service, after all her dedication and searching, she didn't have confidence the agency would allow her to study the Halo, or to learn all its secrets. This might be her last chance.

Footsteps echoed off the high ceiling. Ronnie turned her attention from the photos along the wall to Jane Carter and her husband, who were rushing into the long hallway.

"He's gone," Jane said.

Ronnie was practiced at keeping a calm demeanor but she felt her heart trip against her ribs. Several possibilities flickered through her mind.

"He has to be somewhere in the building," Ronnie said.

"We've looked everywhere."

"And the artifact?" That's when she noticed Stan holding it.

She reached out her hand, "I'll have to take that."

"I could ask you for a warrant—"

She cut him off before he could finish. "And I could give you an argument for not needing one. This is a matter of national security."

"I was going to say 'but I'm not going to'. We all— Nick included—agreed to turn it over to the NSA. We're turning it over willingly. Just for the record."

Stan handed the Halo to Ronnie and, as she took it, she asked, "What is your opinion of this device?"

"Opinion?"

"I'm not naïve, Mr. Carter, I'm sure you've studied it. What is your conclusion? Genuine, or a hoax?"

"Yes, we've studied it, but we haven't had enough time to make an assessment yet."

For the first time, Ronnie thought the couple might be blatantly lying to her.

"I'm not asking for an in-depth analysis. What is your gut reaction?"

"If it's a hoax, then it's a damn good one," Stan said.

Ronnie moved her fingers along the lower rim of the artifact, rotating it as she said, "We need to get the boy home. His mother is worried about him. Do you mind if I search the building and the grounds?"

The observatory was at an elevation of approximately 4200 feet, with rugged terrain and steep drop-offs all around. If the boy had fled on foot, he had put himself in unnecessary danger. She didn't want to call in a search team at night. Even though Mt. Hamilton was largely uninhabited, if she ordered a helicopter search, it would surely draw unwanted attention. The last thing Ronnie needed was for the media to get wind of this story. Her team had managed to keep the press at bay in Michigan, and Ronnie wanted to keep it that way. She made her way outside and told the agent waiting behind the wheel to search the perimeter of the observatory.

The grounds were deserted this time of night. Except for the Carters, the only other personnel on site was the telescope manager. They all volunteered to help search for the boy. None of them liked the idea of him roaming the mountain at night, alone and on foot.

* * *

Nick slipped out the side door situated on the east side of the building near the small dome while the Carter's were talking with Agent Vagnetti in the west entrance foyer. He carefully closed the door so that it wouldn't echo back from the high ceilings. The nighttime November sky was clear and the air cold. It was eerily quiet except for the occasional howl of some nocturnal animal that Nick couldn't identify. A pale wisp of condensation formed in front of him. His breathing sounded ragged in his ears. He didn't stop his forward motion as he surveyed the terrain in front of him. The mountain sloped severely downward but not so much that he lost his balance. Just beyond a clump of evergreens was a drop-off to the road below. Nick scrambled to the edge, kneeled down, and listened. He didn't know how many other agents Vagnetti had brought with her. Maybe they were scouring the area already. He had to be careful.

The only sound was the wind whispering through the evergreens. Gripping the edge of the white concrete-block escarpment that held the mountain back from the road, he slipped over the side, hung for a moment, then dropped and rolled to break his fall. His heart pounded in his chest, more from fright than exertion, as he sprinted across the road and then tumbled down the steep slope on the other side. He noticed a thick cluster of low, widespread chaparral bushes and dived underneath, using the branches as a shield.

He didn't know how long he would have to wait, or if he would have to move farther down the side of the mountain to be safe. His eyes fixed on the back of the observatory. If someone came looking for him they would, most likely, be coming from that direction.

* * *

"I've called in an additional search team." Ronnie was wheezing from all the activity. The thin mountain air didn't help. They had been searching for over an hour but had found no sign of Nick.

Now they were seated around the long table in the library where Jane and Stan first wore the Halo only a few hours ago. Jane had offered Ronnie an aluminum telescope case, with foam padding on the inside, for Ronnie to transport it. The handled case was sitting on the table.

She hadn't told the Carters, but half a dozen drones were being deployed from nearby Beale Air Force Base to do an aerial search.

"The NSA is requesting you don't speak to the press about this."

"Of course," Jane said.

"If you both don't mind, I need to make a few private phone calls."

If this was her last chance, she was going to take advantage of it.

* * *

Nick didn't know for sure but he might have nodded off for a second. He was still lying on the ground beneath the branches of the chaparral when he heard a buzzing noise, a low hum like a giant bee. Alert, he sat up on his elbows, leaned his head toward the noise, and scanned the sky, but he couldn't see anything in the darkness. Adjusting his gaze to slightly behind the noise, he saw the light emitting from the observatory reflect off metal. A drone. And it was very close. He thought of all the news footage he'd seen of police chases taped from helicopters with thermal imagining, and he pushed himself deeper into the thick tangle of branches, hoping for better coverage. He curled into a tight ball. If the drone came nearer, he hoped whoever was monitoring the drone would think the heat coming off his body was from an animal. He didn't know how many drones the NSA had searching for him, but the safest place for him at the moment was right where he was.

It seemed like hours before he heard Agent Vagnetti's voice drift over the mountain air. Then he heard the low rumble of a car engine. He hadn't heard or seen any more signs of drones for a long time but, even though his thighs had started to cramp, he didn't take the risk of stretching his aching muscles. Now, he cautiously moved just enough to see through a small break in the undergrowth. He watched the headlights as they moved like a serpent down the mountain and then fade around a bend in the road. Nick started to turn his head away when something caught his eye. Another set of headlights emerged from the shadows just below the observatory. Nick could see both of them now, one trailing the other from a safe distance.

* * *

Ronnie's driver, Matthew Hogan, was new to the agency, fresh out of training and eager to please. She thought about her upcoming retirement and how quickly her time at the agency had passed. The aluminum case holding the device was sitting on her lap, her hand firmly clasped around the handle.

Instead of making phone calls, she had worn the Halo—as the Carters called the artifact—for twenty-minutes. Emotional shock and dismay replaced any small feeling of smug satisfaction she might have had. How many people had worn it? Ronnie knew the boy and the Carters had. Whoever shipped the artifact from China would have had an opportunity. But Ronnie doubted whoever helped Henry Applegate smuggle it to the United States realized what they possessed, or they might not have followed his instructions. Had Applegate worn it? Not unless he had access to the urn before Nicholas got to it.

The artifact produced many startling images, but the most startling to Ronnie was the chronological depiction of the alien's methodology of altering the DNA of Earth primates. If Ronnie comprehended what she saw, then the mystery to the missing link had been solved.

If it wasn't so disturbing, she might have found a certain degree of ironic humor about it. She thought about how the creationists and evolutionist would react to the knowledge. The human species was both created *and* had evolved. The idea of man having a creator—of being formed in the "image and likeness of God"—was born out in what Ronnie had seen. Man had, indeed, been fashioned after their maker, and a slow natural evolution occurred after the initial manipulation of man's DNA accelerated the process.

The other shocking revelation concerned a horrific time in mankind's more recent history. The truth about the spread of the Black Plague. Now Ronnie understood how the mythical image of the Grim Reaper came to be. In many historical accounts, survivors of the plague claimed the disease spread through their town after seeing black-cloaked men on the outskirts of their villages waving "sickles" before them. Whenever these cloaked figures appeared, the plague followed. Man was not the first sentient being to use biological warfare. What Ronnie had seen verified the recent studies exonerating the much-maligned rat as the major carrier of the Black Plague. There just weren't enough of them, and there was no other physical evidence to prove rats spread the deadly disease.

These two revelations alone could rock the world.

Ronnie knew from experience that, even if knowledge of the artifact and the things it revealed were made public, there would still be doubters. The idea that aliens had visited Earth in the past would move from being a conspiracy theory perpetuated by UFO hunters, to a conspiracy theory perpetuated by those people who did not believe that Man had really walked on the moon.

There was still more to be seen, but Matt had knocked on the library door wanting to give her a report on his search for the boy. No matter, it had been enough time. What she had witnessed was enough to ponder for a lifetime.

They left the search to the expert trackers. The boy didn't have a cell phone or any other electronic device they could trace. He'd either be found by the search team or would turn up on the grid somewhere, she was sure. That he was alone on the mostly uninhabited mountainside worried Ronnie. She would hate for any harm to come to him, but she had done all she could do at the moment.

Again, she thought about why he had run away. It wasn't to protect the device. It was resting on her lap. The Carters claimed they were preparing to turn it over. Then, suddenly, the answer came to her. The only logical answer was that he didn't want to be sent home.

The key to Ronnie's success over the years was that she always asked the question why. And she asked it now: Why didn't Nicholas want to go home? What was his motivation? The answer was: His personal mission had not been completed to his satisfaction. Wherever he had gone, Nick would return to the Carters, she was certain. She realized too, that even though they had gathered enough data to work with, Jane must have been telling her the truth.

They hadn't had enough time to make an intelligent assumption about the artifact's authenticity. They either needed more time to study the data they had and/or needed to find more data.

Ronnie's gaze wandered to the side window and up at the nighttime sky. She was not good at picking out constellations, but she searched for what she thought was the Pleiades star cluster. What did she believe after wearing the device?

"What the…" Matt sputtered.

Headlights illuminated the interior of the car from behind. Ronnie's right hand instinctively tightened on the handle of the case. The other vehicle swung around to the driver's side of their car. An agency issued vehicle, Ronnie noticed, just as the passenger flashed his credentials at Matt.

"What the…" he repeated.

The man in the other vehicle motioned for him to pull over. Matt snapped his head toward Ronnie.

"He wants me to pull over."

"I can see that." The man had a friendly smile on his face. Something wasn't right. They both knew it. She turned and looked out the side window where the road fell off into a deep ravine. *Nowhere to go but down*, she thought.

"Ready your weapon."

She shifted the case to her left hand, unzipped her sweater, and felt for her weapon with her right hand. Ronnie might not be physically fit, but she was an expert shot. Although she had only fired her weapon a few times in the line of duty, and those were at the beginning of her career before she had become tethered to her desk job.

Most of the shooting she'd done during her time with the NSA had been at the practice range.

Matt found a shallow shoulder on the right and pulled over next to the guardrail.

CHAPTER 22

"Where were you?" Jane held him by the shoulders. He was shivering.

"Hiding."

"Obviously," Stan said, a relieved grin on his face. "We're just glad you're okay. We were about to launch another search party to look for you."

"You're not going to tell Agent Vagnetti, are you?"

The Carters looked at each other then back to Nick.

"Why did you hide?" Jane said.

"You know why. I want to go with you to Mesa Verde. I've come this far. You can't make me go home now."

"We told you, Nick, we can't take you across state lines. We'd be in a load of legal trouble"

"Legal? You weren't worried about legal when you brought me up here with the Halo!"

Stan and Jane exchanged a glance.

"We'll keep you informed. Tell you the minute we find anything. There's no need for you to come with us."

"You have to let me come. If it weren't for me, you would have never seen any of it! I brought the Halo to you remember? You didn't want to have anything to do with it."

They stared at him.

"Besides, I already called my mom, remember? I told her I wasn't coming home until I found some answers. She wasn't happy but, in the end, she said okay. There's no reason I can't go with you."

* * *

Jane and Nick made the dizzying drive back down Mt. Hamilton Road in the rented SUV with Stan following in his Yukon. They were more than halfway down the mountain when they saw flashing lights in the distance.

"I wonder what happened," Nick asked.

"Accident. Somebody going too fast and missed a curve, most likely," Jane said.

A police officer appeared in the headlights and held up his hand for them to stop. Jane stuck her head out as the window slid down.

"Hi, Larry."

"Hi, Jane. Why are you coming down the mountain this time of night? Or should I say, day?"

"Places to go. People to meet." She smiled. Officer Carson had the midnight shift patrolling Mt. Hamilton Road all the way up to the observatory. In the past, he'd helped Jane with a few flat tires, among other things. "What's going on?"

"You'll keep it under your hat for a while?"

"Sure, Larry, no problem."

Larry looked back at the blue police strobe lights. "The folks at Lick and the other residences will hear about it sooner or later anyway, I suppose. I just don't want to frighten them for no reason."

"What is it?" She shifted her weight forward, trying to get a better view.

"Found a couple people shot in their car."

Jane's heart thudded in her chest.

"Can you tell me if the victims are a man and a woman?"

"Yeah. How'd you know?"

"They just left the observatory."

"So you know they're—"

"Government." Jane said. "Are they…are they alive?"

"The woman was lucky. But the man …" Larry shook his head. "More like a boy, really."

Jane's right hand flew to her mouth.

"What's gov'ment doing up at Lick?" he asked.

Jane hesitated. "They had some technical questions."

Officer Larry squinted his eyes at her.

"Could you tell the woman I'm here? It might comfort her to have someone she knows nearby."

Jane and Nick were already getting out of the SUV, and Stan was coming up behind them.

"Make it quick," the emergency technician said. At Agent Vagnetti's request, he left them alone at the back of the ambulance. She was lying on a gurney, just about to be lifted into the back. A bloody bandage was covering her left shoulder.

The technician had pulled aside the oxygen mask and now Jane leaned in close to hear the agent speak. "I threw the case over the cliff." The agent wheezed. "Before they could get to it. It went to the right. Landed in a bush. The taillights. It reflected."

Stan and Nick took a step forward.

"Find it. Keep it safe." She coughed and wheezed.

"Now call the technician back. I need a doctor." She managed a weak smile.

They pulled their vehicles off the road and piled into Stan's Yukon to wait together. Officer Carson told them they couldn't go any farther down the mountain until they had secured the area.

"I don't want anyone else shot tonight. Maybe you should go back up to Lick, to wait it out. This might take a while." He suggested.

"We need to get home as soon as we can. We'll just wait here, if that's okay." Stan said.

"Suit yourself." Officer Larry touched the brim of his hat.

A few vehicles were let through the roadblock on the other side of the scene. They headed up the road, the passengers rubbernecking to get a better view of the accident.

"Why do you think she did it?" Jane asked.

"Throw the Halo over the cliff, or tell us that she did?" Stan said.

"Both."

"Obviously, to keep it safe from someone she didn't want to find it. Why us? Because we're here and already involved. We've already studied it, and she knows it, so why not? And we'd already shown our cooperation by turning it over to the NSA without any fuss."

"Who would be ballsy enough to try and rob the NSA?" Jane shook her head.

"Henry said a lot of people would be looking for it. Bad guys and governments," Nick said. "Maybe a foreign government's version of the NSA?"

They continued to speculate until the red light on top of the ambulance started to blink. As it pulled away, Officer Larry walked over to them.

"She's on her way to Stanford Hospital. We've collected all the evidence we can until we get some daylight. Officers have covered the entire road but haven't found hide-nor-hair of the other vehicle. Looks like they got away. For now. You folks want to follow me down?"

"No need for an escort." Stan said. "We'll be taking off in a minute. The boy needs to use the facilities." Stan crocked his head toward the shrubbery along the side of the road. "Hope that's okay."

"Under the circumstances, I think I can overlook it." The officer smiled. "You folks be careful and don't stop for anyone. But I don't think they'll show their faces on Mt. Hamilton any time soon. We have extra squad cars keeping a watch."

Once they saw Officer Carson's squad car and the tow-truck round the bend, they walked to the yellow caution tape that marked the shoulder where the NSA agents' car had pulled over. Stan carefully crawled over the guardrail.

Agent Vagnetti said it went to the right. Stan swept the large beam from his flashlight over the area. The landscape was mostly short grass interrupted every now and again by pines and low chaparral bushes.

Nick and Jane stood by the metal rail and followed the light.

"I see something!" Nick cried.

Stan turned the beam of light toward him. "Point."

Nick raised his right arm and pointed to where he had seen a flash of light in a low bush.

Stan swung the flashlight around. The beam of light jerked as he searched for the bush. It was fifteen feet away, down a steep slope. He would have to be careful, but it was doable.

"Good job, Nick."

* * *

Their original plans hadn't changed. The only difference was now they had the Halo to protect.

When they got near the bottom of the mountain, Jane slowed the SUV down to almost a stop and made a hard U-turn left onto Ridgeview Way. Stan's headlights lit up their car from behind. Within a few minutes, they were driving up the steep driveway toward the Carter home. Nick didn't know what to expect from the house of two astronomers, but he liked it. A lighted walkway led to the front door. Stan keyed in a number on a lock-pad and then led them inside to a stone-tiled foyer area. To the left, on the front wall, was a closet. Just beyond was a short hallway with a little niche on the back wall. It held what looked like some kind of award. To the right of the niche he could see another hallway that he assumed led to bedrooms.

On the other side of the front door was an oak paneled den with glass-paned entry doors. But what Nick liked the best were the huge arched windows on the far back wall of the living room directly opposite the foyer. He could see a small telescope sitting in one corner, pointing out one of the windows. The room had cozy furniture and a two-way fireplace on the adjacent wall to the kitchen. Nick had expected a sloppy house, with books and charts and things everywhere. But, while one wall housed a huge bookcase filled with books and papers, the house looked very well kept.

"Nick," Jane gestured toward the den. "Could you get driving directions from Cortez, Colorado to Mesa Verde

National Park while Stan and I gather up all the equipment?"

Stan had made a phone call to his friend while they were weaving their way down the mountain. A jet would be fueled and ready at the airport. They would fly into Cortez, Colorado, which was the nearest airport to the national park. A leased Jeep would be waiting for them as soon as they got off the plane. Hal had made all the arrangements using his own credit card, so NSA couldn't trace their activities.

Jane was about to walk away, but turned back to Nick. "Get as detailed a map of the park as you can, especially near the area of the Sun Temple. From what I remember, that will be a perfect place to set up our observation. The Anasazi would have built their temple to the sun in a significant location, some place they held sacred. The Cliff Dwellings was where they lived, not worshipped, so I don't think that would be a good spot. We couldn't get a good view of the entire night sky from there anyway."

Nick could tell she was excited. She kept chattering on, looking out at the night sky through the large expanse of windows.

"Petroglyph Point is another sacred spot, but it is down in the valley. The Sun Temple location is perfect. A sacred spot high on the mesa with a great view of the entire night sky."

While searching the internet for detail maps of the park, Nick read about the Anasazi, about the city they had carved in a cliff and about the petroglyphs—strange pictures etched in stone—that Jane had mentioned. He read that the Sun Temple was a stone building shaped like a D and that the Anasazi never completed it. No one knew why.

From the map, he saw it would only be a short walk to the temple from the road. Lucky for them because they had lots of equipment to haul.

Nick joined Jane and Stan in the basement after he printed out the maps. The equipment was sitting in the middle of the floor waiting to be packed. The optical telescope set-up, the laptop computer containing the analytical software, flashlights, binoculars, a handheld GPS, sleeping bags and other camping equipment were all carefully placed into the backpacks.

"What about the Halo?" Nicholas asked.

"I don't think it's safe to leave it here," Stan said.

Nick threw his backpack into the SUV. The Halo, protected by the slightly banged-up aluminum case, was safely stowed inside. He left the camera and Henry's lead-lined pouch filled with film at the Carters. He had no use for any of it now.

It had only taken them a little over an hour to get back on the road.

"You sure you're not too tired to drive?" he asked.

"We work at night, that's when the stars are out," Jane said.

Nick hadn't thought of that, but he was glad to hear it. Being in the car with a sleep-deprived driver didn't sound like a good idea to him. Personally, he couldn't even think about sleeping. He was way too geared-up.

Jane followed Stan's packed Yukon down the steep driveway and then turned back onto Ridgeview Way. They had only gone a few yards when Nick noticed headlights reflected in the passenger side mirror. He turned in his seat and strained to see the car, and who was driving it, but it was too far away and he couldn't see anything around the glare of the headlights, or the dark of the night. *Nothing unusual about a car being on the road,* he thought. *I'm just imagining things.* But he wondered where the car came from so quickly. He hadn't seen it when they first turned out of the driveway. He thought of saying something to Jane, but she was talking about the Anasazi again, and Nick couldn't get a word in edgewise.

Once they left Mt. Hamilton road the area became more populated and the streets more crowded. Nick called his mother again, to check in like he had promised, and then he and Jane drove several miles past the car rental shop where they dumped the disposable cell phone that Jane had purchased the day before. Then they drove to the rental office, where they met back up with Stan, and turned in the leased SUV. Jane's Jeep would have to stay in the mall parking lot for a few more days. Hopefully, no one would notice. Then they headed toward San Jose Airport where the jet was waiting.

Nick kept glancing back to see if anyone was tailing them but, in the early morning rush hour traffic, he couldn't tell. Why were the hairs on the back of his neck standing on end? He just couldn't shake the feeling that they were being watched. It was becoming a familiar feeling.

CHAPTER 23

Nick had never flown on a private jet before. By the time they got in the air, it was early afternoon. Hal had made sure the jet was well supplied with food and drink, and now a lone female flight attendant served them a nice roast beef sandwich with some kind of weird lettuce on it. Nick was hesitant, but after taking the first tentative bite, he decided he liked it.

Stan had made sure the pilot understood the equipment was to be handled carefully and that everything was well secured in the luggage area. The flight was uneventful. When they landed, the four-wheel drive Jeep was waiting for them for the long trip to the Sun Temple.

They had been driving for a little under an hour when Nick called out, "There it is!" He pointed to the sign leading them into the park.

They had stopped in Cortez for a quick bite to eat and at a local grocery store to pick up some bottled water and snacks for the long night ahead.

Nick couldn't be sure, but he thought he saw a hulking black SUV parked down a side street near the grocery store. He turned to look out the back window when they passed, and he watched as it pulled out. The vehicle followed them for two blocks. He forced himself to turn around, thinking he was being paranoid again. When he couldn't control himself any longer and glanced back, the vehicle had disappeared. It hadn't reappeared, even on a long stretch of straight highway where he could see for miles.

"We stay on Highway 10 all the way. It's also marked as Ruins Road." Nick was the designated navigator. The maps were laid out on the seat next to him and on his lap.

"We're heading toward the museum and Spruce Tree House, and then we follow the signs to the Sun Temple."

It was seven pm and dark. The sky was covered with patchy clouds. Even though the park tours were closed for the season, the park itself was still open to traffic.

"If these clouds don't part for long enough, we might have to stay another day and try again tomorrow night," Jane said, peering up into the night at the clouds moving steadily across the sky. "The official report on the GOPEX experiment said that inclement weather 'posed an unacceptable high-risk to the demonstration.' I don't know if clouds will interfere with our data collection, but it makes sense that a clear sky would offer the best chances of getting good readings."

She glanced back at Nick. "Try to find a WiFi signal and look up the weather on the internet. See if these clouds are moving out of here."

Nick flipped open the computer and switched the WiFi connection button to the ON position.

After a few minutes, he said, "I'm not getting a connection."

"See if my phone works." She tossed him the disposable prepaid cell they had purchased in Cortez. Stan had left his cell phone at home. If anyone was tracing Jane's phone, then they were certainly tracing his.

Nick had no luck getting a signal with the phone either.

"Keep trying. If we're lucky maybe we can hit a hotspot, just in case we need it out here in the wilderness." She smiled.

"What about the data for our observation?" Nick asked. "Don't we need an internet connection for that?"

"No, we have a wireless connection from the camera to the laptop. No need for the internet for data collection."

Nick was glad. He hadn't considered that the park might be a dead zone. Luckily, it would have no affect on their search for a signal, but the weather might.

The ride deep into the park reminded Nick of the drive up Mt. Hamilton Road. He was glad both trips had been at night. The darkness prevented him from seeing the steep drop-offs on the side of the road. The drive up the mountain to the observatory seemed like such a long time ago, but it was just yesterday.

It was another twenty-one miles to get to the museum area and then a few more miles to where the Sun Temple sat at the edge of the mesa, about a forty-five minute drive from when they first entered the park. Except for Nick calling out a few directions, they rode in silence, until they finally reached the road running alongside the temple. The tires crackled over the gravel as Stan parked the Jeep safely off the main road.

It was cold. A wind blew across the mesa and bit into his exposed skin. Luckily, the map was right; it was just a short walk across the road to the temple ruins. The Carters had packed the backpacks skillfully. Stan only had to go back to the car once.

Nick had never experienced such quiet. There were no sounds of industry or traffic, just the wind whistling through the spruce and fir trees and the low sage bushes. In the dark, he couldn't get a good view of the temple. All he could see were the rounded brick walls of the ancient structure. The three of them followed the wall until they were on the northeast side.

"This is a good spot," Jane said.

Nick sat in front of a small propane heater, enjoying the feeling of warm air against the cold at his back. He watched as Jane and Stan adjusted the position of the telescope with the camera now attached to it. A few feet away, a laptop sat on a small portable fold-up table, waiting for data to arrive.

The Carters stepped back from the equipment and stared up at the sky.

"We lucked out," Stan said, "looks like there is a break in the clouds."

"Do you want to have a look through the telescope, Nick?" Jane asked. She sniffled in the cold.

"Sure."

Jane directed him to the side eyepiece. "Just look through there."

He leaned forward and placed his eye over the small telescope jutting out from the side of the larger main scope.

"Wow."

"Have you ever looked through a telescope this powerful?"

"No," he said, "That's pretty awesome." He recognized the Pleiades from his astronomy charts. The Seven Sisters, it was called, even though there were more than seven stars in the cluster. They all sat within the bigger constellation of Taurus.

"Let's get started." Stan said, rubbing his hands together.

Nick watched as Stan and Jane adjusted and readjusted the delicate equipment from within the circle of light provided by the lanterns. Even with the warmth of the propane heater, Nick was starting to shiver.

"You're probably very bored right about now," Jane said, "I'm sorry you can't help." She pointed toward her backpack. "Why don't you unroll one of the sleeping bags to keep warm?" She smiled at him. "And, don't worry, if we see anything interesting, we'll let you know."

He was glad for Jane's suggestion. The added warmth of the down-filled bag made him feel very cozy. He lay on the ground and looked up at the sky. Even with the light from the lanterns, Nick was still able to see stars he would never be able to see back home. He started naming the constellations in his head, to see how many he could recognize, while he listened to Stan and Jane's soft murmurings as they huddled over the laptop.

Nick rolled over in his sleeping bag, drawn back to the warmth of the heater. He must have fallen asleep. He sensed, rather than saw, Stan's silhouette standing by the telescope.

"What's going on?" Nick looked into the black void in front of Stan. They had turned off the lanterns. Nick wondered why. Would their light interfere with the collection of photons?

"Shh!" Jane warned from somewhere out of sight. "Stan thought he heard something."

No one moved. He could feel the tension from the adults, and his heart beat a little faster.

"Anybody there?" Stan called out. His voice echoed in the dark void.

In the silence that followed, they only heard the soft wind rustling the shrubs. Then, just a few yards ahead in the blackness, something moved in the low underbrush.

"Jane," Stan whispered. "Turn on your flashlight and let's have a look."

The beam from the flashlight arced across the space in front of them and hit something moving. The beam jerked upward as Jane jumped, startled, and then she settled the light on whatever was out there.

"A mule deer." Stan stated.

"A what?" Nick asked.

"Mule deer. They are fairly common out here."

A deer with a large rack of antlers stood and stared into the beam of light, mesmerized.

"Okay, you can turn it off now. Nothing to worry about."

As soon as Jane turned off the light, they heard the click of the deer's hooves as it crossed over to the other side of the road. At the same time Nick was turning to snuggle back into his sleeping bag, the beam from Jane's flashlight glinted off something in the distance, where the road forked and formed the loop that ran in front of the temple.

"Did you see that?" Nick pulled his arm out from the sleeping bag and pointed, realizing how silly it was, as neither Jane or Stan could see his arm now that the light was gone. "I saw a reflection off something further down the road. Do you think someone is watching us?" Nick asked in a low voice. He was acting paranoid again, but he didn't care. He saw their dim shadows standing, looking down the road into the impenetrable darkness.

"I don't see anything. It could have been anything, a reflection off a rock..." Stan's voice tailed off. "It's probably nothing. The deer just spooked you."

Stan didn't sound as confident as Nick would have liked.

"The sun is going to come up soon. We'll be out of here quick enough."

"Nick," Jane said. "While you were asleep, we captured loads of data. And it's wonderful!"

"Why didn't you wake me?" he cried, as he struggled out of the sleeping bag.

"We don't want to get ahead of ourselves. This is just one test of many to come, but it certainly looks promising," Jane said.

"Look," Stan said leaning over the laptop. "These graphs show what I was explaining to you before. We counted the number of photons that arrived at our camera during a billionth of a second, and we've detected dozens per each time slice. This is clear evidence someone is flashing a signal our way."

"And remember we talked about NASA's GOPEX laser experiment?" Jane said. "Well, our images look remarkably similar."

Nick didn't fully understand the graphs and images on the laptop screen, but the Carters were talking non-stop about the data and what it meant. Apparently, not only did they get images much the same as NASA's experiment produced, but also the photon counter indicated the pulses were almost undoubtedly of intelligent design. It would have been exciting to see the data as it came in, although he wouldn't have known what he was looking at.

"We were about to wake you, Nick, but the deer woke you instead." Stan smiled at him.

Stan looked up at the sky and spread his arms wide. "Do you realize that we three are the only people on Earth who know that we are not alone in the universe? That there is intelligent life out there?"

Nick was sure he saw a glint of a tear in his eyes, reflecting back the faint light from the laptop. He wasn't sure why Stan was so convinced, but he trusted the Carters' judgment.

It seemed that Nick finally had his answer. His dad was not part of a hoax, and he hadn't gone mad right before his death. Even more mind-blowing, they had reasonably concrete evidence that intelligent life existed outside of Earth. Nick didn't know how to feel—excited, awestruck, scared—all those feelings roiled up inside of him. The Carters would perform more tests at different locations in the USA and around the globe. They would try to capture more signals, more evidence of extraterrestrial life. But it was just a formality. They seemed convinced that the Halo was genuine, and the signals were being sent by intelligent design.

The night was suddenly quiet, as if all the creatures had stopped along with them to ponder this moment. He couldn't help but to think about Henry. How would he feel if he knew? His life's work had been validated.

Then Nick looked up at the sky again, trying to pinpoint Asterope. He thought about the people, or the beings, who had brought the device to Earth, and wondered if they would ever return. And, if they did, how would the world react?

* * *

"Hello, Ronnie."

She had just walked back from the bathroom, pulling an IV stand behind her, and was settling onto her hospital bed, adjusting the tangle of tubes so she wouldn't sit on them.

Her head snapped around at the familiar voice.

"What are you doing here?" It was such a pedestrian thing to say, she realized, but he had her at a disadvantage.

"Not happy to see me?"

Ronnie had already regained her composure.

"I don't know. Should I be?"

"Of course." He smiled. "First things first: How are you feeling?"

"Spectacular. I can be out of here tomorrow as long as I promise to take it easy."

"That's good news. Mind if I sit?" He pointed to a chair next to the window.

"Be my guest."

The light streaming through the window cast his face in deep shadow, and through the dim gray light and the fog of painkillers, Ronnie already struggled to remember what he looked like after that first, brief glimpse of him.

"I suppose you're wondering why I'm here."

"After all these years of secrecy, you might say that. Although I have a pretty good idea."

She grunted as she wiggled herself back onto the hospital bed and covered herself with the thin sheet. Not the best first impression, she was sure. The wound she received had been a through-and-through. The bullet had traveled underneath her collarbone, missing her ribs, shoulder, and major blood vessels. A clean exit. Recovery time was significantly reduced. She was lucky.

She glanced back at the man seated in the dark shadows and wondered if her luck had just run out.

* * *

They were subdued. Each processing this newly found knowledge in their own way as they gathered up the gear and carefully repacked it in the harsh glow of the lanterns. The darkness started to ease as they made the short hike back to the Jeep, the wind the only noise as it moved across the mesa.

Frost had formed on the windshield overnight. Jane scraped the glass while Stan and Nick loaded the backpacks and equipment into the rear of the vehicle.

Jane scrambled into the front passenger seat with the heavy-duty laptop. "As soon as I can catch a signal, I'll send the data file to my office as backup."

"Good idea," Stan said.

They were silent on the long ride out of the park, each absorbed in their own thoughts.

Nick's stomach gurgled as he watched the last stars twinkle and fade, causing his attention to turn to more earthly things. Food. He was hungry. He had been too preoccupied and excited by their discovery to eat any of the snacks they had packed. Besides, he wanted real food. They were nearing the exit onto Highway 10 that would lead them back to the city.

He was about to ask Stan if they could stop in Cortez for breakfast as they approached a road that dead-ended on the right. A black Cadillac SUV waited at the intersection. Nick's heart thumped as he caught a glimpse of a shadowy figure behind the tinted glass as they passed. He watched the vehicle turn onto the highway behind them. The passenger moved, and Nick was sure he caught sight of a weapon in his hands. He couldn't be sure but he thought it was a semi-automatic.

"Stan," Nick called out. "There's an SUV following us." There was no doubt this time. "And I think they have a gun."

Stan glanced in the rearview mirror. "A gun?"

"I saw that same car in Cortez. The driver looks familiar to me. I know I've seen him somewhere before."

Jane shot a glance out the back window as Stan's eyes darted between the road and the mirror. The black Cadillac rapidly closed the gap between them.

"My God!" Stan shouted.

They all watched in horror as a herd of mule deer suddenly leaped into the narrowing space between the two vehicles. Stan reflexively hit the brakes, his eyes now riveted to the rearview mirror.

Nick heard a sickening thud as a deer went through the other vehicle's windshield. The back-end shot forward on the icy road, slamming into two other deer, and slewing the front-end to the right. It only took an instant for the SUV to skid across the width of the road and plunge headlong over the cliff.

Nick heard Jane scream. His own throat seized as he turned to see a huge doe leap in front of the Jeep. A bloodied hoof burst through the windshield and the airbags exploded with a loud pop. Nick gasped as a wave of cold air, heavy with the smell of blood and deer, rushed into the vehicle. His heart pounded in his chest. The Jeep crossed the centerline and slammed against the rocky embankment. Sparks sputtered and sprayed while they hurtled forward, the hard granite gouging into the heavy steel of the vehicle. He threw his arm across his face when the Jeep suddenly lurched forward. The shoulder strap bit into his skin as the front end careened off a rock wall, slamming him against the door. Nick let out a gasp when the vehicle momentarily lifted off the road and then fell back, rocking violently from side-to-side, tossing him around like a rag doll. The frantic motion slowed to a sway, until the sound of straining metal and tinkling glass was the only noise. The Jeep finally settled, and everything went quiet.

He felt oddly calm as he watched Stan's hand reach out from the front seat toward Jane. Someone moaned. A hot pain shot through his left leg. The last thing he remembered, before everything went black, was the smell of burning rubber.

CHAPTER 24

Ronnie leaned back in an Adirondack chair on the patio attached to a cottage unit at the Ritz-Carlton Half-Moon Bay Resort that looked out over the Pacific Ocean. A fire flickered in the round ceramic pit in the center of the patio. That, along with the blanket over her lap, provided just enough warmth against the chill, damp air. Inside, a nurse sat reading a paperback novel by lamplight in a comfortable upholstered chair.

Patricia Cruz, her liaison at the NSA, had made contact with Ronnie shortly after she was admitted to the hospital. Patty handled the everyday business details of Ronnie's employment at the agency. Together they had made arrangements for someone at the NSA to personally contact Matthew Hogan's family and arrange for his body to be flown home. Ronnie had liked the kid, but she wouldn't let herself dwell on it.

When Patty asked her if she wanted another agent sent out, Ronnie said no. As far as she knew, Patty was just a facilitator, the person who handled the everyday, mundane operations of her unit. But in her line of work, one could never be sure of anything. Ronnie took her working orders from a disembodied voice over a phone, or the occasional secure email.

"I'm checking out of the hospital. I have more business to take care of. I'll be in contact," she told Patty.

The distant rhythmic sound of waves crashing against the shore below had almost put her to sleep when she heard the rasp of the glass patio door as it slid open. The man Ronnie had first met in the hospital walked to the chair next to her, lifted the blanket resting on the seat, and draped it over his lap after he sat.

"Ah. Cold air. Warm fire. Nice yin and yang, don't you agree?" he said.

"Yes, I've always enjoyed sitting by a fire on a chilly evening."

"Glad you're enjoying it." The man leaned back and took a deep breath, filling his lungs with the salty sea air. Then he turned to Ronnie. "How are you feeling? Is the nurse treating you well?"

"I'm sore, which is to be expected. But I'm feeling remarkably well, and Nurse Carol is treating me like a queen." Although Ronnie had secretly given her the nickname of Nurse Ratched, after the crazed nurse in the movie *One Flew Over the Cuckoo's Nest*.

The man nodded. "Good."

The glass door slid open again. The nurse handed the man a glass of cognac. "How rude of me, I should have asked if you'd like a glass."

If Ronnie were going to drink, she would have preferred Frangelica. "I doubt Nurse Carol would let me imbibe. She's already given me my nightly dose of pain medication."

"A pity." He held the short round-bottomed glass of clear amber liquid to the firelight. "Hennessy. Good stuff."

He took a sip, savoring the taste. "Tell me, Ronnie, have you ever heard of The Bilderberg Group?"

"The Bilderbergs? Yes, I'm aware of them."

"What exactly do you know about them?"

"They are a group of a hundred or so of the world's most powerful people from both the public and private sector: heads of state, prime ministers, royalty, wealthy businessmen. If one were to believe the conspiracy theories, they decide the fate of the world at their annual meetings. They decide everything from the price of oil to who goes to war with whom."

The man nodded thoughtfully and Ronnie continued. She was used to giving dissertations on her knowledge of things.

"Their meetings are very private and, from what I understand, the main objective of the group is to create a new world order. A one-world government."

The man said, "Isn't it strange how conspiracy theories often have a soupçon of truth to them, a tiny element to lend credibility? It's why so many people believe in them, even if secretly."

Ronnie didn't respond.

"I've been rude. It's time I introduce myself." He leaned in close to Ronnie, conscious of her wound, and reached out his right hand. She extended her own. His hand felt soft, but his grip was firm.

"My name is Alec Gordon and I'm a member of The Bilderberg Group, your employer for the last fifteen years."

* * *

Something smelled. Did Mom burn the toast again? He wished she'd stop yelling at him to get up. He didn't want to go to school today. He just wanted to sleep.

Nick cracked open one eye. Wherever he was, there was smoke. And then the rancid odor of burning rubber and plastic blasted him in the face. Everything came back to him gradually, like the last bit of wave being pulled back to the ocean. He turned his head and saw Stan pounding on the opposite passenger-side window.

"Unlock the door!"

Nick coughed and stared at him for a second, still not fully comprehending what was going on.

"Come on, Nick!" Stan tugged on the door handle. "Unstrap yourself and get out of there."

Was that blood on Stan's arm? Nick suddenly came out of his stupor and was fully in the present. Leaning toward Stan, he fumbled with the seat buckle until he felt it give and then pushed himself toward the other side of the vehicle and flipped the door lock. He felt Stan's powerful hand take hold of his shirt to help pull him out of the car.

"Wait!" Nick felt the lump of his backpack under his feet and reached down to grab it. Stumbling out of the car, he landed in a heap a few feet away and sat gasping for air while Stan ran to the back of the Jeep and tried to open the tailgate, but it was too late. The back of the vehicle was in flames, and the door too hot to touch.

"Where's Jane?" Nick called.

"Over here."

She was sitting a few yards away next to a spruce tree, with one hand supporting the opposite elbow. Her laptop sat on the ground beside her.

Nick half walked, half dragged himself over to Jane. Stan followed, and they watched as flames appeared in a soft swoosh and licked the seat where Nick had left the door hanging open.

"Is everyone alright?" Jane asked.

Nick already had the start of a giant bruise on his left calf. He pulled his hands through his hair and felt little pellets of glass.

"I think I'm okay." His voice sounded as dry as wood chips.

Stan had a deep gouge in his left forearm.

"You should wrap something around that." Nick said. All the years living with a nurse kicked in.

He watched the flames fully engulf the seat where he had just been sitting. That's when he noticed a bag lying on the ground.

Nick leaped up, favoring his left leg, and ran back to the car.

"What are you doing?" Jane yelled.

He didn't stop to answer but laid himself flat when he got close to the car and scooted toward the bag. He reached underneath the flames and swatted at the bag until it slide a few feet away from the car. Nick pushed himself backwards until he was clear of the flames. Then he stood up, grabbed the bag, and limped back to where the other two were sitting on the patch of grass near the edge of the road. He thought he smelled singed hair and rubbed his hand over the back of his head.

"Well, that wasn't too smart," Jane said.

"Good goin' kid," Stan countered, raising his eyebrows at Jane. "I could use a drink right now."

The cloth bag was filled with the snacks and water. Stan rummaged through it. "Anyone else?" He held up a bottle of water. They both nodded and he tossed one to each of them.

Stan poured water over the cut on his arm. Then Nick helped him struggle out of his button-down shirt and pull off the white cotton t-shirt he wore underneath. Nick ripped a narrow strip off of it and tied it around Stan's wound.

They fell silent as they watched the flames devour more and more of the Jeep. Finally, the smell got to be too much for Jane.

"Let's move downwind."

That's when they heard the familiar *thomp thomp thomp* of helicopter blades.

They stood and watched as it passed. It took a hard right bank and circled back toward the spot where the other vehicle had gone over the cliff. It lingered there for a few seconds, and then headed back toward them and the burning car on the highway.

"It's military," Nick said. The image of a semi-automatic in the hands of the passenger sitting in the vehicle that went over the cliff flashed in his head.

"What?"

This helicopter wasn't an air ambulance, Nick was sure. This was military, fully loaded. He could see the rockets hugging the side.

They all looked at each other, each knowing what the other was thinking. None of them had yet to figure out why Agent Vagnetti led them to the Halo that night on Mt. Hamilton Road. Why hadn't she just called someone at the NSA to come get it?

"Friend or foe?" Stan asked.

"Foe," Nick and Jane said at the same time.

"Let's get out of here."

There was a thick copse of spruce on the side of the road and they turned toward it now. The cliff was at a gentler incline than where the black SUV went off the road, but it was still steep and they practically tumbled down it. Nick had grabbed his backpack, Stan carried the bag full of snacks and water, and Jane clung to her laptop. They had a little time before the helicopter came back to where they were and before it could find a place to land. Nick thought about the rockets he'd seen loaded on the side of the chopper and quickened his pace.

* * *

It amazed Liz how efficiently and stealthily the NSA had pulled up stakes. If any of her neighbors noticed the unusual activity around her house during the last few days, they hadn't approached her about it yet. The shoot-out between the NSA and the two kidnappers had happened more than a block anyway. No one seemed to have connected the Farradays with the incident. If anyone had called to question the police about it, there was no way for them to connect-the-dots to the Farradays or to Henry.

Frank had gotten word from his boss that he was to keep close watch on them until further notice. Liz had agreed that they could all stay at her house. Upon Frank's insistence, Henry took Nick's room and Frank got the sofa in the living room.

Liz didn't know where the NSA had taken Ming Lin and her cohorts. She didn't much care at the moment. First, she wanted her son back home and, second, she wanted to know that they were out of danger—that this madness over the crown was over. Instinctively, however, she knew there was probably another wave of crazies out there who might come looking for it again.

CHAPTER 25

Sharp stones dug into Nick's hands as he stumbled after the Carters. Stan had noticed a ledge jutting out from the side of the mountain, creating a shallow cove that was covered by a thick copse of chaparral bushes and hidden by the tops of several tall spruce trees. The helicopter probably had heat-seeking instruments on board. If they could stay far enough back, perhaps the heat from their bodies couldn't be detected. They scrabbled into the shelter and pressed their backs against the far wall.

"We don't really know if they're a foe." Jane's chest was heaving with every breath.

"I'd rather be safe than sorry. Before I go waving them down for help, I have to think for a minute." Stan slumped back and touched the bandage on his arm.

"Yeah," Nick said. "I'd like to know if the men in the helicopter are with the guys that went over the cliff."

"Me, too."

Jane said, "I still wonder why Agent Vagnetti told us she threw the Halo out of her car? Why not call the NSA and tell them to come get it?"

"We've gone over this already," Stan snapped. "Maybe she didn't think she had time. Maybe she thought she'd die before she could tell anyone. We were there, and we'd already freely turned it over once. Made sense when we talked about it the first time. Still makes sense."

Nick shook his head. "It still doesn't make sense to me. Why didn't she just ask us to contact the NSA? Give us a number to call?" He knew they were all thinking the same thing.

They were silent for a moment, listening as the blades of the helicopter cut through the quiet of the morning air.

"If we could get a damn signal up here, I'd call my mom and get Agent Vagnetti's number. Ask her if she knows what this is all about. Ask if these choppers are her doing."

Jane raised an eyebrow at Nick's language, but didn't say anything.

"We can't hide here forever."

Stan said, "Nick's right. If we can get in contact with Agent Vagnetti, then maybe we can get some answers. Hopefully, whoever is in the helicopter will give up searching soon and we can move farther down the road and try for a signal."

"This could just be a case of one hand of the government not knowing what the other is doing," Jane said. "Maybe we should just let them see us. We haven't done anything wrong."

"No!" Nick said. "I know this in my gut: Agent Vagnetti passed the Halo back to us for a reason. And I'm not turning it over to anyone but her."

The helicopter was circling the area right in front of them.

"We might not have a choice," Stan said.

* * *

"Not even your superiors at the NSA know who really funds your unit. All outward appearances indicate you are gathering intelligence on what is considered fringe science or unexplainable phenomenon. But we both know your main objective is to look for evidence of both past and present extraterrestrial activity on Earth."

Ronnie wasn't really surprised. She had never met this man before seeing him at the hospital, but she had talked to him many times over a secure, dedicated phone line. She knew there was someone else outside the NSA pulling the strings of her small elite unit. But The Bilderberg Group? Of all the alleged secret societies out there, this one seemed the least likely.

"I wasn't aware there was a permanent membership, just the movers and shakers du jour gathered for an annual meeting."

"It isn't just about the annual meeting. There are a number of people who organize the activities of the group, who create the agenda, and who know our real purpose. You see, Ronnie, layers upon layers of secrecy, and only those at the very top know the truth, as it is with any good secret society." He managed a weak smile. "The majority of the influential people invited to the annual meeting don't have a clue about the true nature of the organization."

"So creating a new world order isn't the main objective of the Bilderbergs?" One corner of her mouth curled up in a sneer.

Alec placed his drink on the small table beside his chair.

"Quite the contrary, that is exactly why the group was formed."

Ronnie's eyebrow twitched up involuntarily.

"But not for the reasons everyone thinks. Not for money or power. But to save Earth."

* * *

They watched the helicopter drop a few men near the crumbled black Cadillac resting at the bottom of the ravine. Then the chopper suddenly banked to the left, and they watched as it carefully landed on the road near the burned-out shell of their own wrecked vehicle. The mountain curved outward where they were hiding and gave them a clear view. Two armed military personnel exited the chopper and extinguished what was left of the flames with a blast of dry-chemicals. The tiny group huddled in the cave and watched through the branches of the chaparral as the soldiers searched through the wreckage. The uniformed men picked what was left of their charred and melted equipment out of the back of the Jeep.

"They're looking for something," Stan said dryly.

Jane let out a soft groan when she saw the melted, charred clumps of her camera and other expensive equipment.

After going back and loading the two, either dead or injured, men from the wreckage of the black Cadillac, the chopper came back and picked up the military men who'd searched through their own vehicle. The helicopter took off again but this time disappeared into the distance.

Nick carefully searched the skies. "That doesn't mean they aren't still looking for us. They had drones searching for me at the observatory. And they don't make much noise."

They decided to stay put for the time being. It was a good place to rest. Their hiding place provided shelter from the wind. The sun filtering through the trees offered them just enough warmth. The Carters hadn't slept the entire night, and Nick had only gotten a little sleep.

"I don't know if it's a good idea for you to sleep. I think you might have blacked out for a minute," Jane said.

He didn't want to admit it, but Nick thought he passed out from fright rather than being hit in the head. He didn't have a headache or any other sign that he'd banged his head.

"My mom always says unless there are some symptoms then it's okay to sleep, but I'll stay up and keep watch. You two can sleep."

Stan said, "Just for a little while. Then we'll start walking out of here. It's a long trudge to the main road, but maybe someone might pass by and give us a lift back to Cortez."

* * *

"If your objective is to save the world, how does this connect with possible extraterrestrial activity?"

"Before I answer that I have to ask you a few questions."

Ronnie heart rate ticked up.

"We know you retrieved the device from the observatory."

Of course he did, Ronnie thought, she'd left a message for him on the dedicated cell phone.

"And we know that, sometime during your unfortunate accident, you lost it."

Ronnie remained silent, waiting for Alec to reveal exactly what he knew.

"Where it is now, we have no idea. What we do know from looking at the police report of the accident is that 'the victim'—that would be you—talked with Jane Carter before being loaded into the ambulance. Very detailed and thorough reporting by the officer in charge, I commend him."

Alec took another sip of Hennessey. "The report also says the gunmen were interrupted by the approach of a police car. The vehicle fled the scene. The officers didn't give chase, as they were attending to you and the other agent."

That he called Matt "the other agent" rather than calling him by his name sickened Ronnie.

"So my question is this, Ronnie: When did these gunmen have time to steal the device from you?"

She moved her gaze to the horizon, where the sea met the sky.

"I blacked out. I never saw the police arrive. I really couldn't tell you what happened until the ambulance came."

"Hmm. Unfortunate lapse of consciousness. But I have a theory."

When he didn't continue, Ronnie asked, "And what would that be?"

"That the gunmen did not have time to steal the device from you."

"And?"

"And you saw an opportunity when the Carters arrived on the scene and passed the object on to them."

"Why would I return it to them after going to so much trouble to retrieve it in the first place?"

"I don't know, Ronnie. You tell me."

"Your theory doesn't hold." Ronnie was good at lying. Something she wasn't particularly proud of, but it served her well in her line of work.

"No?"

"No. I would have called you to have someone come and pick it up. And if the police didn't give it to the ambulance driver to bring it with me to the hospital, then it could very well be sitting on the floorboard of the car at the police impound lot."

"You know we would never let that happen. As soon as we heard about the accident, the NSA took control of the vehicle. The device was nowhere to be found in the car, and it wasn't with your personal belongings at the hospital. We've checked into all of that."

Alec looked down at his hands. "Where is the device, Ronnie?"

"I have no idea." She didn't have to lie. It was the truth. "Why do you think I wouldn't turn over the device to you if I had it? Why do you think I would give it to the Carters and not tell you about it?"

"We've been keeping a close eye on you lately, Ronnie. Did you know that? Some of your activities have been out of the ordinary."

Out of the ordinary? She didn't have any idea what he was talking about. Lately, she had been delving a little deeper into the intel she received out of her own personal curiosity. Perhaps stretching her security clearance to its limit. But she couldn't think of anything else that would lead her superior to believe she was anything but loyal to the NSA.

"You act as if I don't want the agency to find it. I thought we were both on the same team. Of course, it could have been you that sent those goons in the first place. They did flash NSA ID."

Alec's head jerked and Ronnie could see his pupils dilate slightly. Maybe she'd hit a nerve. That wouldn't be in the report. She had not offered that information to the police.

She said, "Maybe someone else got there first?"

Alec shuffled in his seat. She detected a hint of surprise, but he was trying hard to hide it. Ronnie had been certain he was behind the incident; now she wasn't so sure.

"What possible reason would I have?" He seemed to recover. "It could have been fake ID. Just another bunch of opportunistic thugs out to steal a priceless artifact."

Ronnie got the feeling he didn't want to admit that there might be another powerful group vying for the device. A group that not only had knowledge of the object's existence, but the means to successfully track it as well. Alec had been taken aback by her revelation and needed to regain a sense of control, Ronnie was sure.

Finally, he said, "No matter. Make no mistake, we will find it. And I have a sneaky suspicion you've had a chance to wear the device. To see what it does. To experience it. Power and knowledge has a way of corrupting the best of us. It wouldn't be the first time someone went over to the dark side."

You should know, Ronnie thought.

The pain meds were kicking in. Nothing seemed to matter now but the crackle of the fire and the sound of the waves pounding on the surf below. It would make no difference if Alec knew she'd actually worn the crown or not.

"If I took the opportunity to wear the device, it wasn't to gain power." She shook her head. "No, not power. But perhaps knowledge. I'd say it was more like a retirement gift to myself. Working all these years to gather intel, to find mysterious objects or phenomena, but never knowing what it all meant—how it all connected. If the strange things I uncovered were hoaxes or real. I thought I deserved to know before I faded into the sunset."

"I don't blame you. I would have done the same."

They remained silent for a few moments, both staring into the flames.

"So it was worth it?"

"It was extraordinary."

* * *

Despite having said he would stay up to keep watch, Nick had dozed off. The sound of voices woke him.

A police car and a couple of ambulances were parked near their burned-out Jeep.

He shook Stan's shoulder. "Stan, wake up."

Jane was leaning against Stan's chest and his cheek rested against the top of her head. He looked toward the road and blinked.

"Police and ambulances by the car." Nick pointed. "What should we do?"

Jane pushed herself up. "What's going on?"

"Someone must have noticed the wreck and called the police." He nodded toward the road.

"I never did like the idea of hiking out of this park."

"What's our story going to be?"

"The truth. We were in the park conducting experiments and, on our way out, some deer leaped out in front of us."

"What about the SUV?"

"We saw them go over, but there wasn't much we could do. They were too far down."

"What if they ask us where they went?"

"We have no idea. Because we don't."

"And why we were hiding?"

"We found shelter where we could watch the road and wait for someone to come by."

CHAPTER 26

Alec stopped questioning her about the whereabouts of the device. The shock of what she'd told him had thrown him off his game. And maybe he was starting to believe that she didn't know where the Halo was, or perhaps he was trying to convince her that the right decision would be to tell him if she did.

"We've known for years that aliens have visited Earth, and we've been trying to prepare the general public to receive this knowledge ever since. It isn't that we wanted to keep the information secret forever, but we knew the populace was not mentally, or intellectually, ready for the revelation. Think about the implications—from religions to governments—it would create complete chaos.

"There is proof preserved in ancient archaeological sites and in ancient texts from all over the world. In the past, those in power explained it the best way they could: with legends that turned into myth that turned into religion. Once our intellect caught up with our knowledge, we continued to spin the evidence, to explain it away as something else. It was easy to continue with the old explanations, even though our science pointed to a different answer.

"That is until the discovery of this artifact. From what we've previously learned about it, and from what you've just shared with me regarding your first-hand experience, this is irrefutable. It would be very difficult to put a spin on it. What is it the kids say nowadays? *It is what it is*."

Ronnie said, "I might agree, but as difficult as it would be to convince me that it isn't exactly what it seems, there is still a chance it could be an elaborate hoax. Pictures can be manipulated."

"It isn't the images that lend the device credibility. It's the way they are delivered. There is no technology capable of creating an image inside someone's head. Not even close. Believe me, we would know."

She couldn't argue. The object would be difficult, if not impossible, to debunk. Once someone wore the device, it would be hard to convince the wearer it wasn't exactly what it seemed. Only if the general public, and the media, were denied the opportunity to experience it would it be possible to control the discovery through disinformation.

"So it was you who posted the video to the internet?" Ronnie asked.

"Of course. Not me directly, but someone within our organization. What better way to diminish it?"

Ronnie shifted in her chair. Her shoulder was beginning to throb. "You think I might leak the secret. You want to know which side of the fence I stand on. You brought me here because you feel I'm a threat."

"Hardly," Alec chuckled. "I brought you here because I think you know where the device is. In any case, if you decided to go public, we could neutralize your efforts in a heartbeat."

Ronnie snapped her head toward him. "I'm not the only one who's worn it. You don't have to worry about Doug Farraday any longer, but I'm sure his son and the people from SETI have worn it. Did you plan on killing us all?"

Alec let out another short laugh. "We could neutralize your efforts without killing any of you. We have other equally effective, but far less distasteful, methods. Although if push came to shove..."

"Did you kill Doug Farraday?"

"The archaeologist?" Alec shook his head. "No, the earthquake did that. But, you know, he was one of us."

How could she have known? She knew he worked undercover in an offshoot branch of their very elite unit, but she had no knowledge of The Bilderberg Group's involvement.

"We approached him and convinced him to work with Henry Applegate. He was a very altruistic man, but we eventually converted him to our cause. More importantly to him, I think he wanted to know the truth, just like you did.

"That Applegate fellow and Doug were the perfect match-up. If Doug did discover anything of importance, Applegate's reputation would serve as the catalyst to help us discredit it, while still being able to build on our knowledge of the ancients. Why they came in the first place. What they did while they were here, and if they are coming back."

The chime of Alec's cell phone interrupted their conversation, accompanied by the sound of a wave crashing on the shore below them. The chime sounded like the music from the chorus of "My Way" but Ronnie couldn't be sure.

* * *

It was harder climbing up the cliff than going down. They scrambled up the rocky incline, just a few yards beyond where their vehicle lay wasted on the road. Nick noticed an officer taking pictures of the scene. A female officer walked toward them.

"Is this your vehicle?" she asked.

They went through a series of questions that the officer delivered in a manner suggesting she'd ask the same questions a million times before. They gave her the answers they had agreed upon. The police would have to wait to bring in heavier equipment before going down to rescue any would-be survivors from the crumbled vehicle at the bottom of the ravine. Neither the Carters, nor Nick, told them that there wasn't anybody in the car.

All three were treated in the ambulances, and it was determined that none of them had any life-threatening injuries, although they were all feeling very sore and would probably feel even more so tomorrow. Nick already had a big purple bruise on his left calf and smaller ones on both shins.

Jane might have chipped a bone in her elbow, but she would have to have an x-ray to determine that. They gave her an ice pack and a sling. Another emergency tech cleaned and bandaged Stan's cut. They checked out Nick for concussion but found no apparent signs.

"Sure you don't want to go to the hospital?" The woman had introduced herself as Officer Mullins.

Stan said, "We'll get checked out by our own doctors when we get home. We just want to get into town to fill out the accident report on the rental. Then we'll catch a flight home."

"I can bring you to the station. We can fill out our reports there, and you can contact the rental company. They might want to come over and have you sign some papers and get copies of the report at the same time."

* * *

Officer Mullins walked over to where they were sitting with the rental car associate.

"We just got word. No bodies were found in the other vehicle."

The three of them looked at the officer with their best theatrical confused stares.

"And we don't see any evidence of them exiting the vehicle."

Nick realized that the powerful wind from the helicopters must have swept away any trace of the soldier's footprints on the hard rocks and pavement, both near their car and down the cliff by the mangled wreck of the Cadillac. And, even though he didn't witness it himself, he was sure the military was adept at not leaving any traces if that was their objective.

"You're sure you saw this vehicle go over the side just before you crashed?"

What did she think, Nick wondered, *that we're suffering from mass hysteria or something?* But he didn't say anything.

Stan said, "We had been up all night working our experiment. We were all tired. I know we were all sleeping at one point while we were on the ridge after the crash. They could have gotten out of the vehicle then."

"There's blood in the vehicle but no sign of them. They were obviously injured. I doubt they could have gotten far," the officer said.

"Maybe someone picked them up on the highway?" Jane offered.

"It was next to impossible for us to get down there for the rescue. I doubt they could have made it up on their own, especially with injuries."

"Well, I don't know what to tell you, officer, but we didn't see anyone leave the vehicle." Stan shifted in his seat. "Perhaps they got thrown out? They could be quite a distance from where the car landed."

Officer Mullins gave him a sardonic look. "We did a very thorough search of the area. Just wanted to double check with you all."

She turned on her heels. "But we'll keep looking. They have to be somewhere."

* * *

It was clear that Officer Mullins didn't want to let them go. If it weren't for the fact that she had no real reason to hold them, and that she learned the Carters worked for SETI (she was a big fan and an amateur astronomer) they might have all been held overnight. If she had known Nick lied back at the accident scene when he had told her that Jane was his aunt, she might have insisted on calling his mother. But, as it was, she had no reason to hold them.

Officer Mullins dropped them off at the Best Western Hotel on East Main Street and waved as she pulled away from the curb. Jane wrote fake names in the registry and paid with one of the prepaid cards that she had purchased the first day she and Nick met, before they made the trip up to Lick Observatory. She only rented one room. All they needed was a place to shower and hang out for a few hours until Hal could get his jet back to Cortez Municipal Airport to pick them up.

Stan and Nick had finished showering and now Nick stood by the front window. He held the curtain aside. To the left was a gas station, and directly across the street was a coffee shop. His heart sank. There was a black Cadillac Escalade in the parking lot.

He wondered why it always had to be a black Caddie. Out loud he said, "Guys!"

Jane had just come out of the bathroom, towel drying her short hair with one hand, while favoring the other. Her elbow was still red and swollen, and a nasty bruise spread along her tricep.

"Take a look."

Stan walked to the window and peered out.

"I don't see anything."

"The black Cadillac."

"There are black Cadillacs everywhere, Nick. That doesn't prove anything."

"Not like those. If you look you can tell it's been reinforced. I've seen enough of them in the last few days, I should know. That's an armored vehicle."

Jane scooted between the two of them. "Those SUVs all look big to me. You'd think they'd try to be a little more original."

She must have read Nick's mind.

"But, with everything else that's happened, I wouldn't doubt we're still being followed."

They had accomplished their goal. They had found a laser pulse signal from 21 Tauri—from Asterope. Emily and Henry were safe. Nick could say with more than a fair amount of certainty that the Halo was genuine; that his dad hadn't gone crazy right before he died; and that Henry hadn't concocted the entire thing just to sell books. So now what?

Nick suddenly felt the urge to call home, to speak with his mother and his sister. And, more than anything, he wanted to ask Agent Vagnetti why she had told them where to find the Halo after she had gone to so much trouble to get it from him in the first place. And he wanted to see if she could get the NSA, or whoever was tailing them, to call off the dogs. He was tired of being followed.

"I want to call home," he said.

* * *

"Mom, it's Nick."

"You're coming home?"

"No, not yet." Before she could yell at him, he said, "Is everybody okay there?"

"Yes, we're all fine. The NSA pulled up stakes, but Frank is still here with us. Henry too. He's staying here for the time being."

Frank? Nick wondered when they had gotten so friendly. And Henry was hanging out with his mom? She must really be mellowing.

"Listen, I can't talk. I need Agent Vagnetti's cell phone number."

"I don't know if you can get hold of her. She's been in some kind of accident."

"I know."

"You know?"

"Yes, Mom, please! Could you just give me her number?"

She was gone for a minute.

He heard something muffled and then, "Do you have a pencil?"

CHAPTER 27

R onnie watched as Alec listened to whoever was on the other end of the phone. He never spoke, other than to say hello, and then he ended the call and slipped the phone back in his pocket. He seemed distracted, and disappointed, in whatever news the phone call had offered.

There was still a small amount of liquid in his glass. He swirled it around the bottom and then watched as thin ribbons of amber formed on the sides.

"Maybe if I explain a little further, it would make things clearer for you. Where to begin? I should probably start with Hitler."

"Hitler?" If Ronnie hadn't recognized the voice of this man as her contact for so many years, and if he wasn't aware of so many details, she might have thought he was some lunatic that had managed to con her.

"Think about when people first started to report UFO sightings. It started during World War II and increased after. Makes sense, with all that covert activity. Governments were testing new technology and, while most people attributed the sightings to military secrecy, some people mistook the new aircraft for flying objects from an alien planet.

"They weren't far from wrong. The technology required to build the aircraft was from an alien race, but built by we humans on Earth. You are probably aware of this, but I'll repeat it anyway. Hitler hoarded art and antiquities. During the war, he stole even more, stashing it away in secret places. In so doing, he stumbled upon information left by the aliens. Startling information. Information he was using against other nations.

"Luckily, there were a few scientists who understood he meant to use this knowledge for evil instead of good, and they defected to the United States in an attempt to stop Hitler and his followers."

Ronnie had heard rumors of this story. In her line of work, it would have been hard not to. But hearing it from Alec put an entirely different spin to it.

"Only a few people knew where he had obtained this invaluable information and, once the war ended and the Nazis were defeated, most of those privileged few were either imprisoned, executed, dead by their own hand, or hiding with a deep desire to not draw attention to themselves. The information was transferred to the allies. To the victors go the spoils."

He stared at the fire for a few moments, with the hint of a smile lingering on his face.

Then Alec shifted in his seat and said, "But, back to UFO sightings. During and after the war, the number of sightings increased in number and intensity, to the point that the US Government formed a special task force, Project Blue Book, to write down and study all reports of UFO sightings. Most of the sightings could be adequately explained as something earthly. But when they couldn't..." Alec shrugged. "Then they were debunked by whatever means necessary. When the project finally closed, our group created a more clandestine operation to take its place."

He tilted his head toward Ronnie. "Your unit was a manifestation of that operation."

He waited for some response from her, but there was none.

"The bottom line is, Ronnie, the Earth has been visited by aliens in the past, and they left scientific and historical data that, if put in the wrong hands, could lead to disaster. So a group of us, who have enough power and money to make a difference, decided to form an organization to protect this information and to prepare the world for the possible..." he paused and shook his head, "No, not *possible*—the highly probable return of the aliens."

The idea of forming a one-world government would be necessary if, or rather when—according to Alec Gordon—the aliens returned. Earthlings would need a powerful and unified voice. *Earthlings.* Ronnie never liked that term. *It makes us sound like children*, she thought.

Alec continued. "All those rumors you've undoubtedly heard about the Bilderberg Group being behind the H1N1 vaccine as a way to control population? Would it shock you to learn we *were* behind it? Not for population control, but rather to inoculate as many citizens of Earth as possible against the threat of alien viruses that could be brought with them when they return."

Was this to protect them against diseases the aliens might purposefully spread? Or did they think they were protecting mankind from diseases the aliens might, unwittingly, bring with them? Did Alec's group know about the Grim Reaper, about what Ronnie had witnessed while wearing the device? He didn't mention it, and Ronnie wasn't going to share what she knew with him until she better understood his motives.

From his attitude, Ronnie got the uncomfortable impression the Bilderbergs were confident the aliens had mankind's best interest at heart. If so, how could such a powerful group hold such a naive notion? Or maybe Alec was holding back. She wondered if the artifact would change their attitude about how to best prepare the world for the aliens' return.

Then it was her turn to interrupt their conversation, she felt the soft buzz of her cell phone through the pocket of her cardigan.

* * *

"I'll have to call you back," Ronnie said while staring at Alec.

"Are you going to call off your goons?" Jane asked.

"They're not mine."

"They're government."

"Sometimes the right hand doesn't know what the left is doing."

She had cut Jane off before she could say anything about the device. Not only was Alec sitting right next to her, but he might have also bugged her phone. If he couldn't hear everything that was said, he could certainly find out later. She needed to hang on to any small amount of leverage she still might have.

"We need some answers," Jane said.

"I know. Give me fifteen minutes. Should I use this number?"

"Yes."

She flipped her phone shut.

Ronnie needed time to think. Her job had been to gather intel on strange phenomenon or discoveries, scientific or otherwise; and to keep her finger on the pulse of offbeat theories regarding new discoveries, or old ones that had been forgotten but recently rediscovered. It was up to someone else to decide what was done with the information Ronnie passed on. She would occasionally keep up with the more intriguing findings; stashing away in her mental file what had happened to the discovery or to the person who made it. Ronnie didn't question her government's need to either obtain the information or their need to keep it a secret. Was it really for the good of mankind to be in the dark? She had often pondered this question.

Most of what Ronnie passed on could be easily explained away. And why get the populace's panties in a bunch if the source was less than one hundred percent reliable? But this new finding was special. This device was the most believable piece of evidence she had run across in her long career. Even with an infinitesimal measure of doubt, the term *most believable* didn't even cover it. It was irrefutable, as far as she was concerned.

It was the scenes that unfolded inside the mental hologram that gave the real proof. It spelled out in black and white, and all the colors of the rainbow, the ancient history of Earth. Unless it turned out to be an elaborate production by some far-advanced earthly society—like some ancient blockbuster sci-fi movie—then it was an alien-created documentary of what really happened thousands of years ago.

If Ronnie hadn't worn the device, she might not be so convinced. There was nothing earthly about her experience. She knew why Alec had come to her. This new evidence was a game-changer. This was an explanation of all the mysteries that had been plaguing our historians for centuries. A Rosetta Stone of sorts, but far more valuable. It explained everything from how the pyramids were built to why the dinosaurs disappeared from Earth. All the things historians and scientists scratched their heads over and argued about.

There were those who held the belief that our rapid advance in modern technologies came from data left by alien visitors, but there had never been any real evidence to indicate that man's advancements weren't anything other than the results of mankind's own efforts and brainpower. Now Ronnie wondered if the development of some of our technologies was the direct result of previously discovered ancient extraterrestrial artifacts.

Another question that nagged Ronnie: Did the higher-ups at the NSA really know who was directing her small, elite group of analysts and field operatives for the past fifteen years? That was the problem with such a high level of secrecy; there were very few, if any, checks and balances.

Did Ronnie think it was morally right to keep this information from the public? She wasn't sure. But she was sure of one thing. If the Bilderberg Group didn't want the information to be released at the moment, then she wouldn't have any choice but to play along. And neither would anyone else who held intimate knowledge of the device.

She turned to Alec. "What are you planning on doing with all of us?"

"I'm glad you asked."

Alec said, "First of all, I hope you and your cohorts agree that releasing this information, at this time, would do more harm than good."

"I can't honestly say I'm in full agreement with that premise, but my job has never been to question."

"Our goal isn't to keep this a secret forever. Our goal is to slowly prepare the world for the inevitable. Don't you agree that this is the best approach?"

On the surface, Ronnie could understand the need for preparation. The shock of being confronted with irrefutable truth was far different than being presented with speculation.

"I can see the need to prepare the populace."

"What I would like to do is gather all your friends together—you; the couple from SETI; the Farradays; that Applegate fellow—and sit down and have a civilized, meaningful discussion."

He took the last sip of his Hennessey and sat the glass on the edge of the fire pit.

"I've managed to book the rest of these cottages." He swept his arm toward the buildings. "For their convenience and our privacy. Do you think they would accept a friendly offer to have a chat?"

Ronnie's mind was churning, cranking out scenarios like an old time Flicker Reel Animation Viewer. Should she contact her superiors at the NSA even though they probably only had an inkling of who her real boss was, or what her real job entailed? Even if she wanted to, she would have little opportunity to contact them. She knew the woman inside wasn't only a nurse but probably had skills Ronnie could only imagine. And since Alec had first visited her in the hospital, someone had been with her at all times. Alec was having her closely watched.

"Do any of us have a choice?"

She flipped open her cell phone and pressed the last caller icon.

CHAPTER 28

L iz was all too eager to get the hell out of Dodge. Until someone put an end to the rumors about that blasted crown, her family would never be safe.

Frank had received a call from Agent Vagnetti. What they talked about, she had no idea. All she knew was that they—herself, Emily, Henry, and Frank—were headed to San Francisco at the agent's request. Frank said it was for their protection, and she wasn't going to argue. She also realized the SETI Institute was in Mountain View, which was southeast of San Francisco. Her hope was that Agent Vagnetti had arranged for them to reunite with Nick. She'd questioned Frank about that possibility, but he said all he knew was that they were to leave as soon as possible. She'd tried to call Nick using the cell phone number stored in her phone from the last time he'd called her, but no one answered.

They were flying in a private jet, something Liz had never experienced but could certainly get used to. The pilot had just made an announcement that it was okay to unbuckle their seat belts. Ahead of her, the flight attendant was handing Henry a beverage. He had been subdued ever since his rescue. Liz saw him casting concerned glances at Emily every now and again. *The man has a heart after all,* she thought. The fact that Ming Lin had betrayed him in such a way had wrecked him, she knew. She'd never liked the woman and wondered what Henry ever saw in her. She was bright, yes, but there was something underneath that had always bothered Liz. Henry had been blinded by his regard for her father, she knew. Not the first person to ever be fooled by someone. Liz actually felt sorry for him. She knew how painful betrayal could be, imagined or otherwise.

Emily was deep in conversation with Frank near the back of the plane. They seemed to be hitting it off well. Liz knew he was trying to take her mind off the kidnapping, and she was grateful. Like Liz, Emily wondered how many other crazies there were still out their looking for the crown, and who might be willing to do anything to get it.

"Sounds like you have a natural talent for languages," Liz heard Frank say.

"I enjoy it. And, from what I understand, my father spoke several."

"That, combined with your computer skills, might make for a very nice career with the NSA. Those particular skill-sets are always welcome at the agency."

Over my dead body, Liz thought. But she'd deal with that later.

Liz unlatched her seat belt and made her way to where Henry was sitting.

"Mind if I have a seat?"

Henry blinked twice. "Yes. I mean no, I don't mind. Please."

He gestured to the seat on the other side of the round table where his drink sat untouched. Flying in a private jet was quite a different experience than flying commercial.

"What do you think will happen to us?" she asked.

"Whatever do you mean?"

"Even if they recover the crown, I'm still never going to feel safe. They'll always be someone out there thinking we have it. Unless the NSA is willing to make a worldwide announcement—which I doubt they'd do—then this will never be resolved. For us, at least."

Henry picked up his drink and took a sip.

Liz said, "Do you think they'll want us to go into some kind of witness protection program?"

He looked startled. "I never considered that possibility. I...but what about The Antiquarian?" He looked wide-eyed into the empty space before him.

Seeing him that way, Liz suddenly wondered how he was able to handle being on the jet. Either he was well medicated, or his ordeal had cured him of his phobia forever.

He slowly came back to the present and said, "I enjoy my life."

"I enjoy mine too. But having to look over my shoulder every minute of the day and night isn't my idea of a good one."

The conversation was upsetting him, she could tell. She didn't want him to have a panic attack on the plane.

"Listen, Henry. Whatever happens, I just want to say I'm sorry I've been so...harsh with you over the years. I'm not saying we can become best friends just yet. But...I admit, I probably diverted some of the anger I felt toward my husband to you."

"I appreciate you saying that Liz. By hiring Doug, I never meant to hurt you or your family. And I'm sorry about Ming Lin. Truly. A great disappointment to me."

"Seems as if we've all been guilty of misjudging character."

* * *

"Sounds like we don't have a choice in the matter," Jane said.

Stan said, "We have choices, just not very many good ones."

"I don't know about you, but I'm not ready to give up the Halo again just yet."

Jane had heard something in Agent Vagnetti's voice over the phone when she had finally called Jane back. Something that made her think the agent wasn't ready for them to give it up either.

"Did she say she was going to call off the goons?" Nick asked.

Jane shook her head and repeated what the agent had said about the right hand not knowing what the left was doing during their previous conversation.

"That's curious," Stan said.

"And rather scary, if you think about it," Jane said.

"So that means she can't call them off?" Nick asked.

"We should assume the answer is no, and that they probably aren't part of the NSA team," Jane said.

She repeated to Nick and Stan what the agent had told her. She explained that a man named Alec Gordon wanted to have a chat with them. He had arranged for a meeting at the Ritz-Carlton Half-Moon Bay Resort and would have a private jet at the Cortez Municipal Airport to fly them to Half-Moon Bay late that afternoon. It seemed the hotel had its own private airport. That didn't give them much time. A limo would be waiting to drive them to the resort once they landed.

Jane wondered if this Alec Gordon was a member of the wealthy Gordon family who had built their fortune in the newspaper business during the late nineteenth century. They continued to build their fortune in the media communication business and were now one of the wealthiest families in the world. The Gordons owned several magazines, publishing companies, and television stations. She had no idea what he had to do with any of this—with the Halo or extraterrestrials—or if this man was related to *the* Gordons, but she had a suspicion that he was.

Ronnie had offered a low-key suggestion that they agree to the meeting. Whether they wanted to or not. Jane knew this was something bigger than she had ever dealt with before and, unless they cooperated, the outcome might not be good for any of them.

"We can't hide forever, like criminals on the run." Jane spoke to no one in particular.

She had kept her promise to Nick and helped him prove his father wasn't a lunatic. And now she and Stan knew where and how to gather data that would help provide even further proof of intelligent life on another planet. They realized the laser beam came from Asterope, and that the beams held a vast amount of data. They only needed to figure out how to decipher it, which would require significant resources and a lot of time. Would Jane like to see more of what the Halo had to offer? Most definitely. But there were powerful groups looking for it, and they weren't going to sit back and let SETI have all the fun. And she was beginning to realize there was something even bigger to consider.

"Even if we give the Halo back, now that we've seen what's on it, do you really think the government will trust us to keep quiet?"

"Maybe that's what this meeting is all about. To see how trustworthy we are."

"From Agent Vagnetti's own admission when she spoke with us at Lick, no one really knows what the Halo does. All they have is rumor and the YouTube video. "We," she moved her arm to indicate the three of them, "are the only ones who really know how incredible it is."

"Agent Vagnetti might know," Stan said. "She was alone with it for almost a half hour at the observatory. She could have worn it. I know I would have if given the opportunity."

"True." Jane thought for a moment. "But I wonder how much she fully understood of what she saw? I'm sure she's quite an intellect but her learning might not include high-level astronomy or physics. But think about it. We, and most likely Agent Vagnetti also, are the only people who really know the value of the Halo. And now we're all being called to a *meeting*."

"Either she's leading us into a trap, or she's in danger herself. And why lead us into a trap if she freely gave it back to us to begin with? And the comment about the right hand not knowing what the left was doing, that sounds more like a warning than an admission of a government snafu." Stan started pacing.

"But no matter what, as long as we have the Halo, we still have the upper hand," Jane said.

"This Alec fellow must know we have it."

"Not necessarily. Agent Vagnetti didn't ask us to bring it. She just said Gordon was requesting a meeting, and she was urging us to accept." Jane shook her head. "Something in her voice makes me think she doesn't want us to hand it over. Remember she told us to protect it. You'd think she would have at least asked about its safety. But she didn't. Something's not right."

Jane spun around and grabbed the laptop.

"What are you doing?" Stan asked.

She pointed to a card on the table.

"This place offers WiFi. I say we rent a safety deposit box and stash the Halo while we go to this little meeting."

* * *

The ad for the Cortez Vault & Safety Deposit Box Company looked impressive. It wasn't affiliated with any bank, which was a good thing. All it offered was a thick steel-walled vault with safety deposit boxes behind. Perfect. And it was just around the corner.

Jane had google-mapped the area and found the quickest way to get to the vault company, and the best way to avoid the SUV parked across the street. They would go out the conference room entrance toward the back of the hotel, head toward the rear parking lot, and cut through alleyways and side streets.

"I have one more thing to do before we leave," Jane said. She looked at Stan. "I'm sending an email to Jerome."

"Dr. Ellis?"

"Yes. I'm going to tell him to set up an optic laser experiment—just like we did on the mesa—at Stonehenge. I'm not going to tell him why, other than we had some promising results. And I'll insist on his confidentiality until we have more data."

Dr. Jerome Ellis was an old and trusted friend and colleague who worked at Leeds Metropolitan University in the United Kingdom. He'd even attended Jane and Stan's wedding.

"Couldn't think of anyone I would trust more."

After she'd sent the email, Jane stood up and said, "All set. Let's go."

Nick pulled his backpack, with the Halo still safely tucked inside, over his shoulder. Jane picked up the laptop, and they left the hotel room.

A dark-haired beefy man greeted them when they walked through the door of the vault company. He had a precisely trimmed short beard. "Welcome. I'm Bruce Belford. How can I help you?"

After deciding which size box would meet their needs, Jane filled out the appropriate forms. Just to be safe, she made a last minute decision to use the name of the first female astronomer, Maria Mitchell, and the address of San Jose public library. She had her library card in her wallet with the address on the back.

The deposit box came with two keys. They decided Jane would carry one and Nick would have the other. They all signed signature cards and used the library address. After Jane had signed her name as Maria, the other two followed her lead and made up a name they would remember. They all wrote down fake phone numbers.

"So, you people aren't from around here."

"No. But we visit often," Jane said. They shared furtive glances at one another.

"Hey, sorry." He reached his hands in the air as if he was being held up. "It doesn't pay to be nosy in my business. Didn't mean to pry. We're just friendly around here, is all."

"Is there a problem if we're not residents?" Jane asked.

"No problem at all. As long as you pay the rent," the manager said with broad smile. "We don't ask a lot of questions."

They paid for a three-month rental with the rest of Henry's cash.

Bruce led them to a small room where they could place their valuables in the box in private. Once they came out, he led them inside the huge vault and guided them to the empty slot awaiting their bin.

Jane slid the box in place. The manager closed the door, used his master key in the first lock. Jane put her key in the second.

When they were finished, she asked, "Do you have a WiFi connection here?"

"You can catch one down the street at the coffee shop."

The smell of freshly brewed coffee and the sweet smell of doughnuts hit them when they walked into the store. They scanned the area to make sure they weren't being followed. On the walk from the vault, they had discussed what they should do about Jane's laptop. They decided they would ship it, overnight, back to her office at SETI.

"We should send the keys too. What if this Gordon fellow searches us?" Nick said.

"Good idea."

"What will you have?" The barista was a young, thin, college-age male. A latte for Jane, black coffee for Stan, and Nick ordered a small chai.

Stan found a table in the back with a clear view of the large picture window that covered the front of the store. They were sitting for only a few minutes when Stan said, "I think we have company."

Jane looked up from her computer search and Nick put down his drink.

"The black Cadillac just drove by."

Jane said, "I think we can take side streets to get to the shipping store. Let's call for a cab to pick us up there in a half hour. That should give us enough time to get to the airport. Besides, what's the plane going to do? Take off without us?"

Shipping the package was managed without incident. Stan had already called Hal and told him they wouldn't need his jet after all. Once in the cab, they were all silent, not knowing what would be waiting for them once they got to the Half-Moon Bay Resort. No matter how they felt about it, there really wasn't any other reasonable option left for them but to meet with Alec Gordon.

CHAPTER 29

"The evidence is everywhere."

Ronnie and Alec were alone again on the patio. The others hadn't arrived yet.

"Pictures of spacecraft explained away as something else entirely. The Mayan Lord Pakal's sarcophagus holds a carving that is interpreted as a depiction of him descending into the Maya underworld, but on the edges are images representing the Sun, the Moon, Venus, and others constellations. If you look closely, it clearly represents a spacecraft, and Lord Pakal is ascending, not descending. And then there are the carvings on the walls of burial tombs in Egypt showing the use of electrical power for lighting the deep interior of the structures. These are dismissed as depictions of someone holding a flower and the scent radiating outward, instead of what it actually is: an object that throws light. So you see, we have all sorts of nonsensical explanations.

"Yet, these explanations are freely and willingly accepted by the masses. To think otherwise would make one look somehow unbalanced. When someone suggests a more logical explanation, they are scorned. For instance, it is widely believed the Egyptians used a series of copper mirrors to reflect the sun in order to light the deep recesses of the burial crypts while they worked. There are no traces of the smoke from torches, so this is the answer the scientists have come up with. If anyone were to suggest the Egyptians might have known about electricity, that person would be regarded with skepticism."

Ronnie was getting the feeling that Alec Gordon was trying hard to impress her with his knowledge. She'd seen this kind of behavior before. She started to realize he must be a very small fish in a large pond. And, even though he had been the voice on the other end of the phone that guided her for so many years, he probably had someone much higher up telling him what to say. In her experience, this made him unpredictable and dangerous. She listened as he continued with his harangue.

"Look at our friend, Mr. Applegate. Mainstream scientists scoff at his books. But we know that much of what he says in his so-called conspiracy theory books is true. Don't get me wrong; we appreciate Mr. Applegate's notoriety. He helps keep the truth at bay."

Alec paused for a moment and Ronnie thought he was finished, but he continued. "We don't have to go all the way to Egypt. There are also examples right here in the United States. Have you ever wondered how the Grand Canyon was really formed?"

Ronnie's head jerked around at the mention of the canyon. She had worn the Halo and witnessed how it had been formed. What evidence did Alec and the Bilderbergs have regarding its creation? One thing that struck Ronnie, Alec had never mentioned anything about the aliens providing the answer to the missing link. Did his group know about this? Did the Bilderbergs already have evidence? Or was the artifact—the Halo—the first evidence ever found that explained the missing link of man's evolution on Earth?

"We have knowledge that the canyon was formed by mining operations conducted by various groups of aliens. Do you know anything of geology, Ronnie?"

"It isn't one of my specialties."

"Do you know they named a certain rock, one formed in the Grand Canyon millions of years ago, the *Vishnu Shist*? And other types called the *Brahma* and *Rama Schists*?"

Ronnie knew enough about Hinduism to know that Vishnu was considered their Supreme God. How that related to a rock formation in the Grand Canyon, she wasn't sure. But she was certain she was about to find out.

"In the Hindu tale the Bhagavad Gita, Lord Vishnu rides around in a flying craft called the Vimanas. Have you heard of this tale?" He didn't wait for an answer. "Of course you have, you are a woman of extensive learning."

Ronnie thought of the irony of Henry's password. She knew the Bhagavad Gita was a favorite topic among UFO conspiracy theorists. This new twist might be interesting.

"Do you think it is by accident these molten rocks were given this name?" Alec shook his head for emphasis. "The Vimanas caused these black rocks to form in the Grand Canyon by the heat from the powerful engines that lifted them. And why were these Vimanas in the Grand Canyon to begin with? Long before it was a canyon, it was a vast plain that was teeming with precious metals. The Grand Canyon was formed from years of strip-mining. The geologists can scratch their heads all they want and come up with theory after theory. The truth is: The canyon is one great wasteland created by ancient mining activity."

As much as she was irritated by Gordon's long soliloquy, Ronnie wondered how many more odd and otherwise unexplainable things could now be explained. All the ancient mysteries of Earth were no longer mysteries at all. Like a giant Rubik's Cube, the disjointed, previously unexplainable stories of Earth's past were now clicking into perfect alignment.

* * *

At the airport, the limo driver handed Agent Nelson a note.

"This is as far as I go," Frank said.

Liz and Emily turned toward him.

"What?" Liz said.

He waggled the note in the air. "Orders from headquarters."

"But I thought...I thought you were assigned to protect us?"

"Things have changed. But you'll be with Agent Vagnetti."

"Will I see you again?" Liz didn't care how desperate she sounded. She had gotten used to Frank being around. She would feel vulnerable without him.

"You've got my card."

Emily gave him a big unrestrained hug. "I'll miss you."

"I'll miss you too. Take care of yourself. And let me know if you're ever interested in a job with the NSA."

"I will."

Emily turned away and Liz stepped closer. She felt like hugging him, too, but didn't know if it was appropriate.

Instead, she stood on her tiptoes and gave him a quick kiss on the cheek.

"Thanks for everything."

"It's my job."

Liz raised her eyebrow. "So we're just a job to you?"

"You know what I mean."

He stood for a moment and stared down at the note, then turned and walked away.

Liz and Emily watched his back until he turned and smiled, and then they climbed into the aircraft that sat waiting for them.

* * *

A middle-aged doorman with epaulets on the shoulders of his navy jacket opened the limo door and a female concierge rushed up to meet them as they climbed out of the long black sedan. She wore a black pencil skirt, a blazer, a crisp white shirt, and alarmingly high heels. Other than the designer pumps, she looked all business with her blond hair tied back into a severe ponytail. If she was trying to hide the fact that she was pretty, it wasn't working, Nick thought.

"Did you have a pleasant flight?" she asked as she guided them through the lobby with its polished hardwood paneling. The lush room was decorated in warm shades of gold and red, and rich oriental rugs covered the hardwood floors. The room had a regal feel to it. Nick had never been anyplace so luxurious.

"I'm Anna," the concierge said. "I'll take you to the cottages. It's only a short walk." She turned to smile at them. "It's worth it. The view is stunning."

Her heels clicked in a sharp, rhythmic pattern against the wood flooring. Nick couldn't tell if she actually worked for the hotel or if she was an employee of Alec Gordon, or the NSA. Whatever. He was anxious to get this meeting over with.

They walked to the end of a wide hallway and through an arched doorway into the cool night air. Anna led them, like a group of goslings following their mother, toward the cottages in the distance.

When they neared, she walked to the middle cottage, used a key card to open the door, and led them inside.

"Nicholas!" Liz ran to greet him as soon as he walked through the door. She pushed his head into the crook of her neck until he was almost smothering. "I'm so glad to see you."

"I didn't know you'd be here." He had to admit, he was very glad to see her, too, but after a minute of being in such a tight bear hug, he gently pushed away. "Where's Emily?"

"Here I am!" She ran to her brother and gave him a big hug of her own. He hadn't heard her come in behind their mother.

"Em, I'm so glad you're okay." Nick felt tears welling in his eyes but none spilled over.

"Yeah, me too."

Liz had moved around them, giving them time to get reacquainted, and introduced herself to the Carters. Henry had followed Emily through the door and was now taking his turn at greeting Nick.

"It isn't the time right now," Henry said, "but one day I'd like to tell you how sorry I am for putting you in danger. And how proud I am of you."

"It's okay, Henry."

Anna said, "I've taken the liberty of purchasing a change of clothes for all of you."

Nick remembered the flight attendant asking them their clothes and shoe sizes. He thought it odd at the time but now he understood.

She turned to Liz. "Your family will share this cottage. Ms. Vagnetti is staying in the north cottage and," she turned to the Carters, "you will be sharing the south cottage with Mr. Applegate. It has an extra bedroom. You will be very comfortable there, I assure you. Once you've freshened up, Mr. Gordon has arranged for an outdoor dinner. In the meantime, the fire pits on the patios are lit and the view is spectacular."

Anna passed out key cards to everyone, wished them a pleasant stay, and turned to click her way back to the main building.

CHAPTER 30

"**D**o you realize tomorrow is Thanksgiving Day?"

Alec Gordon stood before them. Behind him was a spectacular view of the Pacific Ocean. An almost-full moon highlighted the whitecaps that rushed toward the narrow shore below the steep cliffs.

"We might have our own special reason for giving thanks tomorrow."

A large white tent with high festive peaks had been set up in front of the three isolated cottages. There were several tall portable heaters around the periphery to take the chill out of the night air. Hors d'oeuvres were scattered between them on the round table but, so far, no one had eaten any. While they had sat around the fire pits waiting for their host to arrive, Ronnie filled them in on a few details regarding Alec Gordon—that he was involved with both the NSA and the Bilderberg Group.

"Perhaps I should get to the point," Alec Gordon said, after he had given them a more in-depth briefing, repeating many of the things he had already told Ronnie. "I'm hoping that one of you can tell me where the device is."

The sea wind whipped the sheer drapes hanging down the side of the tent.

"None of you own up to having it? Perhaps going over the timeline of events will help."

Alec lifted his wine glass and inclined his head toward Henry.

"We know it was shipped to the US in an urn containing the remains of Doug Farraday. The urn was then interred in the Farraday's family crematorium, which was subsequently broken into, the urn shattered, and the crown went missing. Agent Vagnetti is confident that it was young Nicholas who took it from the urn."

Alec inclined his head toward Nick. Liz gave her son a hurt, confused look but didn't say anything.

"Agent Vagnetti was able to retrieve the device from the Lick Observatory where Nick had, presumably, gone to get assistance from the Carters in authenticating the device. Unfortunately, the agent had a little accident on the road down the mountain and seems to have lost it."

Nick glanced at the Carters. Agent Vagnetti must not have told her boss what happened on Mt. Hamilton road. She hadn't ratted them out. He saw them shift their eyes toward him, silently acknowledging their secret.

"Exactly who are you to be questioning us?" Liz cut in. "What authority do you have?"

"You are correct. I have no legal jurisdiction over you. I'm not in law enforcement. I'm nobody. Yet I'm someone who wields a lot of power. And, you must trust me, Mrs. Farraday, you have no better friend in this situation."

"Oh, and how's that? So far, all you've done is give us veiled threats."

And not so veiled, Nick thought. There were black-clad guards armed with semi-automatic weapons positioned about twenty yards from each end of the tent. Farther out along the cliff he could see several shadowy figures. Either they were there to keep them safe, or keep them from leaving; Nick couldn't be sure which.

"Our intention isn't to harm you. We don't simply *off* our adversaries or anyone who happens to get in our way like in some Godfather movie." Alec smiled. "We're a bit more subtle. Our approach to problem solving is a little more intellectual, if you don't mind my saying so."

"Let me get this straight," Stan said, "The Bilderberg Group has proof that extraterrestrials have visited Earth before. They also have a pretty good notion that the aliens will someday return. And the group's sole purpose is to prepare the world for this 'second coming' while keeping this knowledge and their motivations secret in order to stop widespread panic?"

"That pretty much sums it up, Mr. Carter. It is not one government, one nation, or one individual, who wants to control this knowledge. We are a group from all occupations, and a variety of nations—people whose life circumstances have put them in a position to make a difference. All with one goal: To protect and prepare the world as best we can for the return of the aliens. No matter what you've heard about us, the majority of it is false information. We are not unhappy about the misconceptions. The further away the world is from realizing our real purpose, the better."

"The Bilderbergs are notorious for having roots in the Nazi movement. Is that false information too?" Stan's voice had an edge to it.

"Our mission throughout the decades has been a difficult one." Alec looked at the candlelight flickering over the deep red of the wine. "The group first formed in

World War II when we learned Hitler had information left by extraterrestrial beings that gave him a great advantage over the rest of civilization. You might have heard rumors that some of our first members were Nazis. The more accurate statement would be that some of our members were spies who infiltrated the Nazi organization. As I said, we like this type of misinformation, it deflects from our real purpose."

Stan said, "Any secretive organization whose members are as powerful and influential as the Bilderberg Group is potentially very dangerous. Just because you think you're on the right side of the good-versus-evil issue doesn't make it so."

Alec turned to him. "You tell me, Mr. Carter. Are we on the right side? What would you do in this situation? At the time of the war, do you think humankind would be ready to learn the magnitude of what we'd discovered? Is the world ready now?"

No one answered.

"If you already know so much about the aliens, why is it so important for you to retrieve the Halo?" Jane asked.

"If our assumptions are correct, it not only contains valuable information, but it is proof positive of alien visitation. From our intel, we understand that once the Halo is—shall we say—experienced, it cannot be debunked. You can understand why we want to secure this object."

"And what will you do with it, if you were able to secure it?" she asked.

"Study it, just like you would want to do. And keep it safe."

"Safe from whom?" Stan said.

"From those who would misuse the knowledge it holds. And from those who might misuse the knowledge that extraterrestrials once wandered this planet, those who might use it as a means to create panic. From panic comes chaos. From chaos comes an opportunity to seize power. And power in the wrong hands can mean disaster for the world."

"Which hands are the wrong hands, Mr. Gordon?" Jane asked. "You expect us to trust your intentions are good just because you say they are?"

"Yes, Mrs. Carter, I do."

* * *

Jane turned her eyes toward her husband. What Alec said made some sense. On the surface, it all sounded noble and principled. Yet, the wariness of the group of people seated around the table was palpable. Alec Gordon was assuring them that he was the good guy and only trying to help the peoples of Earth. At the same time, they all knew that having sole access to a secret as great as this meant the group held an extraordinary amount of power. Chaos wasn't the only way to seize control of the world.

Alec said, "I'm sure you've all aware of at least some of the Swine Flu and H1N1 conspiracy theories?"

The adults all confirmed with various degrees of head shaking. Emily and Nick sat quietly.

"Of course, the theorists got it all wrong. We are trying to inoculate as many of the Earth's population as we can, using whatever means possible. But, our main objective is to protect the world from the potential threat of any viruses the aliens might bring with them. Those who are inoculated will pass their immunity to their offspring, with the immunity getting stronger with each generation.

"We are not evil. We are trying to prepare society and save humankind. We will use any means necessary. And we will continue to do it with or without your cooperation."

The sound of the rhythmic motion of the surf filled the silence. A breeze kicked up and unsettled the curtains inside the south end of the tent, revealing the business end of a semi-automatic in the hands of one of the paramilitary guards posted outside.

"So my theories were not unfounded," Henry finally spoke.

"No, Henry, they were not. And whether you were aware of it or not, you've been aiding our efforts for quite some time."

Instead of being angry, Nick thought Henry almost looked ecstatic. Nick knew what this meant for Henry. Along with his father, Henry had experienced a vindication of sorts.

"The bottom line is: You might not like the idea of the Bilderberg Group. You might not trust us, or agree with our approach. That is not my concern. I'm here to tell you that while we would appreciate your cooperation, and maybe even your help—I will address that in greater detail later—if any of you have the Halo, yet refuse to give it up willingly, we will find it by whatever means necessary. Have no delusions about that. My hope is you will make it easy for us, now that you understand our motivations."

Stan said, "We turned it over to the NSA, Mr. Gordon. You say that Agent Vagnetti lost it after leaving the observatory. Why ask us where it is?"

Alec tapped the fingers of his right hand on the table.

"I've learned that anything is possible in this game, Mr. Carter. In any case, if you don't have it," he shrugged, "then all you have is a story that no one will believe. A great story, with no place to tell it. No one will take you seriously."

He turned to fully face the Carters. "Your reputation and the reputation of SETI will be in jeopardy at the very moment when the institute needs to be making more friends, not less."

He raised his arm toward Henry seated to his right. "Henry here can go on making allegations in his books, and he will have some believers, but mainstream society will still think he is just a greedy capitalist trying to sell books to the gullible. Any one of you could go to the press as a whistle blower, but do you think anyone will take you seriously? How do you think we've been able to keep our knowledge a secret for so long? Anything can be debunked."

"Until now," Nick said.

Alec smirked. "If our expectations of the Halo are true then, yes, until now."

"But what about my dad?" Nick came up out of his chair. "I'm supposed to let the world think he was crazy when he actually made the greatest discovery ever?"

Alec leaned back in his chair and cast an appraising look at him.

"Exactly the reaction I would expect out of someone so young."

Nick felt his face grow hot. "And what's that supposed to mean?"

"Do you think your father is the only person throughout history who has given up his moment in the spotlight for the betterment of mankind? Have you never heard of sacrifice?"

Alec gestured for Nick to sit down.

"In any case, what if I told you that your father would be perfectly happy the way things are."

"What do you mean?" Nick snapped. Emily leaned forward in her seat and shot a glance at their mother.

"Your father was part of our team. How do you think he happened to hook up with Henry here?" Alec crooked his head toward Henry. "We set it up. It was the perfect partnership. If Doug happened to find something and it leaked into the public consciousness, as the Halo certainly has, then Henry's reputation as a wild-eyed conspiracy theorist played right into our hands."

"Disinformation. Hide in plain sight," Henry said.

"Exactly," Alec stated.

"I...I don't understand," Liz said.

"Your husband would want to keep knowledge of this object from the world."

Nick was stunned. His father worked for the Bilderberg Group? That would certainly explain why he had risked his reputation to work for Henry.

Ronnie said, "He didn't realize he was working for the Bilderbergs any more than I did. Don't mislead the boy."

"The NSA. The Bilderberg Group. What difference in a name? The point is, he believed in our efforts to prepare the world for this announcement. He believed revealing it too soon would do more harm than good."

"You don't have any idea what he really thought. The man is no longer here to defend himself," Ronnie said.

"Defend? Interesting choice of words." Alec shrugged and took another slow sip of wine. "Please, eat!" He waved his hands at the platters of hors d'oeuvres. "Try some of these *amuse-bouché*. They are delectable."

They all fidgeted with their drinks, but no one moved to select any of the tiny, colorful finger appetizers. The mood of the group grew even more somber.

Liz finally said, "My first priority is to my family. What about us? You make it sound so noble that you want to prepare the world for some possible future event, but what about us right now? We didn't sign up for any of this. As long as there are people who believe this Halo is valuable, we won't be safe."

"All the more reason for you to turn it over to us," Alec said, "We can contain any speculation and protect you, if you let us."

"We've already told you we don't have it," Stan said.

Liz pressed on, "Do you mean a witness protection program?"

Jane sat her drink on the table. "I'm not interested in a witness protection program. I have a career. I'm not willing to give it up."

"There won't be a need for that," Alec said. "As I already explained, we've been very successful in the past at eliminating any rumors and dissipating any unwanted interest. Let us worry about that. Let us do our job."

"You can't possibly expect us to forget about this," Jane said.

"No. How could you? And I'm not asking you to. What I'm asking you to do is to help us in our endeavor. You are all in a unique position. Each of you, in your own way, can help lead the population of Earth safely into a new age of enlightenment."

"Right now, my only concern is my safety and my family's," Liz said, "We're just ordinary citizens—not like the agents here—and our lives have already been put in danger. My daughter was kidnapped in an attempt to get that Halo. I'm not sure we can even go back to our old lives with people still out there searching for it and thinking we know where it is. What's going to happen to us?"

"Whatever happens to you from this point on is in your hands, Mrs. Farraday."

"That sounds a lot like another threat." Liz instinctively leaned closer to her children.

"Not a threat, just a fact. We protect our assets, and do our best to reduce our liabilities. Simple economics."

"We're not just figures in some balance sheet, Mr. Gordon," Liz said.

"I've given each of you a lot to think about. Now let's enjoy our meal. I'll leave you to think things over tonight. We'll all meet again tomorrow for a Thanksgiving feast."

CHAPTER 31

"Was Agent Vagnetti right?" Liz asked. "Did you take the crown out of the urn?"

Nick shifted his eyes toward Ronnie and the Carter's. He couldn't read their expressions, so he decided to tell the truth.

"Yes."

"And you took it to SETI because Henry told you they could verify its authenticity?"

"Yes."

"But you don't have it now?"

Nick paused. He didn't need the Carters to tell him he shouldn't reveal the location of the Halo. The place could be bugged, and Agent Vagnetti was sitting right there. He still wasn't sure who they could trust. The fewer people who knew were it was, the better.

"Right," he answered. It was the truth. He didn't have it with him at the moment.

"Do you know where it is?" His mother wasn't letting up.

"Even if he knows where it is, it isn't that simple," Jane came to his rescue.

"If anyone here has the crown," Liz said, "then just give the man what he wants and let's be done with it. He said he would protect us, that he would get rid of all the crazies who might still be looking for it."

Jane said, "If he thinks we've 'experienced' it, as he said, then we're still a threat to him. Once we hand it over—if, in fact, any of us knows where it is—we lose any leverage we might have."

Liz turned to Nick again. "Did you wear it?"

"It doesn't matter if he did or not. If Alec thinks he did, then Nick is a threat. Just like the rest of us," Stan said.

"I want to know if my son wore the crown, Mr. Carter. For my own information."

Nick tried to read both Stan and Jane's expressions again. Should he tell her? Jane gave an almost imperceptible nod.

"Mom, it was fantastic. If you wore it, you'd understand why Dad looked so crazy in the video. It's...it's unreal!"

Liz groaned and let her face fall into her hands.

"Why, Nicholas? Why did you have to go after it?"

"I don't regret it. I'm glad I did."

Ronnie pushed back her chair. "Let's all take a little break. We need to think this through.

She stood behind Jane. "Would you walk with me? I saw a couple of Adirondack chairs near the cliff. They look very inviting. And Nurse Ratched," she nodded her head toward the cottage, "told me I needed to walk a little every day."

"Sure," Jane agreed.

Ronnie sent Jane inside her cottage to get a couple of lap blankets and then they walked north, past the tent.

"We're just going for a little stroll," she called out to the guard who shifted his firearm. Alec had said his goodbyes but left behind the paramilitary. Ronnie could still see several dark figures lurking in the distances between the cottages and the main resort and along the edge of the cliff.

Neither of them spoke until they were settled in the chairs. They were far enough away from the nearest guard to give them a small sense of privacy.

"Under different circumstances, this would be lovely," Ronnie stated. They sat looking out over the Pacific Ocean. The steady rhythm of the waves acted like a salve on Ronnie's jangled nerves.

"Do you play poker, Jane?"

"If you count internet poker. My line of work can get pretty lonely."

"Hard to practice your poker face with an online opponent."

"You're right. No way to read your opponents 'tells'."

"Yet you've developed a very good one," Ronnie said.

"My poker face?" Jane didn't wait for an answer. "Yes, I suppose so."

"You didn't tell Mr. Gordon I'd pointed you toward the Halo."

"And neither did you."

"No, I didn't."

"I wouldn't want to be your opponent in a game of Texas Hold 'em," Jane said.

Ronnie's shoulder was beginning to hurt. She wished she'd asked Nurse Ratched for her nightly dose of pain meds.

"Were you able to find it?"

Jane hesitated a moment. Ronnie knew she was weighing her options, knew she was wondering if she should trust her.

"We've been wondering why you asked us to find and protect it. Why you didn't call one of your colleagues at the NSA?"

Answering a question with another question. She was definitely stalling, Ronnie knew. Before she could respond, Jane said, "The only conclusion we could think of was that you didn't trust them."

Ronnie shrugged and stared at the waves in the distance.

"When you locked yourself in the conference room at Lick, you wore the Halo, didn't you?" Jane asked.

Ronnie smiled, not sure if Jane could see her through the darkness. "If you were in my shoes, wouldn't you have done the same?"

Jane let out a puff of air. "Of course."

"So, what do you think of Mr. Gordon's proposal?"

"I wouldn't call it a proposal as much as an ultimatum."

"The Bilderberg Group is a powerful organization, if you can call it an organization at all, more like a secret society."

"I know a little about them. I know they have a yearly meeting that is ultra-secret. I remember reading somewhere that Presidents Clinton, Bush, and Obama attended the annual Bilderberg meeting before they were elected. And I'm aware, as Stan pointed out, of the rumors about their supposed involvement with the Nazis during the war."

"Mr. Gordon wants me to believe that was all a part of their cover story. A way to discredit them and draw attention away from their main purpose."

"And do you believe him?" Jane asked.

"Even if I did, I'm not sure I agree with the Bilderberg philosophy."

"I understand the need to prepare society to receive this information. There would be some level of chaos, at the very least a general unease. And that unease would affect every aspect of daily life on Earth. My one problem with the Bilderberg Group is the amount of power they appear to have, there's always the danger of abuse. Even if they claim their association with the Nazis is a cover, there's danger they could produce a Hitler-like tyrant in their ranks."

Ronnie wondered if Jane had seen the evidence relating to the missing link in man's evolution, but she wasn't prepared to discuss every nuance of what she'd witnessed while wearing the Halo. They both had seen enough of what was on it to know their decision was a weighty one. Right now, they had to determine, as a group, how they were going to react to Alec Gordon's proposal.

"This is what I like to call a conundrum. We both agree with their basic goal but, perhaps, are not as comfortable with the methods they use to implement their plan."

"Yes, it does present a problem," Jane said.

"It's hard to argue with such a powerful group."

"Are you trying to tell me that we don't have any choice but to do what Mr. Gordon tells us? What about your superiors within the NSA?"

"Mr. Gordon was my superior."

"I can't believe there is no one else you could report this to."

"I could. And then we might be right back where we started." Ronnie adjusted her hands underneath the blanket. The damp air was starting to seep into her bones.

"Meaning?"

"Meaning leaders, or at least one very important leader, within the NSA had to know who was running my clandestine group. I have a feeling the Bilderbergs' reach is very high indeed. And, something you didn't know. The men who killed Matthew and shot me? They flashed NSA ID cards at us right before they forced us to the side of the road."

"So what are you suggesting?"

"I'm not really sure myself. I have no way of knowing if they were really NSA or just some thugs out to steal the Halo. Perhaps there is another group within the NSA that doesn't agree with the Bilderberg approach. When Mr. Gordon decides to let us go—if he decides to let us go—I wouldn't know who I could trust. I do know the Bilderbergs aren't going to stop until they find it."

They both fell silent for a moment; each deep in their own troubled thoughts.

Ronnie said, "Something did occur to me. Even though our friend and his colleagues are anxious to get their hands on this artifact, they really have no idea what it holds. They're just speculating."

"Making assumptions after watching Farraday's video?"

"Yes. Even though they have accumulated a lot of knowledge about the alien visitation over the years, there are still holes in what they know. Otherwise, they wouldn't be so anxious to get their hands on this artifact. "

"Those of us who've worn it are the only ones who truly know," Jane said.

"You, Stan, Nick, and me."

They were quiet for a moment, all other sounds drowned out by the steady crashing of the surf as it echoed off the hard surface of the cliff.

"You never answered my question. Were you able to retrieve it?" Ronnie asked.

"And if I said I did?"

"They'll find it eventually, with or without your help. And, as I said, I'm not sure there is anyone out there who can protect us. As long as they think one of us has it, we're all a threat to them."

"And we're worth nothing to them at all without it."

* * *

"This is a fine kettle of fish we're in."

"I don't like that fellow," Henry said. He took a sip of wine. If nothing else, the food and drink had been superb. He hadn't experienced such a great meal in a long time. He was finding that he was enjoying himself, despite his agoraphobia. Every day, every hour, his anxiety appeared to be diminishing. And the medication certainly helped.

Liz turned her back to Henry to address Stan. "If Nick doesn't have the crown, then either you and your wife, or Agent Vagnetti has it."

"You don't know that for sure."

"I can make an educated guess."

"We're all in this together. Let's wait and see what Ronnie and Jane come up with."

Nick and Emily had gone to warm themselves by the fire pit outside their cottage.

"What he says isn't wrong." Stan leaned back in his chair. "The release of this information would change the world forever."

Henry asked, "Did the world fall apart when we discovered Earth wasn't flat? How about when we found the universe didn't revolve around us? That we were just one small planet in one unremarkable solar system in one galaxy of billions?"

"This is a bit different, I think."

"I'm not so sure," Henry countered. "I have more faith in Humanity."

"It really doesn't matter what any of us think," Liz said. "What matters is our future. My children's future. I didn't ask to be part of this and neither did they. Now there doesn't seem to be a way out. All I want to do is go home and forget that crown exists. If that's even possible."

"It might not be. Don't be so sure that once they have it they'll leave us alone," Stan said.

"I think they're more interested in the crown, not us," Liz said. "I'm more worried about all the loons out there who might know about it. Am I just supposed to sit around and wait until one of my children gets kidnapped again? At least Mr. Gordon promised some measure of protection. He said he could make this all go away for us. A group as powerful as the Bilderbergs could pull it off."

They all turned as Jane walked into the tent with Ronnie leaning on her arm.

Jane stopped and glanced around the interior. "Where are the kids?"

"They've gone to sit by the fire," Liz answered.

"I'll go gather them up. We need to have a talk."

* * *

Ronnie shifted in her seat to get more comfortable. Nurse Ratched had come outside to administer her nightly dose of pain meds and then went back inside to read her book by the lamp. Even though the guards were too far away to hear their conversation, they talked in hushed tones. Ronnie warned them there might be listening devices planted nearby.

"One thing we have in our favor is that no one, except a few within this group, really knows what the Halo does, or what it reveals," she said.

"Until Alec and company get their hands on it, they're just speculating," Jane reiterated for the entire group.

Liz said, "Why not just give them the darned thing if you know where it is?" She waved her arm in the air. "Do we look like we're any match for this Bilderberg Group? Is it really important if the peoples of the world know that aliens once roamed Earth?"

"The real question here isn't whether we are in agreement with the basic principle that the world isn't ready for this knowledge. That it would destroy organized religions —"

"It wouldn't necessarily," Henry interrupted Ronnie. "One can still believe in a Supreme Being even if there is intelligent life found someplace else in the universe."

"That's sounds good in theory," she continued, "but it would completely destroy many of the basic tenets of organized religion. It would show that our religions were based on encounters with extraterrestrial beings. Should this information destroy man's faith in God? Intellectually, the answer should be no. But will it? I agree that revealing our true history would be a shock and that it needs to be done delicately. The world needs time to adjust.

"But we're getting off track here. As I said, that's not the real question. The question is: Should we trust one organization, one group, to make all the decisions about this?" Ronnie said.

"Don't you work for this guy?" Liz said. "Why did he lump you in with our little group? For all we know, you could be a mole."

Ronnie smiled. "You're right. I very well could be. But I'm not. And I've been wondering the same thing about our friend's motivations, and I've come up with one conclusion. Mr. Gordon thinks anyone who has worn the Halo poses a threat to his operation. So, until he's sure what my intentions are, I'm the enemy just like the rest of you."

CHAPTER 32

The tent was still up from the night before, the portable heaters turned on. Buffet tables were set up at one end, ladened with a Thanksgiving feast being catered in by an assembly of wait staff.

Since Mr. Gordon was, unfathomably as it seemed, Ronnie's boss, they had decided to let her be the spokesperson. They could see no way out of their current situation. Their only option was to cooperate. The Bilderberg Group's reach extended too far. There was no hiding from them.

Alec dismissed the staff and watched as they climbed in the modified golf carts to head back to the main building of the resort.

"The food smells wonderful. Shall we give thanks?" he said.

No one spoke.

"None of you have anything to be thankful for?" He waited. "No matter. I'd like to say something."

He lowered his head in thought, then raised it and his glass of wine and said, "To the peoples of Earth: Long may they prosper. Today and in the future."

Nick was the first to hear it, that all too familiar sound of helicopter blades whipping through the air. He ran to the edge of the tent and searched the sky. Two Chinook helicopters looked like dragonflies in the distance.

One of the paramilitary guards came rushing up to the tent.

"Are those helicopters here on your order?" he asked Alec, who was now standing alongside Nick.

"No," Alec said, without taking his eyes off the choppers.

The uniformed man turned and said something into his mouthpiece. His team came running from all directions to meet the helicopters head on.

The small group gathered outside the tent, watching as the aircraft lowered onto the ground. The blades slowed but didn't stop. A man in full-dress military uniform stepped out of the lead chopper. Even from a distance, Nick could tell he was someone important. Probably a general, he thought. Dozens of armed military personnel spilled out behind him and then two men in suits jumped down. Nick recognized them immediately. Agents Conner and Nelson.

The black-clad paramilitary stood in front of the general, but no one could hear what was being said over the whirring of the helicopter blades. The general didn't look too happy. The soldiers behind him shouldered their weapons. After a few tense moments, the lead guard fell back and let the general and his team pass.

"Alec Gordon?" the general boomed.

"That's me." Alec stepped forward. "What's the meaning of this? Why are you here?"

"I could ask you the same question."

"You're making a very big mistake. I need to speak with your superior."

"The Commander-in-Chief? I think he's busy at the moment."

"You're interfering with a very important operation." Alec motioned to his guards.

"I know exactly what I'm interfering with, and I'd advise you to stand down. Do you really want your little guard unit to take on the US military?"

Alec waved them off. "Your job is on the line here."

"I'm not worried about it. You and your associates might have power in high places all over the world but right now you're standing on American soil."

Nick caught the eye of the two agents standing in back of the soldiers. Agent Nelson gave him the thumbs-up sign.

* * *

Two men in black suits and crisp white shirts walked up to the counter of the Cortez Vault & Safety Deposit Box Company. Another stood by the front door and turned one of the deadbolts with a sharp click.

Bruce Belford lifted his head from the paperwork on the counter. "Hey, what are you doing?"

The taller of the two men flipped open a bi-fold wallet. Bruce leaned in for a closer look. "Central Security Service? Never heard of them."

"You should keep up with current events, Mr. Belford. We're part of the NSA."

Bruce's hand went to the ID badge pinned to his shirt. It only had his first name on it. How'd they know his last name?

"What's this about? Tiny beads of sweat formed on his temple. Bruce had been involved in some shady stuff in his life, but nothing that would get him into this kind of trouble.

The shorter agent pulled something out of the inner pocket of his suit coat. He held up a key between his thumb and forefinger. "We need to get into the safety deposit box that belongs to this key."

Bruce was starting to think maybe this was a dream. Stuff like this didn't happen in the little town of Cortez.

"I need a valid signature." His voice was shaky.

The taller agent waved a warrant in the air. "Not with this you don't. And, actually, Mr. Belford, we could have come here without one, national security and all, but we thought we'd be nice."

"My business is based on discretion. I can't just—"

The agent holding the key pushed aside the front of his jacket with his free hand, revealing a shoulder holster. He was definitely packing heat.

Bruce swallowed hard.

"You're just going to have to take our word for it. You'll find the warrant is legitimate, but we don't have time for you to verify it."

Bruce stared at them for a few minutes. The agent with the still-visible holster lifted one eyebrow. Bruce lowered his gaze and fumbled behind the counter until he came out with the master key in hand.

It was several minutes before Bruce and the man with the client key emerged from the back of the building. The agent held a slightly battered silver aluminum case in his hand. Bruce noticed the goon at the front door hadn't moved, but the other agent was sitting in front of the company computer behind the counter.

"Hey, what are you doing?"

"Cleaning up your records." The agent smiled. "Bruce, my man, for your own good, none of this ever happened. *Capisce?*"

Bruce bobbed his head. "Understand."

The word came out in a squeak.

* * *

They sat around a wide rectangular conference table in an underground bunker at Beale Air Force Base, just north of San Francisco. Stan, Jane, and Henry sat on one side. Liz, Emily, and Nick sat on the other. General Jasper T. Eastman stood in front of a huge flickering screen filled with a map of the world that was positioned on the far wall. The three agents: Vagnetti, Nelson, and Conner sat at the opposite end, with Ronnie at the head and the agents flanking her on either side.

"We were hoping you would cooperate freely."

General Eastman pointed to Nick. "Could you come with me, please?"

Liz put her hand on Nick's arm as he rose from his chair. "Where are you taking my son?" Liz asked.

"Come along, if you'd like. We're going to administer a lie-detector test."

"Can you do that without a warrant or something?"

"This is a matter of national security; we don't need a warrant."

"I thought you came to save us! You're no better than Alec Gordon and those damned Bilderbergs!"

"We need to find the Halo, as you call it. You'd save us from wasting valuable resources looking for it, but none of you seem willing to cooperate."

Jane said, "We told you about what we experienced when we wore it. We told you about finding the signals on the mesa. And we also told you that we asked a colleague of ours in England to set up a test at Stonehenge to search for a signal there. This was perfectly within our rights according to international protocols. We are required by those same protocols to verify the authenticity of the signal beyond any doubt before we make an announcement. To our government, or to the public."

"We're not here to ask you to keep quiet about the signals or to stop your search. This is more than the discovery of a possible signal from extraterrestrial beings. This is about the Halo. According to what you've told us, it contains information that could be extremely controversial—human cloning and the like. The implications are staggering." The general shook his head. "This is much more than possible communication from some distant civilization, light-years away. This puts into question the entire history and development of mankind. On this count, our concerns are not dissimilar from what the Bilderberg Group claims theirs to be, but our motivations are clearly not the same."

"And how are they different exactly?" Stan said.

The general clasped his hands behind his back and stared at the floor.

"The Bilderberg Group's main motivation, underneath their façade of humanitarianism, is control."

"And you're trying to convince us that the US Government isn't interested in the increased power this knowledge might afford them?"

"I didn't say power. I said control. There is a difference, even if a subtle one. With control of certain knowledge, they could manipulate markets, among other things, and accumulate great wealth. The US Government, on the other hand, is interested in the promotion and protection of democracy throughout the world. Some might find that sinister in and of itself—and you might be one of those folks—but, I can tell you, I think it is far better than the alternative. The Bilderbergs' motivations are no more humanitarian than you consider ours to be. I am telling you that letting such powerful information get into the wrong hands could be devastating to our freedom and the freedom of democracies all over the globe. We'd like to protect the Halo from getting into the wrong hands."

"I keep hearing that. But just whose hands are the wrong ones?" Stan said.

"Use your head, Dr. Carter. Do you really think letting a madman like, for instance, Iran's Ahmadinejad, or others like him, obtain the information contained within this artifact would be in the best interest of the world?"

From across the table Emily said, "Mr. Gordon said they were trying to inoculate the world against possible alien viruses. What's wrong with that? It seems like a good idea."

"If that is even true. Mr. Gordon might have been using an already widespread conspiracy theory in attempt to sway you over to his side. The rumor is already out there, so why not use it to his advantage? And, even if it were true, throughout history evil organizations have often hidden behind seemingly humanitarian causes. Yes, on the surface this sounds very noble. But their motivations aren't for the betterment of mankind but for putting themselves in the best position when and if aliens return to Earth."

"The United States Government isn't trying to do the same thing? Why should we trust them any more than we do the Bilderbergs?" Liz asked.

"I can't answer that for you. Let's just say there are some of us within the government who still think we're working for the people. The influence of the Bilderberg Group spreads wide and far." General Eastman pointed to the end of the table where the agents sat. "They have even successfully infiltrated our own security organizations. But our government is still of and by the people. And is based on checks and balances. Let me just say we're here to make sure one group doesn't get too much control."

"And who makes sure you don't have too much control?"

He gave Stan a piercing stare. "You will."

The room went silent for a moment, the only noise the shuffling of chairs.

"Let's say, for the moment, that in addition to knowing where to find signals, that we also know where the Halo is," Jane said. "What would you do with it?"

"A good question." The general took a deep breath and let it out slowly. "In the past SETI, and other similar institutes around the world, have only been interested in one thing: a signal from ET. All their protocols and rules have been geared toward that one aspect. But now we have hard evidence that other intelligent beings already visited Earth. Not only visited but helped shape every aspect of our development. This puts an entirely different spin on things.

All the rules and regulations that have been put in place concerning the discovery of a signal are moot. Even without the laser signals, the Halo is proof that other intelligent beings exists—"

"Nothing has been proven beyond a doubt yet," Stan interjected.

"Both you and your wife said you were convinced beyond a reasonable doubt of the authenticity of the artifact after wearing it and running a few preliminary tests, and that's good enough for us at the moment. We are going under the assumption that it's authentic. It's all we can do for now."

General Eastman leaned forward, his fists resting on the table.

"What we propose is the International Academy of Astronautics headed by the SETI Post-Detection Committee not only continues to study the laser signals but also takes full control of the investigation into the authenticity and data collection from the Halo."

Jane puffed up her cheeks and blew out something between a snort and a laugh. "This is what we would have done in any case, so what's the catch?"

"The catch? We would like you to set up the committees so that no one person has all the data from the Halo except for the oversight committee, which will be made up of select members of the group."

"Your goons?"

"If that's what you'd like to call them, I can't stop you. But, no, not our goons, but members made up of our allies who we can trust to not misuse the information. If the Halo contains knowledge on how to produce dangerous weapons of mass destruction, we don't want it to get into the hands of the enemies of freedom, or of the United States."

The room fell silent again. An atmosphere of resignation permeated the air.

The general turned away from the table and paced the front of the room. "There is one more thing. We would like to study the Halo prior to turning it over to the academy. Then we'll return it and—"

"Ah, so that's it." Stan said, "And how can we trust you to keep your word?"

"You just have to take that leap of faith."

"What if you find something on it you didn't expect? Something even more horrific than WMDs? Something we humans might never expect? Would you give it back then?"

"We'll have to cross that bridge when we come to it, Dr. Carter."

"So you are not giving us your word it will be returned?"

"As I said, there are no guarantees in life. But I'm giving you my word that our intentions are to turn it over to the international academy. In a sense, we're asking for first rights for a cursory review of the object. It will take years of study by the private scientific community to understand everything it contains, I'm sure. We're just asking for a quick look."

The room was quiet until the general spoke again. "I didn't have to reveal any of this. We could have just returned it when we were good and ready, or not return it at all, and you'd have no say in it. But I chose to be open and honest as a token of our cooperation and, hopefully, as a means to gain your trust. So, are you all in agreement?"

"Again, it sounds as if we don't have much of a choice."

"You're all talking as if Henry isn't even in the room!" Nick said.

"Excuse me?" the general said.

"If it wasn't for Henry, the Halo would never have been found. If laws don't require him to return it to China, then isn't it Henry's? Doesn't he get some say in what happens to it?"

"We don't consider this an archaeological artifact, it was left by aliens, for god-sake!"

A puzzled look spread over Henry's face, as if he'd just realized the truth in what Nick said, and he then leaned forward, "If this doesn't fall under the laws governing the discovery of artifacts, then the Halo does belong to me."

"You could lay claim to it, Mr. Applegate, but do you have the means to study it properly? What good would it be to you, in that case?"

"I could attract investors, people looking to make an investment on any future technologies that might be discovered. Isn't that the American way?"

"Using the Halo for your own personal gain might prove difficult, Mr. Applegate. Wouldn't that be a little like Newton claiming intellectual and commercial rights for the discovery of gravity? Once this cat's out of the bag, there's no putting it back in. And, if that's what you wanted, then you could have made a deal with the Bilderberg Group."

"I didn't have time to make any decision." Henry let out a sigh and sat back in his chair. "But how can we trust you to not mismanage the information it contains?"

"How can you trust anyone not to mismanage it, Mr. Applegate? Would you rather trust the secretive Bilderberg

Group? I think an international committee of scientists from all areas of study is the most agreeable and fair arrangement, don't you? But, in any case, it would be perfectly legal for us to confiscate it under current national security laws."

* * *

"What do you think, Stan?" Jane asked.

He was standing with Nick, looking out the front window of the bungalow. They were still on the base. Their new residence wasn't anything like the cottages at the Half-Moon Bay, but at least it was clean.

"About what?"

"Did we do the right thing by telling the general where to find the Halo?" Jane said. "Can we trust them?"

"Like you said, we didn't have much choice."

"Be careful what you say, this place could be bugged." Henry was sitting on the couch with Liz. They had been separated from the NSA agents, who had either been sent home or were staying at a different location on the base.

"I think the general was sincere when he said they would turn it over to the academy but," Stan turned to look at Jane, "he didn't say when."

"He said they wanted a 'cursory' look. That sounds like they would return it in a reasonable amount of time."

"Yes, but he didn't really say how long they'd keep it before turning it over. How long will they let their own experts study it? It could be a very long time."

"We'll just have to hope they keep their word and return it at some point."

"Of course they'll want some of their own top brass to experience it for themselves. And, of course, they'll have their own team of scientists give it a whirl before they turn it back over to the astronomical community. That will all take time."

"Right." Jane nodded her head.

The refrigerator had been fully stocked. They found all the ingredients for a nice breakfast and Stan had offered to cook.

"That was wonderful, Stan," Henry said, just as they heard someone knocking loudly on the door.

"May I come in?" General Eastman bellowed, as he shoved the door open.

"Sounds like you already are," Nick said under his breath.

"What's going on?" Jane asked.

"Someone posing as CSS agents removed the artifact from the vault yesterday afternoon," the general repeated.

"Posing?" Stan asked.

"No one at the CSS or NSA seems to know anything about it."

"One hand not knowing what the other is doing again?" Liz murmured.

He didn't respond.

"Did you contact Agent Vagnetti?" Jane asked.

"Of course! And she claims that she is not aware of, nor has she been informed of, any operation organized by the agency. The artifact has disappeared."

CHAPTER 33

Ronnie Vagnetti sat under a bright blue umbrella in the Emperor Terrace Restaurant on the sixth floor of the InterContinental De La Ville Roma. The sky above was porcelain blue, the kind that can only be found in Rome. The outer low walls of the terrace were dripping in fuchsia bougainvillea. Ronnie inhaled the scent of the flowers mingled with the aroma of rich coffee and the assortment of fruits and sharp cheeses displayed on the table in front of her.

She closed her eyes and took another sip of coffee, savoring the moment. This was the last leg of her journey through Italy. She had spent the month she promised herself in rural Tuscany, learning the secrets of authentic Italian cooking. From there, she visited the city of Florence, where she stayed a week at the luxurious Lungarno Hotel that overlooked the muddy Arno River. After spending hours in the famous Uffizi Palace, a museum that holds some of the most famous art in the world; and visiting the Florence Academy of Arts, where she saw Michelangelo's David—the real one, not one of the fakes scattered throughout the city—Ronnie was beginning to understand the puzzling condition called "Stendhal Syndrome" that she had read about in a travel brochure. The term was used to describe a physiological phenomenon where the victim becomes emotionally and physically overwhelmed after spending too many hours viewing beautiful art.

Ronnie was thinking about this when she opened her eyes. She almost dropped her coffee cup. Sitting across the table from her was a priest, as evidenced by his clerical collar.

"I didn't mean to frighten you," he said.

"Yet you managed nonetheless."

"I'm sorry. I thought you heard me approach, but you were so deep in thought..." He shrugged and smiled. It irritated her.

She placed her cup in its saucer and looked out at the perfect Roman sky. "Can I help you with something?"

His smiled broadened. "I am your driver."

She had asked the hotel concierge to arrange a private day trip to Castel Gandolfo, the summer residence of the Pope and the home of the *Specola Vaticana*—the Vatican Observatory. Most people didn't realize that the Pontifical Palace, which was located within the city, and the adjoining gardens, enjoyed the same privileges as The Vatican.

Even though she was retired, it was hard for Ronnie to stop working. She was no longer privy to the kind of data available to her as an NSA agent, but she rarely went without her iPad, flipping through magazine, newspaper, and blog articles. She surfed and dove deep into the Net, searching for everything she could possibly connect with the lost Halo.

There was a lot of chatter on the Web about a new group called the IGIS—International Group of Independent Scientists. This newly formed group had made remarkable breakthroughs in the science of interstellar travel.

Maybe the Church was on her mind because she was in Italy, but, whatever the reason, a connection between the Church, the Halo, and the IGIS was starting to coalesce in the back corridors of her brain. During her research, Ronnie discovered a heavily veiled link between the Vatican and the newly formed group of scientists.

She couldn't help but believe the new scientific breakthroughs were somehow connected to the Halo. If it were true, the irony that the church could be instrumental in utilizing some of the most advanced science known, when, just a few centuries before, they had imprisoned Galileo as a heretic for his remarkable findings in the field of astronomy, wasn't lost on her.

One of the other recent and intriguing activities of the Church was the well-publicized announcement that a priest was hitching a ride to the Russian Space Station. The Vatican was not trying to hide its interest in space travel. In fact, the Church made sure the event received full coverage in the news. Ronnie recognized this tactic—publicize related endeavors as a way to conceal the real mission.

She stared at the priest sitting across from her and thought of all these things.

Then she said, "Is chauffeuring tourists part of your priestly duties?"

"When the occasion calls for it," he answered.

Umberto Fusco was a Jesuit priest. His beard was neatly trimmed close to his round face, but his hair was unkempt, like he'd just gotten up from a long nap. His beard was generously sprinkled with gray, but the hair on his head was a uniform dark brown. The priest drove Ronnie to the small village thirty minutes outside of Rome. Castel Gandolfo overlooked the beautiful Lake Albano.

One of the two existing Vatican astronomic observatories sat atop the hills above the lake.

"The observatory was once housed in Vatican City," Fr. Fusco said as they drove. "But urban sprawl happened and there was too much light for good observations."

Ronnie didn't turn from watching the landscape slip by the passenger-side window of the black Mercedes.

"And then it was moved to Tucson, Arizona at the University there." The priest laughed. "Why do I think I can teach you anything? Of course you already know all of this."

One corner of her mouth lifted but she didn't turn away from the view.

"How did you know I was planning a visit today?" she asked, still staring out of the window.

"Just like you, we have our ways."

It wasn't a very long drive and they spent much of it with the priest pointing out places of interest, or in comfortable silence. Once they entered the village, the priest weaved through the familiar streets and finally parked the Mercedes next to a stucco building colored in the ubiquitous light sienna so popular in Italy. Fr. Fusco walked around the car to open the door for Ronnie just as a younger priest came rushing out of the building to hand him two bottles of water that were already beading with sweat.

"If you don't mind, I thought we would go for a short walk. The grounds are beautiful here and, after being in the car, it will be nice to stretch our legs. No?" He offered Ronnie one of the cool bottles of water.

It took a special audience to tour the Pope's residence and the *Specola Vaticana*. When Ronnie first made her plans with the hotel concierge, she realized she wouldn't be allowed to enter either place. But, for whatever reason, she had felt compelled to come to Castel Gandolfo anyway, and she rarely questioned her instincts. She knew she had to visit the village before she left Italy. To get a feel for the place. To intuit anything she could from it. Because, no matter how hard she tried, she couldn't shrug off her interest in the Halo.

When the priest showed up and announced he was driving her to the village, Ronnie quietly anticipated seeing the inside of the Pope's residence and, possibly, the observatory as well. But now she nodded in agreement. Perhaps after the walk Fr. Fusco would give her a tour.

It was cool under the tree-lined promenade. The Jesuit was right. The grounds were magnificent. Not a weed in sight. All the hedges pruned to perfection.

"You are probably wondering why I brought you here," Fr. Fusco said.

"There could only be one reason."

The priest nodded. "You see, we were right in our assumptions of you."

Fr. Fusco took a sip of his water and screwed the cap back on.

"There is a small pond just ahead." He gestured with his left hand. "It is His Holiness's favorite place. Perhaps we can rest there for a while. There is a comfortable bench."

In back of the goldfish pond was a statue of the Virgin Mary. The priest walked over to it, bowed his head in prayer for a moment, and then turned back to Ronnie.

"Please, let us have a seat."

He led her to the bench where he picked up a straw basket full of small chunks of bread. He held it up for Ronnie to see.

"His Holiness loves to feed the fish."

He took a few pieces of bread and then handed the basket to Ronnie.

"We have been following your activities for some time."

Fr. Fusco broke one of the pieces of the bread in two and tossed the pieces into the pond. A flurry of orange-backed Koi formed a writhing circle around the treat.

Ronnie was rarely surprised by anything, but the fact that the Vatican had her under surveillance was intriguing.

"I know you brought me here because of the Halo." She flung a piece of small bread into the water and watched the fish compete for it. "But you're wasting your time if you think I have it."

The priest gave a short laugh. "No, we don't think you have it."

"Then why did you bring me here?"

"We would like your help."

The priest threw in more bread, this time in a different spot. The tight undulating circle of goldfish turned as one and darted toward the fresh bread. Ronnie thought of the Pope sitting there, watching the mindless, hungry fish scurrying and fighting for scraps of food.

"How could I be of any help to the Church?"

"We have known about the Halo, and others like it, for some time. Before the NSA, and other such groups, even existed."

She wasn't surprised. "So there are others?"

"Yes. But none that are as well preserved and fully operational as the Kunlun-Kette device."

How does he know about the functionality of this *Halo?* Ronnie put the basket of bread aside. Watching the fish fighting for their food was making her tired.

"Why, exactly, do you think you need my help?"

"God gives us talents, and we must use them."

"Meaning?"

"We need your investigative talents."

"My investigative talents tell me you already have the Halo."

"Very good, Ms. Vagnetti. Yes, we do have it."

"You took it from the vault in Cortez?"

"I explained to you that we have a facility in Tucson, Arizona?" He said it like a question and waited for Ronnie to nod her head. "We were very near. It wasn't difficult."

He tossed more bread into the pond and turned to Ronnie. "I am telling you this because there is no way for you to betray us. You realize this. I don't have to spell it out for you, as you Americans say."

"You have the Halo secured within Vatican City, a sovereign state."

"Precisely."

"It belongs to the entire world, not just the Vatican."

"I understand your position. *We* understand." He shook his head. "Let me explain something to you. Although you are a very intelligent and well-informed woman." He smiled broadly. Although Fr. Fusco was an otherwise agreeable man, his smile still irritated Ronnie.

"As secretive as the Holy Church is, there will always be those willing to betray. For money. For power." The priest shrugged, as if he couldn't comprehend these motives.

"There are groups who believe they know as much as the Holy Church about the extraterrestrials, but they are mistaken. Your friend from the Bilderberg Group, for example."

Fr. Fusco turned his body to face Ronnie. "But let me get to the point. I see you are getting impatient. I don't have to spell out these things to you.

"I am a Jesuit. Our mission is to explore new territories and to educate. Our mission does not stop at Earth's boundaries. You've had a chance to experience the Halo. Yes?"

Ronnie nodded.

"How much did you see?"

"Enough." Ronnie unscrewed her bottle of water and took a long drink.

"Then perhaps what I am about to tell you will not shock you as much as it once might have. You now understand that it can be said the human race both evolved and was created. No?"

He didn't wait for Ronnie to answer this time.

"What perhaps you don't realize, is that there are those among us who carry the artificially engineered genes the aliens inserted into our DNA, to help speed up our evolution, but there are also those among us who are 'natural' descendants of the aliens. Most of us are a mixture. It seems 'human' nature is the same no matter what far corner of the universe it comes from. Once they created us in their image and likeness, they proceeded to procreate with us. Yes, yes," he nodded his head, seeming to forget Ronnie for a moment. "Original Sin."

Ronnie thought about the implication. Would the direct descendants of the aliens consider themselves superior to the genetically altered humans? Would this cause yet another form of discrimination? Speciesism—where one group discriminated against the other based on their origins?

Fr. Fusco came out of his deep thoughts concerning Original Sin and said, "The Church has known this from the beginning, you understand. Only a select few have been privy to the information, sometimes not even the sitting Pope was fully informed. From the beginning of history, this sacred knowledge has been passed down by shamans, priests, and secret societies. As I said, much of it was not fully understood. Even today, we do not understand everything. But the knowledge was kept intact as much as possible, through oral history—songs and stories—or, later, recorded by scribes. To our ancestors, these extraterrestrial beings were gods. Truth became legend. Legend became myth. Things got muddled."

The priest grew silent. Ronnie had understood this, intuitively, even before she'd worn the Halo. But to hear it from the mouth of the Jesuit was still startling.

"Only recently have we been able to more fully understand the information that had been *qui tutti il tempo.*" The priest had lapsed into his native language. "Sorry. What is the saying in English? Right under our noses the whole time? Yes?

"Though we had this knowledge for thousands of years, we didn't know how to interpret it. Not until the most modern scientific breakthroughs. This is why the Church was so frightened of people like Galileo, who might discover facts that, until that time, only the Church knew.

The Church was not against science, but against the masses learning the truth about potentially dangerous secrets or, perhaps, discovering the key to them before the Church.

"You must understand; this was not done for selfish purposes. The Church was considering the protection and ultimate survival of all mankind. We were not amassing riches and power to control Earth's population, but as a hedge against the return of the aliens."

It seemed the Bilderbergs and the Church weren't that disparate in their motives. Ronnie wasn't sure she believed this. But the papacy was not passed down from father to son, like royalty. It was similar to the American presidency, where an individual was voted into office. The only difference was the President of the United States had a limit of two four-year terms. The Pope held office until his death. Granted, a Cardinal was usually in advanced age when taking the office of Pope. The power of the Church didn't lie solely in the hands of one person but, rather, the entire organization. Even though the priest sitting next to her was sure the Church's motives were altruistic, she was skeptical. All her life, the Church had been a double-edged sword to her.

"We could not have the public becoming too suspicious, too curious, about how this all began." Fr. Fusco looked up at the afternoon sky. "Not before we understood it fully ourselves. We were continually fighting to give meaning to the old myths, the old superstitions, to keep pace with the general public's continual enlightenment.

"The most recent major discovery of DNA has helped us realize many things, Ms. Vagnetti. It contains clues to— and evidence of—our creation. But the Church no longer has to suppress knowledge. The scientific community does it for us. They are not quick to claim evidence of intelligent interference in the development of mankind. It would go against Darwin's theories. No? It would go against the notion of natural selection."

The priest paused for a moment. If he expected some reaction from Ronnie, she didn't offer him one.

"Not all the aliens were benevolent. We knew this. The idea of fallen angels is nothing more than aliens who went against those in authority."

He turned and leaned back in his seat.

"It would take hours, days, to tell you everything. I promised I would..." He paused, trying to think of the American phrase. "Cut to the chase? Yes?"

"We know they visited Earth as recently as the time of Jesus. In fact, this is the last time we were certain of it. To our knowledge, Jesus was the last earthling to interact with them. Why they left and why they haven't returned yet remains a mystery. Perhaps we have evolved beyond their expectations and, therefore, out of their control like in ancient times when they could just send a flood to rid themselves of their mistakes.

"Of course, the return of the aliens is what the 'Second Coming' is all about, you realize? The time is near. If the aliens are coming back, our knowledge indicates they will do so soon. All those people with signs on street corners aren't crazy after all." His smile moved his beard until Ronnie could see his straight, slightly yellowing teeth. He tossed more bread into the water before he continued.

"We need to know when they return, or if they are already among us. Or perhaps they never really left."

He shook his head. "This, Ms. Vagnetti, is where you can help us."

Ronnie said, "You know so much already, and you don't know this?"

"We have never been sure. It is more important than ever for us to know everything we can about possible alien activity here on Earth."

"Why should I help the Church over some other group? Over my own government, or even the Bilderbergs?"

"I cannot help you answer that question, Ms. Vagnetti. But I can tell you the Church holds more information than any of these other entities. And the Church—faith—will be what holds this world together when the aliens return."

"Why do you think the world's populace will trust the Church after it has lied to them for so many years?"

"I knew convincing you would not be easy." He shook his head. "Even if our dogma was flawed, our basic message about fealty to one God has not changed. For we still believe this to be so—that there is one true God, one Divine Creator. The Church does not consider the aliens to be our creators, but merely other sentient beings who interfered with what God intended for our natural progression. As I said, the Church would like to maintain a position of power when the aliens return. Not for the sake of the power itself, but as a protection for our congregation. They—the aliens—betrayed one of us before. Do you not remember what Jesus said on the cross? *My God. My God. Why hast thou forsaken me?* The Church will not stand for it again."

Ronnie had picked up a small piece of bread and, as she listened to the priest, it disintegrated into fine crumbs that fell across her lap. She brushed them away as Fr. Fusco continued.

"Jesus was an advocate for all of humanity. He was betrayed by those he trusted."

Ronnie was stunned by the implication, and even more stunned that she was hearing it from a priest. If he was trying to shock her, he was doing a good job.

"If the world gets news of this—"

"It will destroy the Church? We do not think this will happen. The Church believes Jesus is our Savior. He gave his life so we would understand the power of love. So the peoples of Earth might unite in love. That it was the only way for humanity to survive. Before him, no one spoke of it. Certainly not the beings who came here and interfered with what the True Creator intended for us."

Before Ronnie could fully comprehend what he was saying, Fr. Fusco turned the conversation back to the return of the aliens.

"Perhaps they miscalculated the time of their return. Or perhaps they have become extinct? Who knows? Look how close we have come to mass destruction, and we are not nearly as advanced. Perhaps they did return; but, as I said, they realized we couldn't be so easily controlled this time around. And perhaps it wasn't worth it to even try.

"If they are already here, or if they return in the near future, the masses will not only need military assistance to fight against possible alien tyranny, they will need spiritual guidance as well. What better organization to facilitate worldwide unity than the Church, with its presence, even if sometimes secretly, on every continent on Earth?"

Ronnie stared at the fish, then up at the statue of the Virgin Mary. What had this woman known? Had she cohabitated with the extraterrestrials? Or had they used her body to continue the propagation of a new species without her full understanding? Or something entirely different?

"What would my duties be, exactly?"

"To deliver information to us about possible alien activity anywhere on Earth. To tell us about anything you find suspicious, and to help us locate other Halo-like devices—other devices that might help us understand the aliens so we can better protect ourselves when, or if, they return. And, of course, you will have full access to all the information the Vatican has at its disposal."

Ronnie felt her heart skip a beat. What more could the Church reveal to her? What the priest had already divulged was staggering.

She stared into the shallow depths of the pond. The fish had scattered. Some hid under shadowy rocks and in deep crevices, others swam languidly through the clear, still water.

The Jesuit sat beside her, waiting patiently for the answer she already knew she would give.

CHAPTER 34

"The United States Science & Technology Advisory Board conducted an investigation into the discovery ten years ago of an unusual artifact in a remote region of the Himalayan Mountains by the deceased American archaeologist, Douglas Farraday, who was an employee of the famous author and archaeologist, Henry Applegate.

"The first hurdle the experts had to clear was figuring out which government could lay claim to the artifact. It was found in rugged mountain terrain somewhere near the border between Tibet and China and, therefore, the exact location of the archaeological find proved difficult to determine. What makes this particularly sensitive is the long-standing and ongoing animosity between the Tibetan and Chinese governments.

"In an effort to verify the location, and to follow international terms and agreements involving significant archaeological finds, the board closely examined a sensational video that was posted on the internet last year, which seemed to show Mr. Farraday interacting with the object. The findings of the board verify the video—which had millions of hits, but has now been taken off the internet—was a hoax, and has subsequently been linked to a group whose mission is to debunk

popular UFO theories and were known adversaries of Henry Applegate ... "

Liz, her two children, and Henry, were sitting in the Carter's living room.

"Well, that might help to keep some of the kooks off our backs," she said.

"I hope so." Jane flicked the TV off.

General Eastman had released them shortly after he revealed the Halo had been stolen from The Cortez Vault & Safety Deposit Box Company. He also released the three NSA agents, who worked with Ronnie, back to their desk jobs, but not before Frank Nelson promised to keep in touch with Liz. It seemed the NSA had misplaced Liz's decorative plate that the agents took during their first visit to the Farraday's house. Liz doubted she would ever get it back, but she was okay with it. And Jane knew she had made a friend for life in Ronnie Vagnetti.

True to his word, General Eastman had not interfered with SETI's decision to alert members of the international astronomic community to the possibility of laser pulse signals coming from the Pleiades. SETI had initiated several signal detection studies to be conducted at famous, and not-so-famous, ancient archaeological sites all over the world. So far, they had achieved an astonishing success rate at detecting, what appeared to be, intelligently produced patterns. Of course, there was already speculation that data might be streaming on the beams of light but, for now, the main focus was verifying that the signals were of intelligent design. If data was being sent in the beams of light, it would take years, or even decades, to figure out what it meant. Much like the space race during the 60s, there would be a race by countries to be the first to figure out how to extrapolate and interpret the data.

Even though they had yet to make an official announcement, rumors about the signals had somehow percolated to the surface and out to the public. There was already a palpable undercurrent of speculation in the media. The possibility of signals coming from another planet and the ramifications of the discovery had been addressed by everyone from entrepreneurs, humanitarian organizations, and political and military leaders from every nation, and by religious leaders of every tenet.

The entire world, it seemed, was holding its collective breath waiting for an official announcement. According to protocol, the person or persons who discovered the original signal was given the honor of making the announcement.

"So, Nick, are you ready for the big day tomorrow?" Jane asked. It had been almost a year since she'd first worn the Halo, but it seemed like yesterday.

* * *

The morning sun glinted off the North Dome of Lick Observatory, but it was nothing compared to the flash of lights from the photojournalists. Along with the press, a crowd huddled in front of the observatory waiting for Jane Carter to make her scheduled announcement.

Inside, the crowd was almost as big. Along with astronomers from all over the world, dignitaries, scientists, and even a few celebrities milled around the foyer. Nick, Liz, Emily, Henry, and the Carters were sitting around the tables in the library where Jane and Stan had first worn the Halo so long ago. Jane had invited Ronnie to join them for the announcement, but the agent thought it best she didn't attend. Even Dr. Jerome Ellis, the Carter's longtime friend from Leeds, had made the trip to the United States for the big day.

"This is a great day for SETI," Dr. Ellis had said earlier.

"It's a great day for the world."

It was the last day of the year. Jane thought it an appropriate day for the announcement. Tomorrow would begin a new era, a new age of enlightenment.

The crowd in the foyer was slowly making its way outside. The public relations coordinator, a woman who looked to be in her late thirties, opened the library door and told them it was time. The woman's face reflected the feeling in the air — one of excitement and trepidation all rolled into one. The small group that remained inside the library solemnly made their way to the front steps, each person feeling the weight of what was about to be said.

"Thanks for being so patient and for coming out here on such a cold day," Jane began. The sky was clear blue, but a vapor formed in front of her mouth as she spoke into the microphone.

Nick, Henry, Liz, Emily, Henry, Stan, and Dr. Ellis were standing in a semi-circle behind her.

"Several months ago, we made a startling discovery. We, along with the astronomical community throughout the world, are here to make an official announcement to the public. Even though there has already been much speculation and controversy in the media, we are here to give you the accurate details of what has transpired over the past year."

A volley of flashes made Jane blink. She looked down at her notes to avoid the glare. When they died down, she looked up again.

"So not to keep you waiting any longer, I'll get to the point. As a representative of SETI, I am here to announce the discovery of intelligently designed laser pulses coming from the constellation Pleiades."

The crowd erupted. Flashlights popped in rapid succession. The police tightened their line in front of the steps where Jane stood at the podium.

"How were the pulses first detected?"

"Who was the first to discover the pulses?"

"What does this mean?"

"Is SETI certain the signal is extraterrestrial?"

Some of the foreign journalists were so excited they fell into speaking in their native tongue.

"Please! Let me finish my statement, and then I'll take your questions."

A female journalist near the front turned and shouted to her colleagues, "Please settle down. Be quiet! Let Dr. Carter speak."

Jane nodded her head at the woman, grateful for her effort to help restore control. Now was the time in her speech where she would keep her promise to Nick — the promise to restore his father's reputation. They had devised a plan, and even received approval from General Eastman, on how they would explain the detection of the first signal.

"As some of you may be familiar with, we devised a program called SETI@Home, where everyday citizens can use their personal computer resources to help analyze data collected in our search—data received from radio telescopes. Recently, we at SETI— along with many other international agencies— expanded our searches to include optical signals. After decades of listening, we started looking for possible signals, turned our eyes, rather than our ears, to the skies to scan for possible light signals. Realizing that the NASA had already tested the use of lasers for space communication, we felt it reasonable to assume that ET would be using them as well. So we started looking for extremely brief but powerful pulses of light, rather than listening for the steady whine of a radio transmission."

Jane turned toward Nick and waved him forward. She stood with her hand on his shoulder.

"I'd like you to meet Nicholas Farraday. As many of you already know, he's the son of deceased archaeologist, Douglas Farraday, who has been in the news recently."

A loud murmur erupted from the crowd of journalist.

"This young man was part of our @Home program and very familiar with our work. After reading about our new endeavors, something he read in his father's field journal caught his attention. He contacted us immediately."

She turned to smile at Nick.

"To our discredit, at first we ignored him, due in part to an unflattering video of his father that was posted on the internet."

At the mention of the video, once again the sound of camera's clicking crackled through the air.

"Lucky for us, Nick was persistent and finally convinced us the information left in his father's journal was worth investigating. Because of what we read, we focused our optical telescopes toward the Pleiades constellation. And, as they say, the rest is history."

The flashes erupted once again and both Jane and Nick blinked at the onslaught.

The journalist who had been trying to control the crowd shouted, "The rumor is these signals are hard to detect unless you are at specific locations. How did you know to go to these locations?"

"Good question. When the signals received at our observatories were weak, Nick suggested that the pulses might be more powerful at specific archaeological sites. It was a hunch he had after reading parts of his father's journal. It has long been speculated that some famous ancient structures are linked to astronomy. We know, now, that this assumption is true. The ancients appear to have had knowledge of the universe that was somehow lost to us. But, thanks in large part to Douglas Farraday's studies, and his son's persistence, we might one day catch up to them." Jane turned and smiled at Nick.

"We subsequently organized a field trip to the Mesa Verde National Park and set up an experiment near the Sun Temple of the Anasazi Indians, where we detected the first really strong and steady pulses. That was a little over a year ago."

"Nick!" A reporter near the back shouted. "Are you going to release your father's journal? Are you going to publish it?"

Nick glanced at Jane, wondering if he should speak. She nodded and he moved to the microphone.

"The journal is personal. Right now I don't have any plans to make it public."

"But it's part of history now. A famous document."

"As I said, neither my family, nor I, are interested in making it public."

"What did you feel when you first realized your father had made this great discovery?"

"I was," he shook his head, "overwhelmed? Awed?" Nick was really thinking about what he'd seen when he wore the Halo, but he couldn't tell that to the horde of reporters.

Jane stepped back to the microphone.

"We also need to recognize Mr. Henry Applegate." She waved Henry forward. "He was the financier and planner behind Doug Farraday's last expedition. Without Mr. Applegate's dogged determination to prove his theories in the face of continued ridicule, we might never have discovered these signals. Or, if we had, it might have taken years—or even decades—longer, using a vast amount of resources and money."

Jane paused for a moment during a volley of flashes from the cameras.

"These signals make your theories seem more plausible," a reporter shouted to Henry. "How does that make you feel?"

Although Henry agreed to be present during the announcement, he told Jane that he would not interact with the reporters. Even the mention of it brought about a dizzy spell, and so Jane had promised that he wouldn't have to speak.

"Mr. Applegate isn't prepared to make any statements today. Do you have any other questions?"

She took several more questions from the crowd, then said, "I will be handing out a more detailed written statement. For now, this is all we have to say. We have very promising data, verified by other nations and institutions, that we are receiving laser pulse signals from a distant planetary system. This is an exciting day for Earth! Thank you all for coming."

Someone from the back shouted, "There are rumors the laser beams aren't just a signal, but that they carry data; that they carry a message. Is this true?"

Jane wasn't surprised by the question. She knew there had been many rumors. "All we know for sure is that the pulses are of intelligent design—that they were not produced by nature. If there's information contained within them, we haven't discovered it yet."

They had agreed to only make public the fact that a signal had been found, nothing else.

"This concludes the press conference."

Jane turned from the microphone, but the crowd surged forward and soon engulfed everyone on the steps of the observatory. The throng of reporters and onlookers pushed in on Nick. People were patting him on the back and shaking his hand, reporters were still shouting questions at him. Through the crowd, Nick felt someone grab his arm. A hand pressed against his palm and moved to wrap Nick's fingers around a piece of stiff paper. The crowd continued to jostle and shove him, until the police moved into position to hold them back.

Nick finally pushed his way through and followed the others back inside the building. The crowd would have followed him, but the guards held them back. Once the door was securely closed, Nick leaned against the door to catch his breath, but he was still able to hear the excited horde outside. His tight, sweaty grip had crumpled the card. *A journalist trying to get a private interview*, he thought. Jane had warned him about the possibility. He was about toss it in the trash receptacle sitting by the side of the door when something caught his eye. On the left hand side of the card was an outline of a simple cross with a red rose in the center. To the right of the cross was his father's name and underneath, in a medieval-looking script, were the words:

Knight of the Order of the Rosia Crucia
(AMORC)

"Nick, come on! The party is about to start," Emily said.

His mom said, "I'm so proud of you Nick. Standing up there in front of that huge crowd. You did a great job!"

"I'll be there in a minute. I have to go to the bathroom."

Emily and his mom moved hand-in-hand toward the banquet tables set up against the outer walls of the observatory's foyer. He watched Jane console Henry after the trauma of standing in front of all those people, and the crowd pushing in on them after. He could see the others already toasting each other with champagne.

Nick made his way through the throng of scientists, entertainers, and politicians—all of them shouting congratulations at him or patting him on the back as he walked past. Finally, he slipped into the same control room, where he'd sat with Jane and Stan on that first night and went to the bank of computers on the table. He laid the card down and tried to press it flat.

Alec Gordon's words, spoken so long ago, rang in his ears. *Your father works for us.* But Agent Vagnetti said he probably didn't know he worked for them any more than she did. Why had someone pressed the card into his hand?

Why not just give it to him in the open? He tried hard to remember the faces of the people around him at the time, but he had been looking down at the ground most of the time, trying to find a clear space to put one foot in front of the other.

Knight? His dad? What did it mean? He typed the inscription into one of the computers and came up with a long list of hits. He read a few of them:

"The Ancient Mystical Order of the Rosae Crucia is an organization devoted to the study of the elusive mysteries of life and the universe. The organization is non-sectarian and it is open to both men and women regardless of their various religious persuasions.

"...the ancients believe the cross symbolized man — much like Leonardo Da Vinci's Vitruvian Man, with arms spread out like a cross — the cross representing the human body and the rose representing the individual's unfolding consciousness."

Nick also found a long list of suspected members dating back for centuries. Da Vinci's name appeared on it.

He sat back and studied the crumpled business card, turning it over in his hands. Then he leaned forward and placed the card face down on the desk. He smoothed it again with the palm of his hands. Something else was stamped in gold on the back. A symbol of some kind:

$$\varphi$$

Why was it there, and what did it mean? He struggled to remember where he'd seen it before. Then it came to him.

It represented the Greek letter Phi or The Golden Ratio—1.61803. Nick had learned about it in almost all of his classes: science, music, and art. Artists, like Da Vinci, and architects used this proportion to make their art and buildings more aesthetically pleasing. This *Divine Proportion*, as it was often called, could be seen everywhere in nature.

Nick sat for a long while in the silence of the control room. He felt unsettled. Did the symbol on the back of the card have some special meaning, or was it just a logo?

A small transom window, placed high in the control room, provided a view of the telescope the Carters used during their first attempt to find a signal coming from the Pleiades. Nick stared at it until he heard the door open behind him.

Henry stood in the doorway with a surprised look on his face. "Nicholas, what are you doing in here all alone? You're missing the party."

"Do you know anything about this?" Nick pushed the business card toward him.

Henry studied it and then sat in the chair next to Nick.

"The Rosea Crucia."

"What does this mean? It says my dad was a knight of some sort."

Henry glanced at the computer screen. "I probably know as much about it as you've already read on the internet. Did I know if your father was involved with this organization?" Henry shook his head. "No. But nothing surprises me any more."

Henry held up the card to the light.

"Where did you get this?"

"Someone passed it to me while I was being pushed around by the crowd after the announcement."

"Did you see who it was?"

"No, I didn't. Do you think this organization is part of the Bilderberg Group? Was Alec Gordon telling the truth when he said my father worked for them?"

Henry shook his head again. "If you believe all the conspiracy theorists, then all these secret societies are somehow connected. I've heard rumors, but never heard of a firmly established connection between the Bilderbergs and the Rosea Crucia."

"What about this symbol on the back?"

Henry turned the card over. "The symbol for the Golden Ratio. Threes. The Trinity. The Father, the Son, and the Holy Ghost." Henry shrugged.

"What do you think it means?"

"I don't know Nicholas. I'm sorry I don't have more answers for you."

They were both quiet for a moment, then Henry said. "It seems there has always been a group of people on Earth who knew the truth. Those who knew aliens had visited here. And they all agreed that this knowledge was too powerful to reveal to the general public. Was it to protect us, or for their own profit and power? I don't know. I thought I knew the truth but I was just speculating. To be honest with you, I never thought I would live to see the day my theories were proven to be true. Was your father working toward revealing these truths to the world, or continuing to perpetuate the lies? I don't know. All I know is that someone wanted you to know he was part of this society."

"Do you think they'll come back, Henry?"

"Who? The Bilderbergs?"

"No," Nick almost laughed. "The aliens."

"Again, I have to admit that I don't know. Hopefully, the Halo will resurface so it can be studied further, to find out what the aliens were really doing here. Why they came; why they left; and if they intend to come back."

"We need to find it, Henry. My dad died finding the Halo, and we've lost it!"

Henry pushed his chair back and stood. Nick felt Henry's hand rest on his shoulder as he stared at the card.

"I know, son. But now isn't the time to think about all that. Now is the time to celebrate.

"Come. Let's join the party."

~ The End ~

Acknowledgments

When I was in high school, I read a book by Erich Von Däniken titled *Chariot of the Gods*. With his simple question—*Did unknown beings from the infinite reaches of the cosmos visit the earth in the remote past?*—Von Däniken sparked my imagination. Over the years, as our scientific knowledge advanced and we sent men to the moon and ships deep into space, the more intrigued I became. Suddenly, his question didn't seem so outlandish.

While the archaeological and scientific communities continue to ignore Van Däniken's question, I would like to thank him for having the courage to voice his unconventional ideas, which allows us to ponder the "what-ifs."

In addition, I would also like to give special thanks my husband, for being so patient and being my biggest supporter. He read many drafts of this book and always provided excellent guidance and suggestions. I give a big hug to my grandchildren, for giving me inspiration, and to my children and their spouses for having them!

I would especially like to thank the writing community of authonomy.com, the digital imprint of HarperCollins. Through this community, I met many wonderful writers and made many friends from around the world, who gave me support and invaluable advice during this process.

In particular, I would like to thank John Saxon, a wonderful human being and talented writer. Without his encouragement and great advice, this book would not have been written. I also thank Melissa Conway for reading both a first and final draft, and pointing out things I had grown too blind to see.